WHAT'S GOING ON IN CHILTON?

Something isn't quite right in the town of Chilton. When George Kenner, a hard-boiled investigator, arrives from New York to visit his daughter, he finds she has changed. Like the town itself, she possesses a strange calmness, a serenity that is so dreadful, it jangles George's nerves. What can it be?

He starts asking questions. And step-by-terrifying-step, he learns the dark, horrifying, unspeakable truth lurking behind the manicured lawns, white picket fences, and clean, safe streets of Chilton, New York

THE
HOMING

Jeffrey Campbell

BALLANTINE BOOKS • NEW YORK

Library of Congress Catalog Card Number: 79-17477

ISBN 0-345-28793-2

This edition published by arrangement with
G. P. Putnam's Sons

Manufactured in the United States of America

First Ballantine Books Edition: April 1981

*With love and thanks to Eileen and Lorna
as well as Helena, Iain, Keiron, Lisa and Stephen
for putting up with moods and absences*

1

By the time Kenner reached the Chilton exit he suspected that it might be happening again, whatever the hell it was. Unless the heat was doing it: six straight hours on a hot day in a car without air. That could make your hands sweat and your head ache, could even confuse your thinking. Hell, he'd covered more miles today than in the entire eleven months since the wreck, most of them on the Interstate, land-grabbing with every gas-drunk crazy between Manhattan and Lake Ontario. His body was probably telling him he couldn't take the lifestyle anymore. Bodies talked a very physical language, right?

And then there was a moment, as he eased the overheated Chevy around the ramp, a calm, lucid moment when it didn't matter anymore whether the symptoms had immediate or deeper causes, because suddenly he understood his daughter's decision to live here, where nothing moved faster than a growing pumpkin and there were no pressures; a moment when, finding himself on a quiet, narrow country blacktop darkened on either side by thick trees, he considered quitting his job and moving upstate himself. He'd buy an apple farm near Chilton, near Katherine, and freewheel the rest of his life, spraying the damned apples, doing whatever the hell apple farmers did.

The moment passed, though, as suddenly as it had come, displaced by the old anger. He rolled down his window to empty the car of cigarette smoke, then wound it directly up again, preferring the smoke to the humid, sluggish air that flowed in, all silted up with mosquitoes and smelling of vegetable decay and overripe fruit. It reminded him that Katherine wasn't adapted either to apple fumes and the growing cycle, that two years ago she'd sent him a viewcard of the lake inscribed: *Air's great up here, for as long as you can breathe out.* And that reminded him why he was angry: not just because she'd wasted her education and junked her career, but because she'd done it so damned casually, in the unthinking way of other people's kids.

If he insisted on blaming himself (and he insisted) he could go back two years, to when Katherine had thought of Chilton as a kind of working vacation from graduate school. It seemed to Kenner that everything had started to go wrong then. He couldn't remember an onset, a first time, but he guessed that was when he'd started getting the sweats and the headaches. Somehow it was all connected, all interdependent. A chain of ifs. If he'd wrung a few days out of the company in the summer of '76 and driven up to see her as she'd wanted, she'd be home with him now, and he'd have declined the Pennsylvania job, and there wouldn't have been an accident, and every thought in his head would be his own. But he hadn't pressed Worldwide for time off two summers ago, and after that things had happened too fast, faster than they had a right to happen in the hick time zone, with its 120 seconds to the minute, twice as many on Sundays. Two years without Katherine. How had he let two years slip away like that?

A sign came up, one of those weathered local signs that identified the small towns amongst the woods. A place called Kanga Falls lay to the left and Chilton was twenty-three miles ahead. He was just half an hour's easy driving from Katherine now, and just sixteen months too late. Like one of those zany news items in the long, kooky letters she used to write. *Flash: Chilton, N.Y. Just heard President assassinated by unidentified nut. Let you know when we find out who.* A day later, on a postcard: *Now known to be President McKinley. Opinion here Teddy Roosevelt will make fine successor. Flash ends. P.S. Do you have the new longspeakie machine there yet?*

He'd called her the same evening. It had been a scratchy connection. "Hey," he'd said, "you really do have an antiquated phone system up there, don't you? Hang up. I'll redial."

"It's okay," she'd answered. "Just slacken off the string your end. The soup can's cutting my ear."

"Jesus, I miss you," he'd said. "It's driving me crazy being the only screwball in the house."

"You'll get me back soon, Dad. Meantime, how about coming for a visit?"

"Kath, I can't. It's Arsonists' Convention time again. I swear I'm lighting cigarettes with claim forms."

"Burn the office and get up here. My need is greater."

"Why don't you come home for a weekend?" he'd suggested. "Schools close weekends, don't they?"

"It's kind of awkward," she'd said. "I have to design my stupid experiments weekends. Write notes, stuff like that." She'd taken a deep breath. "The truth is, I want to switch from Learning Theory and I don't know how to break it to Elaine Stromberg. She did the original study when these kids were first-graders."

Kenner had said, "I know who she is, Kath. And I know who you're supposed to be—the whiz kid doing the follow-up study, right? So what are you switching to? Quitter psychology?"

"Thanks for the understanding, Daddy."

He'd softened his tone then. "Okay, I'm sorry. What is it you want to switch to, anyway?"

Another deep breath. Then, "ESP."

"What?"

"Extrasensory Perception, dummy."

"Jesus Christ, Kath. That isn't psychology."

"Beautiful," she'd said. "Your mind's about as open as the Kremlin executive washroom. It's parapsychology and it's pretty respectable."

"It's medieval and it's crap," he'd said. "I'm not—"

"Hey," she'd interrupted, "I didn't tell you my big news, did I?"

"Kath, ESP is—"

"David Hensel asked me shyly for a date. Isn't that cute? It's like a rerun of high school."

"Back up," he'd said. "Who's David Hensel?"

"I told you six weeks ago who David is, Daddy. He teaches most of the kids in the group I'm studying."

"The polite one?"

"That's him. Helps a girl down from the buggy. City boys don't do that anymore, you know."

"We never did, lady. I used to make my girl rub down the horse."

There had been a pause. "I'll write you, okay?" she said then.

"I'll wait for the mail coach."

Two years ago.

Then the letters had begun to dry up. She'd started sending hastily scribbled notes instead, always promising to write more next time. When Kenner called her on the phone she seemed hurried and distracted.

"How's the research?"

"Okay."

"Come on, Kath. 'Okay' is bullshit. Did you tell her yet?"

"Did I tell who what?"

"Professor Stromberg. About switching."

"Oh, that. No, I didn't. I was wrong about that."

"Wrong about switching or wrong about ESP?"

The line had started to crackle. She'd said, "This means of communication has absolutely no future, you know that? Look, why don't I write you instead?"

"Good question. Kath, is something wrong up there?"

"I'm fine, Daddy. Really. I just have to tape some stuff right now, that's all."

"We'll talk at Christmas, okay?"

"Sure."

But she'd stayed in Chilton that Christmas, spending it with the Hensels. And he'd dreamed that she'd called him in the night, begging him to come and take her home, warning him about something that hadn't happened yet but was going to happen. She'd been vague about what it was, and his memory of the dream vaguer still. Next day he'd called her in Chilton "The Hensels are really nice people," she'd said. "I'm having a great time." And he'd said, "I dreamed about you last night." And she'd said, "I dreamed about you too. I dreamed you came to Chilton. You liked it here."

Then, at the beginning of February, she'd married David Hensel.

Now she lives in a jungle, Kenner thought, as the woods which lined the empty road grew denser by the mile, unbroken as a rail fence. It gave him a strange sense of loss to think that, as though she'd taken holy vows and he was pursuing her to some fly-swarming mission in the remotest region of earth. He felt an urge to hurry, a crazy conviction that if he traveled quickly enough he might yet catch up the past. It made him want to straighten the curves and bulldoze the trees in his impatience, as he'd longed to do in his dreams; and, as in the dreams, he fought the lunatic impulse with hands clenched bone-white on the wheel, desperately, like somebody else's hands, not George Kenner's hands at all. All he knew for certain was that he mustn't lose control of the wheel, mustn't brake, whatever happened, as he'd done one wet night in northern Pennsylvania eleven months ago.

But that didn't explain the other dreams, or the intrusions into his waking life of alien thoughts, the sense that he'd picked up the wrong head in a bus station, some madman's brain; and it didn't explain why sometimes he felt there was a dangerous, angry, goddamn animal loose inside his skull. Nothing explained that. Not skull X rays or EEG traces, or Freud, or Katherine's undergraduate texts, which told him a lot about the psychology of rats, nothing much about people. He was shrink-bait, or would have been if he didn't draw the line at having the inside of his head reamed in a psycho ward. He'd find a way to get the bastard out himself. First, though, identify your bastard.

The little newsstand guy on Lexington Avenue helped. Kenner had no idea how he helped, but he had long, crazy conversations with the man, who believed in UFO invasions and psychic auras (they glowed at night), and in secret time-travel techniques that involved knowing the right nerves to hotwire, and that LEE HARVEY OSWALD's being an anagram of HE SELL RADYO WAVE pretty well proved the CIA conspiracy theory, and that Kennedy's brain was being kept alive in an electrically heated mason jar. What worried Kenner was that he listened to the little screwball, stood on the sidewalk and actually *listened*, as if it all made perfect sense. "You know, you're the smartest customer I got," the guy said to him once. "This country needs guys like us, right?"

"Right," Kenner had said. And he'd meant it. God help him, he'd meant it.

Now *that* he really worried about.

He got a three-line note from Katherine, announcing her marriage, and a photograph of his son-in-law, a slim boy with a pleasant, grinning face and short blond hair parted neatly to the side. It was the wholesome look of all those Chets and Tads in family shows of the fifties, the look of a kid who thought grass grew in fields and Coke came in bottles. It was as if she'd married into an endangered species.

The note said: *This is David, my husband. He's a good, uncomplicated person, Daddy, and I think that's what I was always looking for. Please accept it and come and see us soon.*

He didn't accept it and he didn't want to see them soon. He used the severe winter as his excuse for not making the long trip upstate, went on a binge instead, telling himself that in a few days everything would be back the way it was, that the marriage had to be a practical joke she'd let get out of hand. Any day she'd be sending him a bunch of phony news clippings from *The Chilton Republic:* HENSEL BOY WEDS CITY GAL, and beneath it, in smaller print: TITANIC SINKS. HUN-DREDS DROWN. Then she'd probably call and say, "You really bought it, didn't you dummy?" And he'd say, "Are you kidding? The *Titanic*'s unsinkable." But at the end of the holidays there was no letter, no phone call.

After a while, when he'd still heard nothing from her, he started to worry. She was in trouble, she was sick, she was dead. He called her, but she said everything was fine and how was everything with him? And he said fine, and she said that was fine, and he hung up convinced that nothing was fine, that she was lying to him and in bad trouble up there. Yet in his dreams she told him more, something too technical for him to understand, too confused for him to remember in the morning.

He planned a visit for the summer, wrote and told her he'd be coming. It didn't commit him, didn't mean he accepted her decision to drop out of school and live in the wilderness. It was just a visit. But when the Pennsylvania job came up that summer, he took it. Too bad about the visit. Some other time. He felt relieved.

There had been some storm damage to a factory in Scranton and a few flood claims had been made further north. The regular Philadelphia investigator, whose territory it was, had been sick, so Kenner went. And on the way back it occurred to him that he wasn't too far from Lake Ontario, and if he turned north he could make it to Chilton before dark, surprise Katherine. Then it had started to rain heavily, slowing him up, and he'd been tired, just as he was now, only careless-tired, because in thirty-six years' driving nothing had ever happened to make him careful. He didn't remember much about it, except that the rain and the lights had blinded him, and the sweat running into his eyes had blinded him, and his brain had swollen as the animal inside woke up, and he'd known he wasn't going to make it to Chilton, not this time, not yet, because the time wasn't right and she wasn't ready; but it didn't matter, because he'd make it one day; and the hands on the wheel had been somebody else's hands, and it had been somebody else braking, losing control on the slick, dark road, so that the car rolled over and slid, on its roof, halfway into a river.

That was why he hadn't visited Katherine last summer. She didn't visit him either, in the hospital in Taquanna, Pennsylvania. "David needs the car to get to work," she told Kenner on the phone. "Anyway, he doesn't like me to drive long distances on my own."

What the hell kind of excuse is that? Kenner thought. But he said nothing.

"Will you come and see us when you're better?"

"I'll sure as hell try," he told her. Sweet Christ, he really needed to.

Now he was trying.

Almost a year later, a lot of dreams later.

Dreams in which the grinning boy enticed and promised, promised nothing less than the future to Kenner.

Dreams in which Katherine gave him warnings, told him where to look for his answers. There were books he could look in, but the books didn't seem to be available and in any case he couldn't remember the references. "Why don't I just take you home, Kath?" he suggested, but that, apparently, was naïve of him. There was a good reason why he couldn't, and for some reason she didn't even want him to. The problem, whatever it was, seemed to be in Chilton. It had to be solved in Chilton.

"I'll try, baby," he told Katherine night after night. "I'll get there."

Sometimes there was help. A troubled, disbelieving Elaine Stromberg would enter his dreams some nights when he asked for help, and Kenner would say, "How can you be in my dream if we never met?" And Elaine Stromberg would say, "Come on. Do you really believe in telepathic dreams? That stuff went out with Joseph." And she'd explain about dreamwork and puns and hypnagogic hallucinations and the chemical composition of the brain, cholinesterase and serotonin, anything that could explain his dream without recourse to magic. "It amazes me," she'd tell him, "that a hard-headed guy like you can believe in ESP."

"Okay, then how come you're in my dream?"

"You dreamed me."

"How could I dream you if we never met?"

"So we met someplace. Or maybe Katherine told you about me, what I look like. You reconstructed an image that looks like me."

"Do you ever dream me?" he'd ask, and she'd reply, "I never remember my dreams."

Kenner remembered his, most of them. But then he had no behavioral ax to grind. He'd believe whatever seemed most believable.

Even if it was unbelievable.

And this time he made it. He didn't know how, because the pain in his head was worse now than he'd ever experienced it and he'd apparently covered the last twenty miles in a state of near-paralysis. Yet he'd made it. The sign came up telling him he'd made it, a freshly painted sign announcing: CHILTON CITY LIMITS—SPEED 30 M.P.H. He moved his foot quite easily to the brake then, slowing the car, and wondered as he did so why that had ever seemed such a difficult maneuver.

The woods thinned out on his left, gave way to a sidewalk; and soon there were houses, frame houses with white-painted porches and clean-cropped lawns. A second sign said: CHILTON—A GREAT LITTLE PLACE TO LIVE.

It was all pretty much as Kenner had imagined it: the clean, orderly gardens growing flagpoles, the uncluttered driveways, the dollhouse uniformity of the residences. It was a cliché of a place, almost a self-parody, wearing its civic pride like a hand-me-down Sunday suit; neat, respectable, but a joke to everybody except the wearer.

And now he was on Main Street, trying to recall Kath's directions. South to Fourth, then a right to the corner of Elm. It wasn't possible to go far wrong in a town this size, though. Like a kid's toy town, it probably had one of everything, and most of it here on Main: the Exxon station, the A & P market, the row of small family-owned stores that had hung on to business during a time of conglomerate cannibalism: Fred's Drugs, Canale's Leather Goods & Shoe Repair, Jenny's Diner; as if you were expected to know good old Fred, homely little Jenny, to have gone to school with them. These places were like that, though; like old families, fine if you were born into them, damned cold if you married into them. And the winters, he thought, passing Lombard's Tavern, where a pale orange sign hanging in the small window advertised a brand of beer he'd never heard of—Christ, how did she survive the endless months of snow they had up here, the cold that ripped you like broken glass, the sheer soul-stewing dreariness of such a place? He shook his head. Accept it, he told himself. This is what she wants. Maybe the only mystery was how she'd kept that side of her character suppressed all those years. Maybe there was no deeper mystery. He passed a man in a plaid hunting jacket who was standing beside a parked van, filming a storefront across the street with a hand-held camera. Kenner could imagine the eventual screening: a bunch of mud farmers gathered eagerly in a darkened room to watch *Window on Chilton*. Hot stuff. He smiled to himself, then glancing in the wing mirror he noticed that the guy had turned and was pointing the camera along the street, tracking him. Hey, I'm a movie star. I've got the lead in the Chilton Chamber of Commerce production *Tourism: Chilton's Future*. Or was it a real estate blockbuster? Whatever.

Kenner located Fourth and turned right. Here, without the neon, it was darker. The streetlamps weren't lit yet, but there were lights in some of the houses, more of the same frame houses, the same porches, as if some frenzied architect had worked out his private obsession on the town, never quite getting it right; and in some windows the paler light of illuminated fish tanks, television screens.

And then Elm, truly elm-lined, as advertised. He turned slowly into the street and cruised along it until he found 330, a white house with a nearly new station wagon in the driveway. The Hensel house.

He got out and almost at once the porch light was turned on—a subdued amber glow around which a cluster of moths fluttered—and the front door opened. Katherine was standing at the top of the porch steps, her features indistinct, barely lit by the lamp. But he'd have known her by any kind of light.

He walked quickly across the lawn and up the steps, and he put his arms around her, needing just to hold her a minute or two in silence, to fill the space between them. It was only then that he realized how much he'd missed her, not simply her companionship but her softness and her grace and her warmth, the way she moved and the way she laughed, all her habits and gestures, her entire physical presence. "I missed you like a limb," he said. And for a moment it didn't seem possible that it was two years since he'd seen her.

Gently she pulled herself free of his grip. She half turned, with a little embarrassed laugh, and David Hensel stepped onto the porch, his hand already extended.

And now she was no longer his child but this man's wife, Katherine Hensel, a stranger.

"Mr. Kenner?"

Katherine moved to her husband's side and curled her arm around his waist, and Kenner thought: Why not hit me on the head with him, Kath?

"Daddy, this is David," Katherine was saying.

Kenner felt the boy's hand cool and heavy on his own. "David," he said, but the name alone seemed to drain his mind, exhaust conversation.

Then Katherine excused herself and went through into the kitchen and Kenner followed his son-in-law through the screen door into the living room, which was painted in dull colors and full of dull, mass-produced things, as if a blind man had furnished it from a Montgomery Ward catalog with a pen. Kenner glanced around for signs of Katherine's taste, some little, unmistakable Katherine touch, but there wasn't anything. It was all Hensel.

"Nice room," he said, sitting where David indicated, on a sofa with plastic-covered cushions. The plastic squeaked as he shifted his position, then squeaked again as David Hensel sat down. "I hope Kath isn't going to a lot of trouble in there," Kenner said. "I ate on the way up."

"You'll like what she's making," the boy said, leaning toward him slightly. "Chicken's her specialty." His breath was mild, like an infant's, and he smelled faintly of soap.

"Are we talking about Katherine?" Kenner said. "Her specialty used to be caterers. She'd call caterers to make toast."

The boy said, "That's a joke, isn't it?"

"That's a joke," Kenner confirmed. "I kid around a lot."

"I like it. I don't mind if they're city jokes."

"City jokes are my whole act," Kenner said. "I grew up thinking Central Park West was the Continental Divide."

David grinned and shook his head. "You really remind me of Kathy. Anyone can see you're related."

"Yeah," Kenner said. "We used to be a double act."

"I know."

Kenner waited for more, but there wasn't any more. Instead David started to chew at one of his fingernails. Kath, you married a conversational pioneer, Kenner thought: a man who loves wide open spaces between his sentences. For Christ's sake, why?

"Katherine seems to like it here," Kenner said eventually.

The boy nodded. "I guess it grew on her. It'll do that." David Hensel was picking his thumbnail now. Nervousness or agitation? Kenner wondered. "You could get to like Chilton, too, I bet," the boy said.

"How long will it take?"

"You'd have to stay awhile, get to know the town. You'd like it though."

"You're pretty sure, aren't you?"

"Most people want the same things."

"That's right," Kenner said with a smile. Yeah, he thought, and they're all in New York City, beating each other to death for 'em.

"Things like good neighbors," David said. "Do you have good neighbors, Mr. Kenner?"

"Why don't you call me George?" Kenner said. "I've never seen or heard my neighbors, David. That's how I know I have good neighbors."

David shook his head again. "I find that very sad." He leaned back on the sofa and the plastic squeaked again. That's it, Kenner thought. That's every corner of the kid's mind explored in six minutes and some odd seconds. He had the feeling that if he waited long enough the same conversation would start over again, like a recorded message. Jesus, what did these two find to talk about of an evening? Maybe they didn't need to talk. Maybe they just cooed at each other. Ah, the hell with it.

"It's important to get along with other people," the boy said.

Kenner nodded, as if recognizing some great truth simply uttered. "What's the farthest you've been in your life?" he asked suddenly.

David looked bewildered for a moment, then said, "I guess, Chicago. I went there once when I was a kid."

Kenner said, "Katherine's traveled a lot. Did you know she's been to six European countries?"

"I know. You can see those places on television."

"I've seen *Ben Hur* on television," Kenner said. "That doesn't make me an expert on ancient Rome."

"I didn't say I was an expert on anything, sir," David said quietly, and Kenner realized he'd been bullying the kid; which was strange, because he was a nice, old-fashioned, small-town kid, and Kenner almost liked him.

Katherine came in with a tray of food. "I thought we could eat in here," she said. "You guys can have the trays, I'll use nature's table." The tray had little legs, which Katherine unfolded, setting the table over Kenner's thighs. "There," she said. "David, that isn't your place."

The boy got up, fetched a second portable tray from a drawer, and settled himself in an armchair. "My TV chair," he said, grinning. "See how she keeps me in line?"

They sat apart, Kenner thought. He sits in that chair and she has the sofa, and the television completes the triangle. Christ!

"Take us as you find us, Daddy." She tucked her skirt under her, balancing her plate carefully on her lap. "Go ahead. Try it."

Kenner looked down at the food, pieces of reddened chicken on a bed of limp pasta, then up at Katherine. She was watching him with the eager, expectant look of a small child anxious to please. He picked up his fork.

"Chicken cacciatore," David said. "Kathy's specialty."

Kenner forked some of the food into his mouth and

chewed it. The chicken was slippery and tough, the sauce tasteless. It reminded him of airline food. "Fine," he said, and wiped his lips with his napkin.

"Didn't I tell you?" David said happily. "She's a terrific cook."

"My agent," Katherine said. "Daddy, you're not eating."

"What am I doing with my mouth?"

"Pretending."

"Savoring." Once he'd have said, "You know how I can tell this chicken isn't undercooked?" And she'd have smiled and said, "How?" Then he'd have said, "Because it just tole me." But he sensed that he couldn't get away with those routines anymore. Something had changed between them, something more than time and absence. He wasn't sure what. He just knew they weren't a double act anymore. He ate a few more mouthfuls of chicken, then said he'd eaten bad hamburger in a coffee shop on the way up and his stomach was still paying. And Katherine said, "Poor daddy," and let him off the hook.

Afterward she made Sanka ("Caffeine keeps us awake") and Kenner asked for ice water and aspirin, then sat sipping the water, wondering when somebody was going to say, "Okay, let's cut the crap and say what's on our minds," but nobody did. Instead, David said, "Mind if I watch the game?" and turned on the television set.

Kenner lit a cigarette and sat listening to the steady pain rhythm in his own head and to the TV commentator giving somebody's batting average for the season, feeling that something—he couldn't put his finger on it—was out of place, not as it should be.

"Ashtray, hon," David said, without looking up from the ball game, and Katherine went dutifully out and came back a moment later with a sparkling, never-used ashtray.

"You ought to quit that," she said.

"I know. Willpower, right? I'd get along fine, never miss it."

"I wasn't going to say that, Daddy."

Nò, but Kenner had sensed that David was about to say it. He looked at the boy. David shook his head and smiled, perhaps at something that was happening in the ball park. I'm going nuts, Kenner thought.

"You looked tired," Katherine said.

And David, as if on cue, said, "We made up the spare room for you, Mr. Kenner. Want me to show you where it is?"

They wanted him out of the way. He wondered why. The boy didn't seem about to leave his game for anything more urgent, so why did they want to hustle him off to bed?

"It's okay," Katherine said. "I'll take him up. You watch your game."

Take him up. The way you'd talk about a child, or an invalid, or an old man. "I'll find it," Kenner said, but Katherine said, "Hey, what kind of establishment do you think I'm running here?"

He followed her up the stairs, suddenly dreading the spare room, the visit, the whole idea of being in this house with Katherine and her husband.

"This is it," she said. She turned the light on and Kenner stepped into a narrow room containing a single bed and some functional furniture. Two of the walls were painted pink and two were blue. "For when we start a family. Male or female—we're ready."

Kenner looked closely at her, searching her face for a sign, a clue, a hint as to what she might be trying to tell him. He noticed that her hairstyle was altered, changed from the central parting she'd always favored, brushed back now and held by two brown plastic clasps at the side. That was all, though. Her face was the same. She was smiling, a happy, beautiful smile that he might have taken as proof of her contentment with David, with her life in Chilton. All he had to do was believe the smile. He didn't believe it.

"Are you happy, baby?" he said.

"Wonderfully happy," she said, laughing.

"Tomorrow I want us to talk. Just us. A long talk, okay?"

"First get a good night's sleep. Bathroom's along the hallway."

"And your room's next door, right?"

She pulled a face. "That's so we'll be able to hear junior crying. Relax, grandpa. We haven't started production yet." She leaned forward, kissed him lightly on the cheek, then went back downstairs.

He didn't know how long he'd slept, or if he'd really slept at all. There were no sounds from downstairs, nothing that could have disturbed him. He tried to read his watch by moonlight, but fast-moving clouds kept covering the moon. All he was sure of was that he had to use the bathroom.

Feeling his way to the door, he opened it and stepped out into the hallway. At first the darkness was total, depthless. But as he stood there the moon broke free and a column of pale grayish light became visible just along the hallway. Their room, with its door open. For a moment he considered returning to bed, but there was no way he could sleep with a full bladder, and what the hell was he afraid of anyway?

He moved tentatively forward until he was opposite the open door of the Hensels' bedroom. He wasn't going to look inside, he didn't want to see inside. The light, though; those soft explosions of pale light drew him to the doorway.

He looked in.

Katherine was lying supine on the bed, her arms spread out across both pillows, her eyes wide open; David was a darkly moving shadow on top of her, soundlessly and in slow rhythm penetrating and withdrawing, penetrating and withdrawing, while she remained passive and motionless and silent. And all in the pale flickering light of a small portable black-and-white TV, its sound turned down, Johnny Carson laughing soundlessly; and even the bed, foam-mattressed like his own, made scarcely any sound, part of the same silent communion. Watching, Kenner felt something yield inside himself, like a pulse stopping.

No, he thought.

I shouldn't be here. I shouldn't be seeing this.

He closed his eyes a moment. When he looked again he saw that they'd finished and, still silent, had turned away from each other.

He continued along the hallway, found the bathroom, and locked himself inside. He was trembling, sweating. He splashed his face with cold water, thinking: You saw what you had no right to see. It made him feel dirty, stained by a primal sin. Why? Why did you have to look? Then he thought: So what? Married people screw. What did you expect? A pillow fight?

He looked down at his hands, clenched against the edge of the washbasin. Then at his reflection in the mirror—the blue eyes that were still sharp and clear, the short dark hair that was only now beginning to streak with gray, the face lean and firm; a face Katherine had once described as a contradiction of the powerful and the determined and the gentle.

Katherine.

Forget it, he thought. You saw nothing. Not a damned thing.

You saw nothing and you heard nothing.

And then it struck him that it was true—he hadn't heard a thing. There had been nothing to hear. Whatever had gone on in that room was still inviolate, private, as private as thought, inaccessible to any observer.

Private. Passionless. Silent.

Somehow they'd protected themselves from him, gone deep inside themselves to a place where he couldn't intrude. And that was why it hadn't mattered to them that their door was open. Sound was irrelevant to them.

He was irrelevant to them.

There was something weird about that.

Something dreamlike.

2

For a few seconds, disoriented, Kenner thought he was back in his own apartment. Then he opened his eyes fully and remembered that he was in Katherine's house, in Chilton. What he wasn't sure about was what he'd seen in the night. Had he dreamed that? No, that had been real. He'd checked the time before getting back into bed and it had been close to one o'clock, which tied in with Johnny Carson. And he remembered what he'd decided then, to check into a hotel in the morning.

He dressed, packed his suitcase, and took it out to the car before the Hensels were up. It was the moving-train principle, momentum. With his case already in the car he'd be harder to stop. Then he took a walk on Fourth and along Oak, a block down, enjoying the air before it turned sweaty in the sun and the subtle smell of dewy lawns before the power-mowers got to them. Some people waved to him as he walked. A kid on a skateboard pulled over to let him pass, and an old man walking a dog asked what he'd thought of last night's ball game on TV. So it's a friendly town, Kenner thought; it depended on how you liked your strangers. If you liked them glad-handed and your daughter distant, Chilton was fine. He happened to prefer living where his daughter had been warm and a smile from a stranger was a good reason to call a cop.

Katherine was in the kitchen making coffee when he got back. She poured him a cup and they stood in the kitchen, not saying anything to each other at first. Then Katherine said, "You're leaving, aren't you." And he said, "I can't take any more of your coffee," and smiled to show it was a joke. "Hell, I'm only going to a hotel," he said. "The visit isn't over."

She busied herself at the stove. "David saw you take your bag out to the car. We thought you were running out on us."

"Is that what you thought? Don't you know me better than that?"

She shrugged. "People change," she said.

"Not me," Kenner said. "I don't change."

"Did we do anything wrong, Daddy?"

"Jesus, no. You didn't do anything wrong. I just like to make my own house rules. I keep crazy hours. I get up in the night and broil steaks. That makes me a lousy houseguest, Kath."

David came into the kitchen then. He was holding a coffee cup in one hand and a folded newspaper in the other. EAR, MAYOR PREDICTS, Kenner read. It made him think of Joseph's dream and ears of corn. Maybe the mayor was predicting the harvests. It would make a hell of a reelection program.

"We didn't hear you," the boy said. "Did you get up in the night?"

"Not twenty times," Kenner said, "but I got up."

"We didn't hear a thing," David repeated. "Did we, Kathy?"

"No," she said, and Kenner thought: That's like saying to a prowler, "What prowler? I don't see any prowler in here." And he saw that she was biting her lower lip, her childhood talisman against lies, which made it worse, somehow, made it embarrassing for him to be standing there with a coffee cup in his hand and those unwelcome night images in his head, knowing as he stood there that in both their heads the same blue movie was playing.

Then David said, "Whatever you want to do is okay

with Kathy and me. Room's there for as long as you want it, Mr. Kenner." That told him a lot. It told him that he was making them as uncomfortable as they were making him. They were not fighting him. They were relieved to see him go.

It was Saturday. David had papers to grade, which left Katherine free to show Kenner where the hotel was, saved him the trouble of maneuvering to get her to himself.

Kenner drove slowly along Main Street, looking at the storefronts, bright in the sunlight, at the thin scatter of shoppers trying to be a crowd. They passed the Exxon station, where a black Lincoln Continental was getting the treatment from an attendant, and Lombard's Tavern, then a fruit and produce stand with hand-lettered signs. APPLES SQUASH TOMATOS one sign read, like a sports result.

" 'Tomatoes,' without an 'e,' " Kenner said. "The sign back there."

"I didn't see it."

He shook his head. "Jesus, Kath, is this it?"

"Is this what?"

"Happy Valley." He gestured at Main Street. "Is this really where you want to live?"

"What's wrong with it?" she said, and something in her tone, not simply pride or defensiveness but a hint of petulance, infuriated him.

"Come on," he said. "We're talking about the entire unexpired portion of your life, Kath. In a place where 'tomatoes' is suddenly a Spanish word, for Chrissake."

"Why are you getting so mad about the letter 'e'?"

"I'm a *Sesame Street* freak. Dammit, you know what I'm talking about. You. This place. David Hensel."

"I don't think I want to go on with this," she said. "I happen to love my husband. And he loves me."

"Look," Kenner said, "I don't have anything against him personally. He's a nice kid. But he's dug himself a damn foxhole here. He's never going to move, Kath. He likes it here."

She said, "It obviously hasn't gotten through to you, but so do I."

"Sure, but he can't imagine anybody not liking it here. Listen. There's a religious order someplace. Monks or nuns, whatever. Everybody in the order sleeps in a special customized coffin every night of their life. Are you listening?"

"No, I'm not. Somebody has to watch the road. And I don't want to hear any jokes right now."

"This isn't a joke. These people exist. And the reason they sleep in the coffins is to remind themselves of death. Then, when they die, somebody comes along—one of the nuns comes along and screws down the lid. Open coffins with people living inside them. Sneak previews of death."

"That's a sick idea. Is that how you see this town?"

"How do you see it, baby? Is this the life you want? Honestly want?"

"It's what I honestly want," she said.

"How about David?" Kenner pressed. "Is he what you want?"

"He's what I want, too."

"The hell he is," Kenner said. "I'm going to pull over and we are going to talk to each other. Remember that old pastime where the two of us would sit opposite each other and say words? Remember that? It must be a while since you did that with anyone."

"Daddy—"

"It was like television, but with feedback. We called it conversation."

She didn't answer. There was a stoplight ahead and Kenner pulled up at it. He rolled the window down, put his arm out, drummed his fingers against the side of the car. He had the feeling that Katherine's mind was elsewhere, that he wasn't reaching her. He was about to offer something conciliatory, some small verbal salve, when he felt a touch on his arm and he turned.

There was an old guy standing beside the car.

"Saw your dealer's logo," he said.

"Nice," Kenner said without expression.

The old man leaned toward the window. A pulse flickered under one eye and his hands trembled slightly. "Could you give me a ride?" he asked.

Kenner glanced at Katherine, saw that she was shaking her head.

"Could you please?"

"Where do you want to go?" Kenner looked back at the old man, the hair cropped close into the scalp, the eyes watery, staring. The light was changing and Kenner repeated the question.

The old guy looked up and down the street. "Out of town," he said.

"We're not going out of town," Katherine said. Her tone of voice was sharp suddenly.

"I can pay," the man said. He reached inside his coat pockets and Kenner could hear the rattle of coins. "I can pay. I've got money."

"Sorry," Kenner said. The light was green now and he was starting to move forward. In the rearview mirror he saw that the old man hadn't moved, was standing in the middle of the street, staring after the car.

Katherine said, "We have to take a right here."

"Who was he?" Kenner asked.

"I don't know. A drunk, I guess."

A drunk, Kenner thought. In this town, who can blame him?

They headed down a narrow, leafy street which after a few blocks opened out onto a prospect of the lake, a great flat disk of gray water that diffused the sunlight without reflecting it. There was something gloomy about the view; Kenner couldn't decide what exactly. It had to do with the absence of rowboats, yachts, anybody fishing. He couldn't imagine anybody wanting to paint that view or live within sight of it. In fact, he couldn't picture life here—the change of seasons, the passage of generations as people got born, grew up, died. His imagination gave him no sense of time or place, and again he wondered what was the attraction for Katherine.

He pulled over to the curb and parked facing the

lake, opposite a row of old frame houses with peeling paint.

"The motel's just around the corner," Katherine said.

Kenner turned in his seat. She was looking out through the windshield, avoiding his eyes, and in her profile he could see her mother: the familiar look of detachment, disdain, condescension. He wondered if Katherine was still in touch with her, if Barbara, growing old in style in Palm Beach, knew or cared about her daughter's marriage to Mr. Zero. She hadn't cared about ditching the two of them ten years ago for some character who owned half Florida. "Do you know anything about him?" Kenner had asked Katherine then, and she'd replied, "He owns things. Like companies, and Florida. Don't worry, Daddy, he doesn't own me. I'm holding out for California." Then. Ten years ago, back in the Middle Ages, when he'd open the cans and Kath would tip the contents into a pan, and twice a week they'd jointly wash the dishes. Now maybe she, too, couldn't take any more of him. Maybe all she'd wanted was out, and Chilton was out.

"Two questions," Kenner said. "You won't feel a thing. Then you get a stick of candy."

She gave a faint smile. "I'm counting."

"Why did you give up your career?"

The question seemed to startle her. "We went into that, Daddy. David—"

"David, my ass. I don't buy David and simplicity and that whole Walden bit, but that isn't what we're talking about. Why drop the research?"

"That," she said. "I had to decide between two full-time careers and I chose marriage. That's what it is, you know. A career, not a hobby. It's like karate or high-wire, Daddy. You can't dabble in it. You have to be expert or forget it."

"Did David teach you that speech?"

"I write my own material. It happens to be what I believe."

"I seem to recall," Kenner said, "that there's been

some slight reaction to that viewpoint recently. Like a revolution. Hasn't the news reached here yet?"

"It'll swing back," she said.

"Jesus. He's really done a job on you, hasn't he? It's like goddamn ventriloquism. Your mouth opens and it's David's voice I hear. I'll bet you read the Bible, too."

She was silent. Kenner pulled out a pack of cigarettes, shook one free, and lit it.

"Daddy, why do you find it so hard to accept that I've changed some of my ideas? I'm two years older. I've matured. Or do you want to keep me a child forever? Sweet little Kath, just the way she was at age seven, daddy's little girl. I grew up, Daddy. And I married."

Kenner picked a grain of tobacco from his tongue. "Some switch."

"What?"

"When you switch you really go all the way, don't you?"

"You've lost me."

"You wanted to switch to ESP, remember? Parapsychology."

She shook her head. "I don't know where you dreamed that up. My subject was *Learning and Retrieval Patterns in 32 High School Students*. Strictly behavioral, empirical research."

"I didn't dream anything up," Kenner said. "You told me. You told me on the goddamn phone. I remember it."

"I guess you misunderstood the context or something," she said. "Are we through now? Can we go?"

"In a minute. How did Professor Stromberg take it, Kath?"

"You've had your two questions, Daddy."

He reached over and touched the back of her hand. "I'm not trying to put you through the wringer, baby," he said placatingly. Her hand was shaking, though, and she drew it back.

"Well, it feels like second spin," she said. "Only

hers is high-speed. I guess I should be grateful. At least you think up your own questions."

"You're talking about Stromberg?"

Katherine nodded. "She drove over from Ithaca a few times. Last time with a bunch of Personality questionnaires. She thinks I'm sick, Daddy. She wanted to give me the Minnesota Multiphasic—M.M.P.I. It's a diagnostic test for abnormality. Do you think I'm sick?"

"I think you're crazy," Kenner said, smiling. "But then I think I'm crazy, too. What did Stromberg say?"

"Daddy, nobody puts ideas in my head. I do what *I* want, not what David wants. Why won't you and Elaine accept that? I'm fine. I'm a normal, sane, healthy, independent person. And I quit school because I wanted to quit school. That's all."

"Okay," Kenner said. He stroked her cheek gently. "Okay, sweetheart. No more questions."

The motel called itself the Chilton Lake Lodge. It was one of a chain of motor lodges Kenner had used from time to time—about a dozen small cabins and a front office with a green neon vacancy sign in the window.

"Don't tell me," Kenner said, as they got out of the car. "The best motel in town."

"Best and only," Katherine answered, smiling. "Chilton doesn't get a lot of tourist trade."

I'll bet, Kenner thought, hauling his suitcase out of the trunk and following Katherine up the steps to the office. A dough-faced middle-aged woman, her hair in a dark net, sat behind the desk reading a folded-over newspaper (HIS YEAR, MAYOR PREDICTS). She stood up and smiled broadly, as if at old friends dropping by. "Welcome to Chilton Lake Lodge," she said. "You name it, we have it. Air-conditioning? Have it in every cabin. Color TV? Every cabin. And we have a heated pool and courtesy coffee, which is on account of we don't have a coffee shop. Know what our slogan is? 'You won't want to go home.' My late husband thought it up, but he's passed on, so I run the place. Bertha MacKintosh. You just call me Bertha."

"We just want to use your phone," Kenner said.

"It's a joke," Katherine said. "My father's a joker."

Bertha waved her hand at Kenner. "Is he a salesman? A lot of my guests are salesmen, marketing people. I get to hear all the jokes."

She set the newspaper down and rummaged through a pile of registration forms. NO TAX RAISES T, Kenner read. The other half of the headline. The paper was *The Chilton Republic.* "Any idea how long you'll be staying with us?"

"Why don't we leave it open?" Kenner said. "I may want to spend the rest of my life here. Do you have a special rate for that?"

"That's a new one," the woman laughed. "We have a weekly rate, though." She finally found a blank form and Kenner started to fill it out. Katherine was making a phone call on the pay phone in a corner of the little office, but she was talking softly and he made a point of not trying to listen. He completed the form and slid it back across the desk.

"Fine," Bertha said. She worked her way through the information Kenner had given, nodding and saying, "George O. Kenner. Fine, that's fine."

"I flunked the last one," Kenner said, and the woman chuckled.

"You're going to be fun to have around, I can tell." She handed Kenner a key. It was attached to an outsize plastic tag with an outsize 10 inscribed on it, and the slogan: *Chilton Lake Lodge—You Won't Want To Go Home.* "It's Cabin Ten. On the left as you go out, Mr. Kenner. Right next to Cabin Nine."

"I'll find it."

Katherine finished on the phone. "David's picking me up in ten minutes," she said. Then they went outside. The morning air seemed humid after the air-conditioned office, and Kenner was already beginning to sweat. Tuesday, he thought. I'll go home Tuesday. I can stand it three more days.

The cabin was two small rooms and a bathroom, Standard Motel, cloned from some tacky original and reproduced across the continent. He knew exactly what to expect and where to find it—air-conditioning unit under the window (he found it and switched it on), courtesy coffee on a shelf in the bathroom, Gideon Bible in the bed-table drawer, and that little harbor snow scene on the wall; how many hotel rooms had he seen that in? Ten? Twenty? Was it snowing in motel cabins from San Diego to Augusta, Maine? He looked for the frayed bedcover and the cigarette burns that were probably Standard Motel design features, built in to provide a little thrill of recognition, make guests feel at home. He couldn't find the frayed threads or the burn marks, but they'd be there somewhere, he'd bet. He pulled off his jacket and lowered himself into a chair. More plastic upholstery. Jesus, home.

"Remember the Excelsior?" he said.

"The Excelsior?" She was standing by the window, her face in shadow, the sun bright in her hair. He wanted suddenly to walk over and take her by the hand, as he'd done when she was a child, and say, "Let's go home, baby. What do you say we go home?"

"In London," he said. "That snobby place you were crazy about. Where you weren't supposed to use the towels."

"Oh, right. That place. I remember."

"That was a great summer, wasn't it? The new wing." He laughed at the memory. "Christ, they were apoloogizing for it. 1746, and it was the new wing."

She smiled. A polite, dutiful smile. I'm trying too hard, Kenner thought. But if I don't try we'll be coughing to break the damned silence, and it'll be worse. It'll be like a couple of actors forgot their lines and never learned how to improvise.

Outside, a gleaming station wagon had drawn up. David Hensel's car, Saturday-shined. Kenner crossed the room and put his arm lightly around Katherine's shoulder. The station wagon's horn sounded twice, quickly.

"We'll be back for you at one," she said. "Is one okay?"

"If you want to."

She looked accusingly at him. "You forgot. David's parents?"

"I didn't forget," he lied. But visiting the Hensels hadn't appealed, so he'd mislaid the memory, and that's how easy it was. He found himself wondering if Katherine had forgotten the Excelsior for the same reason, if her excitement at London had been just an act to spare his feelings.

"You'll like them, Daddy," she said. "They're truly nice people."

He watched her from the window, remaining there until the car was out of sight. Then he sat on the edge of the single bed and absently picked up a thin Chilton telephone directory from the bedside table. Thirty-five white pages and about as many yellow. He began turning the yellow pages. Air-conditioning contractors, attorneys, auto dealers: two of each. Noah's Ark. He turned more pages. Cemeteries, clinics, electric contractors, fish farms, food distributors and packers (Whsle), funeral directors, hospitals: one of each. Then six pages of farmers, two insurance agencies, a pest control specialist, seven physicians, four restaurants, a couple of gas stations, three taverns, a TV rental service, and a Youth Organization. Nothing was listed under "Z." Zero, Kenner thought. The whole town belonged under "Z."

He lay back on the bed, wondering if he should shower first or jog first. It was a habit he'd got into last summer, a way of losing some of the pounds he'd put on in the hospital; now he did it for pleasure. But there was something else he had to do first, something that had priority. He quickly ran his mind back over the morning until he remembered what it was. Professor Stromberg. Ithaca, Kath had said.

He got the number from Information and dialed it. The phone rang for a long time before it was picked up.

Kenner said, "Professor Stromberg?"

A playful sigh came down the line. "I hope this isn't about a rat taking a wrong turn in the maze." She sounded young, attractive. Kenner liked her voice.

"I don't know any rats, Professor."

"Terrific," she said. "That tells me you're not a student."

"Is that what they do? Call about their rats?"

"Among other things. You wouldn't believe some of the things they call about. Which is why I usually leave the phone off the hook weekends." She paused, then said tentatively, "Do I know you?"

"I'm George Kenner. Katherine Kenner's my daughter."

She didn't respond immediately. Kenner was about to elaborate when she said, "Really? Are you really Katherine's father?"

"The blood test was positive," he said.

"I didn't mean that the way it came out. It's just that you kind of caught me off-balance. I was thinking about Katherine not half an hour ago. Then I thought you were somebody else for a minute. Mr. Kenner, did we ever meet at one of those faculty shindigs or somewhere like that?"

"No," he said, suddenly uneasy. "We never met."

"That's what I thought. I guess I have a strong impression of you from Katherine. She talked about you a lot." There was another pause. "Actually, I was thinking of driving up to see her this weekend. I do that from time to time."

"I know," Kenner said. "She told me."

"Did she tell you about the last time? The personality tests?"

"She mentioned it."

"Okay. I think I have the picture now. You're calling to tell me to butt out, right?"

"That isn't why I'm calling," Kenner said. "You think my daughter has a problem, don't you?"

She hesitated. "Without pressing the panic button,

I'd say 'problem' is a little mild, Mr. Kenner. This may sound crazy, but how well do you know Katherine?"

"How well does anybody know anybody?"

"About as well as we know Alpha Centauri," she said. "Look, I know this doesn't concern me. I have to say it, though. I think you should forget whatever quarrel you may have had with Katherine and go up there and see for yourself. Maybe we can talk again after you've done that."

Kenner said, "We can talk right now, Professor."

"Go see her first. Please."

"I saw her fifteen minutes ago. I'm calling from Chilton."

She was silent for a moment. Then she laughed. "I think I just found out how the rat feels when it takes a wrong turn. In future I'm home to students weekends."

"How about fathers?" Kenner asked, liking her, liking the sound of her voice.

"Fathers in particular. Okay, Mr. Kenner. How can I help?"

"Could you start by getting in your car?" he said. "You'll find me at the Lake Lodge. Cabin Ten."

He ran along the shore of the lake. Dead fish lay on the pebbles, swarmed over by clouds of flies, stinking in the oppressive heat. He ran past the frame houses that faced the beach, conscious of faces watching from the shade of porches; then along grassy dunes, outgrowths beyond the pebbles. Gulls circled overhead. And as he ran Kenner thought about the death cycle, a place where effluence poisoned the water, and the water poisoned the fish, which in turn would poison the gulls. He wondered who or what came next in the chain.

Weeds, slivers of shell, flimsy splinters of driftwood snapped beneath his running shoes. The ache had gone from his calves into his thighs, and the dull pain would soon start low in his stomach, then move to his chest and on up to his head. His brain would begin to expand in the heat, threaten to touch bone, but he wouldn't quit. Not yet. You didn't quit until you'd done at least three miles, until you proved your endurance, satisfied your craving for pain. Three miles, three days. Maybe he'd go home Tuesday. Jog. Don't think. Just let the body work.

The wet heat was sucking at him. He moved through the long grass of the dunes and then he stopped, his lungs aching; he was hurting for oxygen. All he wanted was to lie down in the shade somewhere. And then he became conscious of voices coming up through the long grass, whispered voices carried upward to him by the faint breeze that blew the stench of dead fish against his face. Just below him, hidden by the grass stalks, a young man and girl sat side by side. Their faces were turned toward the lake—empty, gloomy, a great stretch of dead water. Kenner realized they hadn't heard him, they were unaware of him standing above them on the slope. It was some mixture of fatigue and curiosity that made him linger.

And then the conversation, fragmented, stifled.

He strained to listen. They were disagreeing over something, that much was clear, only they didn't look at one another when they talked, they just sat staring out toward the water.

". . . a lot of other places . . ." the young man said.

The girl said something back, a phrase Kenner couldn't catch. He watched her pluck a long blade of grass and raise it to her lips.

". . . doesn't have to be here," the young man said.

The girl nodded her head emphatically. "It does," she said.

The young man turned his face now so that Kenner could see the profile clearly. Sharp and clean and troubled. He leaned toward the girl, as if to kiss her cheek, but he didn't. Kenner moved very slightly, conscious of himself standing there, awkwardly trying to tune in a conversation that had nothing to do with him.

But still he didn't leave.

The young man was saying, "After we're married . . . Chilton . . ."

Damn, Kenner thought. Why was it important to listen to this? He tried to catch his breath against the sickly breeze.

"My family is here," the girl said.

Now the young man was shaking his head from side to side. Something to sigh over, Kenner thought. Being a voyeur could be depressing as a pastime.

". . . too . . . not your family . . . marrying," the young man said.

The girl glanced at him. She said nothing.

"There's nothing here for me," the young man said.

Go to it, Kenner thought, smiling suddenly. A kindred spirit.

". . . nothing . . . anywhere else," the girl answered.

The young man moved abruptly, rising to his feet and gazing out across the lake as if that dark, unreflecting surface might solve his problem. Leave her, Kenner thought. Leave her, kid. She has no sense of adventure. She probably thinks a day trip to Syracuse exhausting.

The young man shrugged loosely. "So many . . . to see."

"No," the girl said. "It just doesn't make any sense."

"Why doesn't it?"

"It just doesn't. . . ." And she added something else, something Kenner couldn't hear, but the tone of her voice was obvious. She was happy here. She was contented here. She would marry here and give birth here and die here, as if her whole life was a tent designed to be erected in one spot and never moved, never once moved. The young man stuck his hands in the pockets of his pants. Kenner couldn't take any more of it.

He jogged up through the grass and away from the shoreline, thinking about the kid. My advice to you, sonny, is to cast her off. Haul both anchor and ass out of this place and see what the rest of the globe has to offer. Leave her here and make your exit swift. Now he was moving across a small lakeside park. Barbecue pits. Sun shelters. Trestle tables. He was hurting again. He stood against a tree, struggling for breath. Hell. This air. This lack of air. He sat down, his back to the tree.

Then he heard the music coming from the far side of the park where some kind of marching band was practicing, kids in black and gold uniforms. He wiped sweat from his eyes and watched. There were maybe forty teenage kids marching in an ornate, precise design. Their instruments burned silvery in the sunlight. A squad of drummers followed them and out in front was a blue-uniformed figure twirling and throwing and deftly catching a baton. They're good, Kenner thought. Damn good.

Beyond, a crowd of adults were watching the movements of the band. Sometimes the adults would applaud a specific maneuver, such as the way the column broke, dispersed, then reunified itself, as if its integrity were preordained like that of a chemical chain. Kenner closed his eyes and just listened. It was a catchy tune, the kind you might find yourself humming in the bathtub.

The band moved into a circling pattern and the baton went up and came down a few times while the crowd gave wild applause. Then the music stopped. The kids stayed in line while an older guy spoke to them through a bullhorn, telling them they were still a little sloppy in places but otherwise pretty good. He didn't tell the kids where they'd gone wrong, though, and Christ, how good did they have to be when they already had timing like a quartz watch? "Okay, let's try it again," the trainer said, and Kenner, thinking once is enough, was up, jogging back across the park, more slowly this time, turning to glance briefly at the shoreline where the two lovers, if that was the word, had walked down through the carcasses of fish to the water's edge and were standing slightly apart from each other as if anything closer would be too much of a temptation for them.

Then he was gone from the lakefront down a side street.

He stopped at a lemonade stand run by a teenage boy and a girl about nine years old in a pink Snoopy T-shirt. Both kids were freckled, with reddish hair and straight teeth, like a living TV commercial. A hand-drawn sign said 10 CENTS EACH. Kenner laughed, wiping streaks of sweat from his forehead with the sleeve of his track suit.

"Is there a jingle to go with this?" he asked, pointing to the lemonade pitcher. The kids looked at him. "Okay, you sold me," he said. "I tried to resist, but you guys are way too high-pressure for me." He gazed at the ice in the pitcher and at the inverted Styrofoam cups, and the kids gazed at him.

"Energy," the girl said.

"Shows, huh? You guys take Master Charge?"

"She's only a kid," the boy said as Kenner dug into the pocket of his track suit. He came up with a dime and a couple of nickels, put the coins down on the small wooden stand, and accepted a cup of the lemonade from the little girl. It was weak stuff, but cold and wet: he'd have drunk it if horses had been bathing in it.

"That's too much, Sis," the boy said, taking the dime from the girl's hand and holding it out to Kenner.

Kenner pointed to the sign. "Ten cents each."

"Each cup," the boy said wearily. "It's her stand. I just look out for her."

"Keep it. You saved my life."

The boy shook his head and the girl did the same. Kenner shrugged and took the dime back. "You run an honest business here," he said. "I'll put the word around."

"You don't know anybody," the girl said.

Kenner wiped his lips with the back of his hand and jogged slowly to the street corner. Then, sweating, he stopped and turned to look back. The kids were staring after him as if they had never seen anybody jog before. An alien in a track suit. He raised his hands to his forehead, feeling suddenly dizzy, disoriented by the density of the heat, the cloying humidity.

What had the girl said?

You don't know anybody?

He rubbed his brow. His hand was covered in perspiration. He wanted to wave to the kids before he turned the corner and went out of sight, but he didn't because he had the uneasy feeling that they wouldn't wave back, they would just continue to stare at him like they were doing now. A stranger in town. That's all it was. Don't take candy from folks you don't know. From strangers that don't know you.

Strangers that don't know anybody.

He closed his eyes and fought the dizziness back. When he looked again he saw that the kids were still watching him. He turned and jogged wearily away.

3

DAVID HENSEL's parents lived away from the lake, where Chilton started to rise in a series of narrow streets built round the shoulder of a hill.

They went in the gleaming station wagon, David driving slowly, with exaggerated caution it seemed to Kenner, like some blond second-feature movie hero landing a crippled B-29 in a forest clearing. No sweat. Kenner, in the back seat, studied the boy's movements —minimal, precise, economical—and the back of his head, where the hairline was squared off and the hair, evenly trimmed, glinted whenever the car turned broadside to the sun. It was a back view he could really get to dislike, Kenner thought, the way he already disliked the boy's superclean house and the car. Kenner lit a cigarette, and David Hensel immediately rolled down his window.

"This is the older part of town," Katherine said, without turning.

Kenner grunted.

"They built on the lake," David said, "before they started building closer to the lake."

No shit, Kenner thought. Tell me more. He caught his son-in-law's eyes a moment in the rearview mirror, and they flicked across him quickly, then returned to the road. "You probably find Chilton pretty dull after New York," the boy said.

"It's growing on me already," Kenner said.

"See, I told you it would."

They pulled up outside a frame house indistinguishable from all the others Kenner had seen. It didn't even have a number on the door, and he was reminded of the dream town where sometimes he ran all night, knocking on door after door, looking for Katherine. A plump woman in a cotton print dress came out to meet them. The Hensels pecked at each other and did a lot of smiling, and Kenner stood on the sidewalk and did his share of smiling; at David's mother, her gray hair bunched at the back of her skull; at her husband, in bifocals that made his eyes seem slightly askew, halved where the lenses joined. For some reason Kenner wanted to say, "I liked you as Tab Hunter's mother," or, "Weren't you in *It's a Wonderful Life?*" That was how they struck him.

And he wanted to laugh when Katherine, a word away from the classic line, said, "Mother, this is my father." It was all so stagy, somehow; phony and funny and embarrassing.

Then David's father pumped his hand, saying, "George Kenner. Delighted, delighted," and they were moving up the steps and into the house, all at the same time.

It smelled of disinfectant and furniture polish, fresh pine. Flowers stood in vases, and the vases stood on white cloths, the cloths on lustrous surfaces.

"George," the man said, "May I call you that?"

"Sure," Kenner told him.

"Family," the man said, smiling. "Folks call me Dick."

I've stepped into somebody else's life, Kenner thought. Dumb mistake. As if David had drawn up outside the wrong house after all, and everybody was too polite to comment on the error. Be nice, you bastard, he instructed himself. Get used to it. But he was never going to get used to it. He was always going to feel this way.

"I hope you're hungry," the mother said, then went into the kitchen without waiting for an answer.

Dick Hensel said, "How do you like it here, George?" and worked at the bifocals with a small white rag.

"Nice. It's real nice."

"Isn't it that? We've lived in Chilton all our lives. Folks raise their families here, George. It's a way of life all by itself, and we're mighty proud of it. Hope you'll want to settle here one day."

"Not enough lead in the air," Kenner said. "I like air I can get my teeth into."

Katherine said, "Daddy's making a joke."

"Oh, sure," Dick Hensel said. "I know that. I'm no rube, Kathy, and I'm old enough to have figured out that what suits some don't always suit others." He smiled at Kenner, replacing his glasses carefully. Kenner turned the phrase over in his mind a moment. Crackerbarrel philosophy yet. It was going to be a slow afternoon. He felt for a cigarette, then realized with sudden panic that he'd run out, that the crumpled pack in his shirt pocket was empty and he was trapped in a house full of nonsmokers.

Hensel was still holding the smile, waiting for the powder to flash and freeze him in sepia. "You're in the insurance line, David tells me."

"Right," Kenner said. "Claims investigation."

"Solid. People need insurance all the time, don't they? Isn't seasonal, I mean."

"I don't sell it," Kenner said. "Somebody makes a claim on a policy. I check it out before the company pays. It's supposed to discourage exaggeration."

"Is that a fact?"

"That's the way it works," Kenner said.

"I didn't know that," Hensel said, jerking his head.

Kenner said, "Happens all the time. All the time, Dick." Hensel jerked his head again and it suddenly occurred to Kenner that this could go on for a long time. It intrigued him. The thought of feeding Dick

Hensel meaningless platitudes and having him jerk his head all afternoon was suddenly incredibly funny. "That's about the size of it," he said, thinking: Jesus, doesn't he know what I'm doing? Hensel nodded and Kenner said: "Insurance investigator. That's what the job's called, Dick."

"Sounds like interesting work," Hensel said.

Kenner didn't believe it was happening. How long could they keep this up? It was as if they were playing some kind of esoteric game, some hick form of verbal poker whose object was to bore the other guy into submission. "Nice day," you said, and the other guy said, "Yup, nice day, all right," and then you raised with, "Sure is a damn nice day," and the other bastard beat the crap out of you with, "It's one helluva goddamn nice motherfucking day, you boring sonofabitch."

There was silence now. Hensel seemed to be meditating. Kenner could hear Mrs. Hensel out in the kitchen, calling Katherine. He watched his daughter go out of the room in answer to the summons. David was staring from the window out into the front lawn, as if waiting for somebody to come. And Kenner thought: what the hell is going on here? Something. Something they all know about, didn't have to whisper about but all knew. That was crazy, though. Why should he think there was some conspiracy between his daughter and the Hensels against him?

He looked up and saw that Hensel was watching him. "Like a drink, George?"

"I'd like that," Kenner said. "I could use a cold beer."

"Beer." He glanced at his son, who turned briefly from the window. "We might have some beer somewhere. David?"

The boy went out of the room to look. Kenner found himself staring at a photograph on the mantelpiece, a young man's face beneath glass, surrounded by a tin frame. A tiny wreath, a miniature of the kind you might lay on a grave, was propped against the picture.

"That's Edward," Hensel said. "My other boy. Two years older than David. Killed in the service of his country."

What did you say? Not, "I'm sorry." People didn't really say that in life, did they?

"I'm sorry," he said.

"No need to be. Chilton's only son to lose his life in Vietnam, more a cause for pride and honor than for sorrow. That's how we feel about it."

"That must be a comfortable way of looking at it." He'd meant to say "comforting," but it had come out as "comfortable." What difference? Hensel wouldn't notice. Irony was a language nobody spoke in these parts.

"It is," Hensel said, nodding, and Kenner relaxed. Because now he could get away with anything.

David came back carrying a glass of milk. "Couldn't find any beer," he said, handing the glass to Kenner.

"I thought we had some Genesee Cream," Hensel said to his son.

"I looked, Dad."

"I thought we picked some up at the store the other day. Thursday, would it be?"

"I guess not," the boy said, shaking his head. "I didn't see any."

He's doing it again, Kenner was thinking. They're both doing it. They'll go on discussing the beer until somebody stops them, until somebody holds up his hand like a cop and says, "Okay, that's enough about the beer." There was something weird about the scene. Kenner could imagine them sitting up late on winter nights talking about the missing beer, attributing the blame to this or that member of the family, accusing one another, blaming the state government, the White House, the Commies, the weather, Satan. Satan would carry the can a lot in this house. Maybe *The Chilton Republic* would send a reporter round, and a photographer. HENSEL BEER STILL MISSING—ELEVENTH DAY. He gazed at the milk. He hated milk. Milk was the drink he hated most in the world, and the boy had brought him milk. What they're really doing, he thought, is apologizing to me; clumsily, obliquely *apologizing* for a minor infraction of hospitality. No beer. So sorry. Oh, so sorry.

"Milk is fine," he said. "I like milk."

Then Katherine appeared in the doorway and said, "Food's ready," and Kenner looked at her, thinking: Baby, I'm sorry for you. I'm honest-to-God sorry. And the sorrow was something he didn't want to think about, the sense of loss something he couldn't deal with.

The meal was an ordeal of silences and forced conversations, of unseasoned food and unfathomable glances. The Hensels looked at him and they looked at each other, reading sign, like animals. And Katherine was a part of it. He was the only outsider.

Something wicked began to stir in him. For a while he pushed it down, but it wouldn't give him peace. It nagged him like a bored child. An impulse, feeding on his brain, fattening itself until he couldn't contain it, until it had become a full-grown compulsion, too powerful to oppose. A compulsion to devastate these people and their insipid world, to destroy it.

"Some salad, Mr. Kenner?"

He looked up, uncertain who had spoken.

"Plenty left." It was David's mother, poised over the salad bowl. The others were watching him anxiously, as if salvation, not salad, depended on his answer.

"I'm fine," Kenner said, working the dry wad of food in his mouth. He pointed his fork at his plate. "Very nice."

"Mother taught Kathy to cook," David volunteered. "That's why she's so good." Katherine gave him a pleased but slightly reproving glance.

Kenner said, "My wife taught her to open cans. She never quite got the hang of it, though, did you, Kath?"

"Oh, Daddy."

"A girl needs a mother," Mrs. Hensel said. "A boy needs a man to raise him, but a girl needs a mother."

"You're so right," Kenner said. "Katherine here

was raised by wolves. Her mother's plane crashed in the jungle."

"Daddy, don't," Katherine said. And to the company: "Mother's in Florida."

Mrs. Hensel made a clucking sound. Her husband looked down at his fork, loaded with ketchup-smeared potato. "As long as ye both shall live," he said. "That's an oath taken before God."

Okay, Kenner thought, here we go. He said, "God couldn't make it to our wedding. He was in Korea at the time, cheerleading for our side."

"Do you believe that, George?" Richard Hensel said.

"Do I believe in a partisan God?"

"That your marriage was not blessed by the Lord?"

"My marriage wasn't blessed by a damn thing," Kenner said evenly, "except a Justice of the Peace and a twenty-dollar bill."

He waited for a reaction but nobody screamed, nobody threw pie in his face. Richard Hensel brought the loaded fork to his mouth and sucked off the mashed potato, slapping his jaws. Somebody's knife scraped on a plate.

"Divorce is a fad," David said, then wiped his lips with his napkin. "Marriage'll survive it."

Kenner said, "What else is a fad, David? Gay liberation? Black power? The women's movement? How about night baseball?"

The boy grinned. "I guess night ball's here to stay."

"How long do you give the others?"

David shrugged. "I don't have a crystal ball, sir. I hope that didn't sound rude. What I mean is, nobody can tell the future, can they? History teaches us that the pendulum always swings back."

"I thought that was physics," Kenner said. "Or Edgar Allan Poe." The pendulum always swings back. Christ alive. Katherine had used almost the same phrase earlier, in the car. It gave him an uncomfortable feeling to hear the boy's words in her mouth, yet when he'd accused her of being David's mouthpiece what was it she'd said? "I have my own ideas." Something like that. It wasn't the impression he got. He got the impression the two of them were interchangeable, almost as if they shared one mind, used it alternately, like something out of a folk tale.

David drained his glass of milk. It left a little silky mustache on his upper lip. He's a child, Kenner thought. That's what's wrong with him. He never grew up.

Later, when the meal was over, Richard Hensel turned on the TV and everybody pulled up chairs.

"This is important, George," Hensel said, arranging a chair for Kenner.

Sure it is, Kenner thought. *I Love Lucy* or *Hogan's Heroes*. As long as they didn't ask him to decide which was more important.

But it was a local newscast they wanted to watch, some warning about mosquitoes along the lakeshore and equine encephalitis. Wasn't that a disease horses got?

Hensel whispered in his ear, "Had a case of that here in Chilton a couple of years back. A boy died. Bad business, George, a terrible business."

"The Dumas boy," Mrs. Hensel said. "Joey. He was only seven."

"Eight," David said.

"Eight?" Mrs. Hensel said. "I thought he was seven."

"No, he was eight."

Kenner looked at their faces, their earnest, introverted faces, and he understood that it really mattered to them whether the poor dead kid was seven or eight, it made a difference to their lives. He imagined it would be more important to them to get Joey Dumas's age right than the year in which John F. Kennedy was killed, as if whatever happened beyond the city limits of Chilton were of only some marginal significance, like a star exploding in a distant galaxy. If it didn't happen in Chilton, it wasn't worth a damn. What was it? Some oddly concentrated sense of community imposed by the hardships of long dark winters? That claustrophobia of being boxed-in, snowbound?

David Hensel said, "Equine encephalitis is terrible.

Convulsion. The spaces between the bones in the head bulge. The pain is agonizing. Delirium. Usually followed by coma and death."

Kenner stared at his son-in-law a moment; that flat tone of voice suggested somebody quoting from a textbook of symptoms. Learned by rote, trotted out almost meaninglessly.

"That's what happened to Joey Dumas," Dick Hensel said.

There was a long silence in the room.

They're sharing something, Kenner thought. Something I can't grasp, can't get a hold of.

Like a memory of some old tragedy.

A memory of the Dumas boy.

He shifted uncomfortably in his chair, staring at the TV.

The announcer was still talking about mosquitos and the spraying of pesticides that would have to take place.

"I'm glad they're going to spray," David Hensel said, leaning forward in his chair and concentrating on the picture.

Kenner shut his eyes and listened to the drone of the announcer's voice.

It was almost dark by the time they dropped him back at the motel. David stayed in the car and kept the motor running. Katherine got out with Kenner but kept close to the car, as if afraid to be alone with him. "Sure you won't come over to supper?" she said. Kenner shook his head and she said, "Okay," just a shade too readily, then turned toward the car. "Pick you up tomorrow."

Tomorrow. Wreath-laying on Edward Hensel's grave. Something else Kenner had let himself be talked into. "Kath?" he said as she reached for the handle of the car door. "Take this on faith. There's nothing, nothing I can't get you out of." She frowned and started to say something, but he cut her off. "Police trouble, money trouble, any kind of trouble. This town, your marriage—just say it, baby, and I can get you out."

"But I'm okay," she said, opening the door. "Really I am."

"Sure you are," he said.

She waved. Then the wagon bumped over the forecourt's speedbreak and when it turned and went out of sight she was still waving.

He wasn't ready to face the motel, the dreariness of the room. A drink—maybe a drink was what he needed. It was a long walk to Lombard's Tavern but the night was warm and he told himself he could take a cab back later if he had to. If he could find such a thing as a cab in these empty streets. Only once did he see a car and that soon turned off into a driveway. Nobody was out walking. A slight wind rising from the lake shifted and stirred through the trees, rustling leaves. He turned onto Main Street, thinking: It's eight o'clock on a Saturday night, on Main Street, and I can hear the goddamn leaves rustling. *On Saturday night.* He walked past the row of small storefronts, all of them darkened, all with CLOSED signs in their windows.

A couple of blocks away he could see Lombard's sign, a pale blue glow of neon. He stopped, looking the length of Main, waiting as if for something to happen, something to move, something that would suggest life and not this weird sense he had of pausing inside a vacuum.

Nothing. Saturday night and zip. A zero.

He realized that if he shouted aloud he would hear only the dry echoes of his own voice rushing back at him. And then he was thinking of Katherine again, Katherine saying: *But I'm okay. Really I am.*

Sure you are, he thought. Sure you're okay and I'm okay and so is everything in Chilton okay. Then what the hell is wrong? What is this feeling of something being out of place? You're itching, Kenner, and you just don't know where to scratch.

He moved forward, stopped again.

At first he thought it was the distant sound of the

lake, the motion of water across stones. Then he thought it might be the wind dragging a sheet of newspaper across the empty street. But when he turned his head back the way he had come he saw something indistinct and shadowy and blurry move in a doorway. A mugger, he thought. Here in *Chilton?* That was New York City thinking—here the streets were clean and safe and empty.

Not a mugger.

Somebody. He stood motionless, watching, tensed.

And then a cop car cruised around the corner, passing Kenner slowly, braking, swinging back in a leisurely arc toward him. It stopped at the edge of the sidewalk and Kenner watched the window being rolled down, wondering if maybe he'd broken some hick law, some antiquated statute about loitering without purpose after dark. Maybe they had a curfew in Chilton, something to do with the citizenry being in bed by a certain hour.

The cop was young and had a light scar over one eye. He touched it as he looked at Kenner through the open window.

"Everything okay?" he asked.

"Just dandy," Kenner said. He glanced a moment in the direction of where he'd seen the shadow. Nothing moved now. "Just taking in the nightlife."

The cop watched him silently for a time. He licked his lips and fingered the scar as if it irritated him badly. Then he lowered his hand to his side and said, "You staying long in town?"

Not if I can remedy it, Kenner thought. "Couple of days," he said.

The young cop nodded. "Not much in the way of night life."

"Right," Kenner said. He looked along the sidewalk. This time he caught only the smallest impression of movement, somebody hurrying quickly away around the nearest corner. Damn. Whoever it was, the cop had scared him off.

"It's a nice town," the cop said. "But, like I said, not much in the way of night life."

"Lombard's looks lively," Kenner said, moving away from the car.

"Lombard's is just fine." The cop smiled at Kenner and then rolled up the window, raised his hand in a final casual wave, and the car pulled away from the sidewalk. Kenner watched it disappear along Main, then he went toward the tavern, pausing a moment to look at the neon sign in the window that said: SENTRY BEER. Inside, it was small but not intimate; as if somebody had converted a store into a bar on a whim. A few people sat on stools by the bar and, here and there, couples talked quietly at tables. The barman— about forty, tall, slim-built, with heavy-framed glasses— looked up as Kenner came in, and Kenner waited for it: the small-town suspicion, the sudden silence, the stares that fully clothed people give the naked. He had sensed it in the cop, he had caught it in the cop's question: *You staying long in town?* What did they do around here—did they *smell* a stranger? Did they just take one look at you and know you didn't belong in Chilton?

But the barman was smiling, a big, welcoming smile, and nobody else even looked up. So I'm paranoid, Kenner thought. Maybe there was nothing out of the ordinary in a cop pulling over. Maybe it was all, perfectly natural. Maybe even the shadow scurrying away was nothing. A figment, Kenner, he told himself. Just that and nothing more.

"What can I get you?" the barman said, wiping bar space with a cloth. "Anything except a Jake's Elbow. I make the world's worst."

"I never even heard of a Jake's Elbow," Kenner said. "Give me a beer."

"Coming right up," the barman said, reaching for glasses. "Any brand in particular?"

"It doesn't matter," Kenner said. "What's Sentry? Is that some local brew?"

"You got it. You want to try it?"

Kenner nodded and put a five down on the bar, but

the barman pushed it back. "I'll run you a tab," he said. "Pay me when you leave. This is a trusting town."

"You from Chilton?"

"Me? I'm imported. Been here four years. I was raised in Vermont. You know it?"

Kenner reached for his beer. "How do you like Chilton?"

"It's okay. Nice people, no action. That's Chilton. Fine if you're used to it. You're from the city, though, so to you it's off the map. Right?"

Kenner watched the barman for a time. "How can you tell?"

"Ah," the barman said, looking pleased. "A whole lot of things. First, the way you came in the bar. Like you expected a bunch of red-necks to stare at you. Then the way you said, 'Give me a beer.' A Chilton person would say something like, 'Could I have a . . .'? or 'I'd like a . . .' whatever it is they want. Plus I know my regulars, and you're not one of them. Psychology. Comes with the job."

"Okay," Kenner said. "It figures." He sipped his beer for a moment: it had a faint metallic taste and no body, no bite. It was insipid. He put the glass down, pushed it away, made a face.

The barman laughed. "That bad, huh?"

"Worse," Kenner said. "I need something better than that."

The barman took the glass away, returned with a fresh glass and a bottle of Canadian beer, Molson's Golden Ale. "You'll find this stronger, I think. How long you in town for?"

The same question, Kenner thought. It keeps coming back to that. He said, "When I run into the street to watch the traffic light change I'll know I've been here long enough. Visiting my daughter."

"Maybe I know her. Most people get in here sometime or other."

"Katherine Hensel? Married David Hensel?"

The barman poured the Molson into the glass and

Kenner drank. "Sure. Dick Hensel's boy. Teaches at the school. Nice family. Respectable."

Nice, Kenner thought. Christ, they have a way with words around here.

"They lost a kid in the war," the barman said.

"I know."

"They're kind of quiet. The family. Don't come in here much."

"They drink at home," Kenner said. "Genesee Cream, when they have it."

"Yeah," the barman said. "That'll do it. Losing a kid'll do that to a family."

"I know just what you mean." Kenner slid off the stool, drained his glass, and went through a door marked RESTROOMS. He was in a disinfectant-smelling hallway without light. A cigarette machine stood against one wall, its illuminated selection buttons glowing faintly in the darkness. He groped his way to the Men's room, then came out and stopped at the machine. None of the buttons was for his brand and one said TEST ONLY. What did you test a machine for, for God's sake? Cirrhosis of the lever? He punched the button but nothing happened. He fed in his quarters, selected Chesterfield, then went back to the bar.

The barman was fiddling with a TV at the far end of the room. Kenner noticed that his glass had been refilled from a fresh bottle of Molson in his absence. He sat back on his stool and stared at the TV, which was repeating the newscast he'd seen earlier at the Hensels', the one about equine encephalitis. The barman came back and said, "They're spraying tomorrow. They should've been doing that years ago."

"Big local issue, huh?"

"Every summer. You'd know why if you saw what the disease can do to a kid—"

"Agonizing pain. Convulsions. Coma. Then death." Kenner said.

"You've been reading your stuff," the barman said.

"Something like that." Kenner reached for his glass and drank some of the cold beer. Then the newscast finished, the picture changed, and there was a series of quick random flashes like the numbers you see at the end of a reel of film. Kenner blinked, then saw the marching band he'd heard that same afternoon. They must have been filmed in the park by the lake—same setting, same scenery, same tune. He watched the picture, the precise movements of the band, noticing the adults in the background. Then he looked round the bar, conscious suddenly of how there was silence, as if all the quiet conversations had broken down at exactly the same moment, all the faces turned toward the TV. The tune played out, then there was a fat guy in a loud plaid suit selling used cars. Kenner looked at the barman and said, "It's like the national anthem or something, that tune."

The barman smiled at him. "The high school band means a lot in this town. You'd call it small-town pride, I guess."

Kenner watched the barman top up his glass from the bottle. He drank steadily and slowly for another hour. The barman found friends at the far end of the counter, returning every now and then to freshen Kenner's drink. A good bartender, Kenner thought, he knows by instinct when his customers are ready.

"How many's that?" Kenner asked on one of the barman's visits.

"Six, if you don't count the Sentry," the barman said.

"I don't count the Sentry," Kenner said. "I think I'll have a Jake's Elbow."

The barman looked pleased. "No such animal."

"I don't get it," Kenner said.

"Psychology. I say you can have any drink, but not this one drink you never heard of, right? So what do you think? You think I can fix any drink you ever heard of. Right? Which makes me look pretty good."

"I still don't get it," Kenner said.

The barman smiled. "And if you don't get it when it's explained, that's the time to go home."

*　　*　　*

The wind had gone now and nothing at all moved in the streets, not even the air. It hung thick and hot and unbreathable. Kenner walked slowly, his collar loosened, feeling slightly nauseous. Six beers, he thought. When six beers get to your gut like this you had to be out of practice. But sleep was still a long way off and his head was still clear.

Clear enough to realize he must have taken a wrong turn somewhere, because it occurred to him that the trees were different. Not the houses. They were the same construction-toy frame houses, but the trees were fat and bushy; before, they'd been thin and sparsely leafed. So what had he done? Turned left instead of right? He tried to form a mental picture of Chilton, but the darkness didn't help him. Where then? Where in all these streets that looked alike?

He was considering stopping to ask at one of the houses when he heard the car. It was moving slowly, a couple of streets away, but getting louder, heading his way. He stood still and turned toward the sound and he thought maybe it was the young cop anxious to make sure he got back to the motel safely. He saw its lights first, then, as it swung around the corner, a light-colored station wagon. It slowed, then stopped, a hundred yards from Kenner, and his first thought was: David, it's David's wagon. That was beige. In daylight the car he was looking at could be beige but the driver didn't sound his horn or get out of the car or make any move at all. He just sat there, and Kenner stood there, a hundred yards away, thinking: *What the hell?*

Then Kenner stepped into the road and started walking toward the wagon, holding up his arm in what he hoped would look like a friendly wave, not wanting to call out in case it wasn't David.

The station wagon began to reverse.

"Hey," Kenner called. "Where's Lake Lodge? How do I get there?"

The wagon didn't stop, though. It went backward, gathering speed, until there was no point in going after it. Dumb bastard, Kenner thought. What does he think? I'm a mugger?

He walked on. Soon the houses gave way to woodland, and that had to be wrong. It meant he was going away from the lake. He felt like an idiot, like somebody who'd got himself lost in the parking lot, and more of a damn fool still when he came up against a high brick wall. The roof of a house—not a frame house, but the older brick-built kind—was visible on the other side of the wall. A gravel driveway led around to an entrance, a pair of ornate iron gates, and on one of the gateposts Kenner found a brass shingle that told him where he was: OUR LADY OF HOPE CLINIC, LAKESHORE, CHILTON, N.Y.

He knew where Lakeshore was. He'd driven along it with Katherine that morning. All he had to do was go back the way he had come, maybe a mile, and look out for Maple. The strange thing was he must have passed the corner of First and Maple about twenty minutes ago. Why hadn't he seen the neon on the lodge sign?

He turned and went back through the dark streets and for a while it was like being alone on earth because he didn't see or hear anybody. And then there was another sound, like dead leaves stirring, like something plodding through brittle chips of dry cut grass, and he turned to look—seeing nothing against the darkness of the houses, the blackness of the trees. Seeing nothing, sensing something. Something. He paused, stared through the night, waited.

There's nothing, Kenner. Nothing at all. It was the same as on Main a while back, imagining a shadow moving in and out of a doorway. You can't hold your beer anymore. You're sick in this dense goddamn heat.

He continued to walk. He didn't look back until he reached the motel where the sign wasn't lit, which explained why he hadn't seen it the first time, but the lights were on in the office and in the cabin next to Kenner's, Cabin Nine. A little white Alfa Romeo sports car was parked outside. Sure, it was the tourist season, wasn't it? This was where the dead came on vacation to get away from it all.

He let himself in, made a plastic-tasting cup of the courtesy coffee, then took a cool shower. He felt fresher afterward but there was still an uneasiness in his stomach, like something heavy he'd swallowed and hadn't digested. When he came out of the shower, he sat listlessly on the edge of the bed and waited for the feeling to pass. Then his telephone was ringing and the first thing he thought of was that Katherine was calling, but when he picked up the receiver he heard nothing for a time, nothing but some labored breathing, an asthmatic sound.

"Who is this?" he said.

"I needed that ride," the voice said. "I needed that ride real bad."

The old guy. The sad old guy. Katherine's drunk.

"You were following me, right?" Kenner said.

"I needed that ride," the man said.

"Look, I wish I could have helped, but I'm tired, I don't feel too good, and I recommend maybe a bus—"

"No," the man said.

There was a soft sighing noise and Kenner realized the line was dead suddenly. He put the receiver down. He rubbed his face gently with the palm of his hand and thought: Why pick on me? Christ. Why not get a Trailways timetable and find your own way out, friend? DT's, the shakes, the sad old story. And some lunatic obsession that Kenner could drive him out of Chilton. I don't blame you for wanting out, he thought. It's just that there's got to be an easier way.

He sighed and sat down in the armchair and watched the late show. *Psycho*. It figures—I just come off the telephone with a nut and I get *Psycho*. I just took a shower in a motel room and I get Janet Leigh cringing behind a plastic shower curtain.

Halfway into the movie there was a knock on the door of his cabin. He opened it, somehow expecting it to be the drunk, but it wasn't.

It wasn't the drunk.

He felt an odd tingling sensation. A hot flash, a rush of his blood. A savage pulse at the side of his head.

She was standing in the doorway, a pretty smiling blonde of about thirty-five, wearing a white pantsuit.

"I'm Elaine Stromberg," she said. She held out her hand.

Kenner looked at her. "I dreamed you," he said. "You were in my dream."

4

SHE laughed, then looked closely at him. "You mean it, don't you?"

"I dreamed you. Seriously," he said.

"I should be flattered," she said as she stepped past him into the room.

He closed the door and turned to look at her. She walked across the floor, stopped, swung round, and smiled at him.

"How could I dream you?" he asked. "Is that crazy?" He watched as she wandered around the room, looking at everything, feeling the drapes, stroking the carpet with her toe.

"Do you have clout here or what?" she said. "This is a better room than mine." She looked up at the ceiling. "And you have sprinklers. Want to trade?"

Kenner glanced up at the sprinklers. He knew they were there. He'd seen too many burned-out hotel rooms not to check that his cabin had fire protection. "Don't you have them?"

"I don't even want a sand bucket. Do you suppose they had a fire?"

"Precautionary," Kenner said. "Would you like some coffee?"

She nodded and they sat drinking in silence for a time. How could you dream somebody you never met?

Kenner thought. What kind of sense did that make. You remembered old stories—a guy arriving at a house where he'd never been before and knowing exactly how it was laid out inside, right down to the last stick of furniture. He said, "It's crazy, but how the hell could you have been in my dream?"

Elaine put her coffee down and smiled at him. "Maybe we can discuss your dreams in depth some other time, but right now we have to talk about Katherine. I have to be back for a class Monday morning. So we have exactly one day for this."

Kenner turned off the TV and Elaine pulled a pack of cigarettes from her purse, gave one to Kenner, lit one herself. "Okay," she said, blowing out smoke. "Let's start with why you're in Chilton. Why now?"

"No," he said. "Let's start with the fact that something's wrong. Why don't we find out what?"

She watched him a moment, then said, "Is it okay to ask why you're at the Chilton Hilton? I know Katherine has a guest room. I slept in it once."

"Me, too," he said. "One night. How was it for you?"

She tilted her head thoughtfully. "Comfortable bed, uncomfortable house. The conversation was above my head. Ball scores. But then I'm an outsider. You're family."

"You answered your own question," Kenner said. "I felt like an outsider, too."

"Did you get the feeling they were cutting you out? Switching to a private channel all the time?"

"Exactly."

"How did they take it when you left?"

"They didn't fight me. I kind of intruded on their privacy in the night and I think they saw me. We were all embarrassed and nobody put up any fences to keep me in this morning."

"Okay," she said, and touched her lip. "Tell me what you think is wrong."

"I don't know," Kenner said. He ran his hand through his hair. "Something's changed Kath. I guess it has to be David, but he doesn't seem to fit. A nice kid, a little on the dull side, but pleasant enough. There has to be another dimension to him, something she can see but we can't."

"You'd have accepted a more forceful type, a more domineering kind of man, is that it?"

"Maybe," Kenner said. "But David Hensel doesn't fit the bill. I don't know. It doesn't make sense. She isn't Katherine anymore. That's the bottom line."

Elaine put her cigarette out. "Katherine's version is she matured."

"I don't buy that."

"Nor do I. I've seen a lot more of her than you in the past two years, and I've probed. And Katherine was more mature, more ego-stable in graduate school than she is now. She was what you probably know as an autonomous personality—independent, self-reliant, internalized. Obviously I haven't tested David, but my guess is he'd score pretty low on those traits. He'd need motivation from outside, group identity, authority figures—God, nation, town, school principal. What does all of that suggest to you?"

"A nice dumb kid who'd die for his ball team."

"Can you see him influencing Katherine radically?"

"It ought to be the other way around," Kenner said.

"That's what I thought," Elaine said. "I used to just think she was answering the Call of the Diaper, which is still pretty common. After a couple of years they want to come back to school. But that isn't happening to her. This is more than a phase."

"How much more than a phase?"

She paused for a second. "It's a radical personality change."

"Is she sick or what?"

"Whatever 'sick' means. No, that was the first thing I thought of. You've got to remember, Katherine was one of my favorite students, and professors aren't supposed to play favorites. But nothing abnormal showed up in the M.M.P.I.—that's a test for diagnosing maladjustment. She wouldn't answer all the questions, but enough to show a normal pattern. Only not normal *for Katherine*. She could have gone through a values crisis, I guess, a reaction against your values."

"That's garbage," Kenner said.

"Maybe," she said, smiling. "Your sensitivity zone's pretty large, isn't it? You're angry. The suggestion makes you angry."

"A lot of things do that. You analyzing me makes me pretty angry, Professor."

"Elaine. It's the weekend, remember?"

He raised a hand in apology and grinned. "Okay, okay. I'm George. To everyone except my son-in-law. He calls me 'Mister Kenner.' "

"I'm not an analyst, George. I don't have enough of a clinical background, and even if I did I wouldn't want to work this up into some kind of psychothera-peutic trip. We're here to talk about Katherine, because we both care about what's happened to her, so let's not get sidetracked."

Kenner was quiet for a time. He rose and walked around the room, rubbing the palms of his hands to-gether. He stopped by the window and said, "Want to know something? I think I'm afraid. I think I'm afraid of whatever her problem is. I'm tempted to check out in the morning, go home, forget the whole damn thing."

"But?"

He smiled at her. "I don't operate like that. I guess there's a lot of the cop in me at that." He paused, peered through the window at the darkened parking lot. He said, "Before Kath quit school did she ever say anything about wanting to switch to a different subject?"

"Subject of research or a different discipline?"

"Either. Both." Kenner shrugged.

She shook her head firmly. "The whole point of her being up here was to update my work on those kids. She was about the only grad student I wanted to trust with that project."

"And David Hensel taught most of those kids."

"That's how they met." She squinted at him, half-smiling. "You're getting at something, George. What is it?"

"Did she ever mention ESP to you?"

She laughed aloud. "Oh, God, is that what all this has been leading up to? You are *way* off. I didn't train Katherine to get her involved in that kind of mush, George. How can I explain this? Being a behaviorist is like being a Jesuit. You have a system of belief. You have a world view. It colors just about every opinion you have. Her getting seriously interested in ESP is like the Pope buying Marxism. It's inconceivable."

"Something was getting her interested," Kenner said. "I don't buy that spoon-bending crap either, but she told me on the phone, and it was just around the time David came into the picture. She never mentioned it to you?"

Elaine looked thoughtful. "No, but she was borrowing a lot of periodicals from the department library around then. I remember wondering about it because I couldn't see why she wanted them. But she wasn't reading *Spook Quarterly*. We're talking about *J.E.P.*, *J.M.S.*, regular mental science publications. We don't even *take* the funnies."

"Do regular psychology journals ever have articles on ESP in them?" Kenner said.

"They touch on it occasionally."

"Do you remember if there were any in the batch Kath had?"

"From two *years* ago? There wouldn't even be a *record* of the loans after she returned the books."

"Did she return them?"

"Sure. Look, what are you saying? Is she supposed to have discovered the elixir of life and then burned her notes? Dropouts do it all the time, George. It's a gesture. An update of burning your boats."

"She did that? She burned her notes?"

"I thought you knew that."

"Christ."

"I wouldn't make anything out of it. She probably did it out of spite. I was disappointed and angry when she quit and maybe I was more rough on her than I had any right to be."

Kenner thought for a moment. "Then why did she lie about it? Why did she lie about it this morning? I asked her if she ever made the switch—to ESP—and she lied, Elaine. A damn stupid lie, too. I know what she told me on the phone."

Elaine shrugged. "I wouldn't make too much out of that either. Bright students like Kath go off on tangents, then they forget what yesterday's tangent was."

"She didn't forget. She found something. She found something in that school and it scared the hell out of her. Or why cover up? When did you do your study there?"

"1967. And, no, I didn't find any telepathic six-year-olds or anything else abnormal. Those kids were entirely unexceptional."

Kenner was already thinking out the chronology of it all. 1967: Elaine's study of first-graders; 1976: Katherine's follow-up study of the same kids, now high school sophomores. Today those kids were seniors, still in Chilton.

Somewhere there was a piece that fit between, a piece that connected unexceptional kids, normal results in '67 with whatever results Kath had got nine years later; with whatever made her burn her notes and marry David Hensel and settle in this spooky backwater . . . So what happened in Chilton during those nine years?

David Hensel happened. Somewhere between the two studies David had started teaching at Chilton High. And the reason Katherine found what Elaine hadn't found was that in 1967 it hadn't existed. Whatever it was. Whatever.

"For God's sake," Elaine said, when Kenner told her his thoughts, "what are we supposed to go looking for? Ectoplasm?"

Kenner smiled at her now. "Why not start with dreams? Do you ever have really weird dreams?"

"We're back at that again," she said. She got to her

feet and stared at him for a while, then she added: "Who remembers dreams anyway?"

It was a hot night and he lay naked, loosely covered by a sheet, kept from sleep by noisy air-conditioning and an aching brain. Elaine had returned to her cabin about an hour earlier, a little before one. He'd found himself hoping for some sign that she might want to spend the night with him, hoping for the relief of physical comfort, but the sign hadn't come and now, with his head hurting the way it was, he was glad. The headaches were something he never got used to, and when he had them he couldn't function properly.

He thought about tomorrow instead. Tomorrow Katherine and Mr. Clean would come for him in the Glossmobile, dressed in their Sunday suits, and they'd all drive out to the cemetery to honor Edward Palmer Hensel. Everybody would look sad and proud in equal measure, himself included, because that was how you had to look at the grave of a war hero, even one you'd never met. Afterward . . . He couldn't think about afterward, but it would be about as interesting as hibernation. The Hensels could make the first manned starshot boring. "How is it out there, Dave?" Houston would say, and five years later David Hensel's answer would come back: "Real nice. Kind of like my hometown, only a lot busier." Kenner looked out at the dead, forlorn landscape of the new planet, and it reminded him of Earth. There was a forest nearby, and the patrol was crossing a narrow strip of land muddied by half-tracks. Then, as if zooming in for *NBC News,* he saw the sniper in the tree, drawing his bead. Angle through Charlie's sights now, the head of Edward Palmer Hensel in the cross hairs, and then the sniper's finger very close up, the yellow-white fingernail with its dark-brown crescent of dirt, the nail whitening with pressure on the trigger as the sniper squeezed off his shot, and a cut to Eddie's head exploding, the thought: Nobody can survive a brain shot, nothing more final. Kenner seemed to feel the wetness of his own brains dripping down his back as he lay there.

He must have kicked the sheet off because he began to cool rapidly, and when Katherine knocked on the door he had to wrap the sheet around himself for warmth as well as to cover his nakedness.

She was holding her coat closed at the neck, standing out there in the dark with the station wagon behind her, its motor idling, two figures inside the car.

"I'm not ready," Kenner said. "It isn't tomorrow yet."

Katherine clucked with annoyance. "You don't have time to change now," she said. "They only hold the table five minutes."

"I guess I fell asleep," he heard himself say.

Then they were in the car, driving along Main Street. He knew it by the blue neon sign in Lombard's window and the cop carrying a lidded cup of coffee from Jenny's Diner to his car, parked out front. It didn't feel like the middle of the night, somehow, but it had to be. He hadn't fallen asleep. He wasn't dreaming. Dreams had a different quality from experience; crazy, out-of-sequence things happened in them. Like going out to dinner in the middle of the night with just a sheet wrapped around you. Crazy things like that. He thought of asking Elaine, who shared the back seat with him, if she'd somehow found her way into his dream again, but he didn't seem able to communicate with her. It was as if a screen of glass was between them.

"Where are you taking us?" Elaine asked, and David replied, "I thought the country club. Their food's pretty good, and it won't be too crowded on a Sunday."

That explained it, Kenner thought. It was Sunday evening. He'd slept the day through, that was all. The realization didn't bother him. He hadn't been looking forward to a Chilton Sunday anyway.

They drove up a long hill and parked near a low brick building. Kenner noted the geography of the place—bar to the left of the entrance, restaurant to the right. Kenner had some trouble getting in (the club had some stupid rule about dress), but when that was resolved they were shown to a window table. The waiter seemed very respectful, gave them the best table in the place, though it was hard to see why a window table was so desirable; it was too dark outside to see the golf course and the table was close to an air-conditioning vent with a noisy fan. For some reason that struck Kenner as significant. He couldn't think why.

There was another hassle soon after, over the wines this time, and then *Moon River* was playing softly in the background and Kenner was saying, "The hell it's coincidence," whatever that referred to. It felt as if somebody else was saying it.

Some time must have gone by. Suddenly they were all eating and drinking. He could see the golf course now; it wasn't dark outside anymore. He puzzled over that, asked what time everybody had. "Daddy has a time hang-up," Katherine said, and David said that was the pressure of city living, and if he lived in Chilton he wouldn't have that problem. In a sense David was right. He had no awareness here of the passage of time. Nothing seemed real, not even the present moment, particularly not the present moment. He wasn't aware of what he ate, only of an eating sensation, dry, badly cooked food, and of Katherine eating crab. He didn't trust the crab, wanted her not to eat it; but she was making a big deal out of showing how independent she was, so he didn't force the issue. Hell, it was only a dream, after all. Nothing could happen to her in a dream. "A *dream?*" Katherine said. "Is that supposed to be a reason?"

Then it was out in the open, the fact that it was all a dream, not reality at all. Nobody would admit it, but Kenner knew. "You got your line wrong," he told somebody. Then he told them to come clean, but nobody knew what he was talking about, pretended not to know. So he stood back from himself a while and started observing, testing, testing to find out what was real and now. They were so damned good at it though, so practiced. Okay, he told himself, get tough.

He started getting tough with Katherine, figuring that she was the weak link. He questioned her about her notes, yelled at her to tell him what she'd done with her goddamn notes. Elaine was trying to calm him down and David was protesting, too, but he went on. People at other tables were listening, forks poised as everybody waited to hear where the girl at the window table kept her research notes. At last Kenner got through to her. She gave him a long, tearful look and said they were in a pigskin box. He didn't give a shit about the box. All he wanted was the notes. Before he could tell her that, though, David said, "She burned them. She burned everything. So will you please leave it, Mr. Kenner? Will you, please?"

Time passed. He must have let it drop. Coffee was brought, drunk in silence. Katherine sobbed intermittently, and David touched her as you'd touch a dead bird if you thought it might suddenly flutter back to life in your face. Yet it seemed to calm her. Kenner was aware of himself sitting there, smoking cigarettes and drinking coffee, trying to grasp some idea too incredible to be taken seriously; and aware of himself watching George Kenner from the outside, unable to get into Kenner's head to find out what the impossible, unbelievable thing was. Somebody at a nearby table was saying that sick people ought to stay home instead of coming into public places. He looked at Katherine, saw that she looked pretty sick. Her face was pale, and she had her hand on her forehead. "I'd like to go home now," she was saying. "If nobody minds."

Nobody minded. David drove in slow motion down the hill, stopping once so that Katherine could throw up, then took her directly to the hospital. She was very sick now. Shivering, clammy, faint.

Kenner found the hospital a disquieting, strangely non-urgent place. They waited a long while. Then, when a doctor finally came, he didn't bother to examine Katherine, just nodded and then had her wheeled away on a gurney. Kenner didn't like that. There was something about that he didn't like at all. It surprised him, in fact, that when the doctor told him to go home (he'd be informed how his daughter was), he went. He could always come back, he rationalized. They knew what they were doing. It was only a dream. He rationalized.

That was why he let David drive him back to Lake Lodge.

In his room again, Kenner wrapped the damp, fetal position on the bed to wait for news. He didn't expect to sleep much. The air conditioner was noisy; he was cold and anxious. Yet he must have dozed at least, or when the phone rang it wouldn't have woken him up.

"Mr. Kenner?" David Hensel's voice. "It's bad news, Mr. Kenner."

He found himself kneeling with the phone in his hand, weeping, shivering, his hair soaked with sweat, the damp sheet around his shoulders, his insides threatening to break loose.

Bad dream.

His mouth was dry, his lips and tongue sticky. Sleep did that.

He ran shakily to the bathroom and retched over the toilet bowl. The floors and walls pulsed and spun, so that he had to press his face to the cool, tiled wall to steady the room. A little fluid came up.

When the nausea had passed, he filled the washbasin with cold water and dunked his face in it, thinking: Nothing solid came up. I threw up and there was no undigested food in my stomach.

It was a dream.

But it had felt so real, like an actual, physical experience. So real that even now he couldn't accept that it hadn't happened. Jesus, how did you ever begin to check out a thing like that? What did you do? Did you call your daughter in the middle of the night and say, "Are you dead or did I dream it?" Or did you simply lie waiting for morning to see if she came to take you to the cemetery (Christ, the cemetery)?

Think.

Time. What time is it? He checked his watch. It said three-thirty. An hour since he'd gone to bed, two hours since Elaine had gone back to her cabin. No way it could have happened in an hour.

Elaine. He could go next door and wake Elaine. And say what? "Look, I know it's three in the morning, but did you dream we went to dinner at the country club and then to the hospital?"

God, he didn't even know if it was Sunday morning or Monday morning. It had been Sunday evening in the dream. He crossed to the window and looked out. Elaine's Alfa was still there. But that only proved she hadn't checked out, not that it was Sunday. Maybe she planned to drive back to Ithaca after breakfast.

He was going nuts. One day in Chilton and he was ready for the funny farm.

Then he thought of the night clerk. Almost at the same time he thought of the TV. All-night time checks. And that led him to all-night gas stations, hospitals, cops. God bless insomniac America. You could wake from a nightmare and pick up the phone or flick a switch on the TV and somebody would tell you what reality was.

First he dialed the motel desk. Nobody answered. Lake Lodge probably didn't even have a night clerk, not enough guests to justify one.

He turned on the TV set and got wavy lines and buzzing noises. Angrily, he tried all the channels on the dial. The major networks were showing movies, but reception was bad and he didn't have *TV Guide* to help him identify the day or check the time. A sticker on the set told him 5 was the local channel. He tried that. Station ID and music over, but it was soothing music. He left it playing and went back to the phone.

I'm panicking, he told himself. Like a little kid waking from a nightmare. It was night that did that. It disoriented you, regressed you. Communications shut down for a few hours and suddenly the universe was such a hostile, lonely place you were ready to believe anything. Anything. That a dream wasn't a dream. That someone had turned your watch back, pumped out your stomach. That if you called the hospital they'd lie to you. That you'd seen tomorrow in a dream; part of you had stayed in bed and part of you had experienced tomorrow. Any damn thing your mind threw at you, you'd believe. Sure, that was why the Gestapo and the KGB made their arrests at three A.M. And he'd bet that was when most UFO sightings took place, most conspiracies were dreamed up. And now, for God's sake, did he check what fucking day it was?

He called the hospital. The phone rang twenty-two times, and then a girl's voice drawled, "Chilton Samaritan Hospital."

"Suppose this was an emergency call?" Kenner snarled. "What did you do—finish your sandwich first?"

"What is the nature of the emergency?"

"My daughter," Kenner said. "My daughter was admitted to your hospital this evening. A little while ago. Katherine Kenner. No, that's Hensel, Katherine Hensel. H-E-N-S-E-L. Could you tell me how she is?"

He waited, twisting the cord around his finger, while the girl looked through some papers. He could hear the papers rustling.

"Nobody by that name has been admitted, sir."

Kenner almost wept with relief. "Thank you," he said. "That's okay. That's really very okay. I keep thinking it's Monday."

"Sir?"

"But it's Sunday, right? Early Sunday morning?"

Silence. She thinks I'm a screwball, he thought.

"Yes," the girl said. "It's now Sunday. When was your daughter admitted?"

"It's okay," Kenner said. "Wrong hospital. And I'm real sorry I woke you."

To double-check he called the Chilton police, and they, too, were asleep and slow to answer. But they, too, had Sunday on the calendar and ten after three on the clock.

Dream.

Kenner went to bed and slept.

This time the hymn-singing woke him, and the bells. Chilton Sunday. Bells outside and hymns inside, from Channel 5, which he'd forgotten to turn off.

He silenced the singers and temporarily drowned the bells in the shower, but they were still ringing when he came out, monotonously, maddeningly, shattering thought into fragments. Kenner opened the phone book and turned to the Yellow Pages again, to *Churches—By Denomination.* There were nine of them, serving around ten thousand people, and evenly balanced among the denominations. It explained the bells, anyway. In Chilton religion was still the religion.

He put on slacks and a sports shirt, then went outside. Elaine's car was still there. She didn't answer her door when he knocked, but he walked around to the back of the cabin and heard the shower running. He tapped on the bathroom window.

"Who is it?" she called.

"Tony Perkins," Kenner said. "Mom sent me."

"Now I remember why I locked the door. Give me fifteen minutes, okay?"

Kenner walked over to the motel office, and that was like a replay of yesterday, with Bertha behind her desk reading *The Chilton Republic,* Sunday edition. DEAD HORSE FOUND IN RIVER had squeezed the mayor from the front page. Another job for Chilton's finest, Kenner thought. The Equicide Squad. A stack of *Republics* and a cash box stood on the desk.

"Beautiful morning," Bertha said.

"Nice," Kenner said, feeling in his pocket for a quarter. "Where can I get some breakfast around here on a Sunday, Bertha?"

"Jenny's opens ten sharp on Sundays," she said. "That's on Main Street."

"I'll try not to be late."

He bought a *Republic* and took it back to his cabin. He had nineteen minutes to kill. Sunday Chilton Time, though—two hundred seconds to the minute. Maybe that part of his dream, the lost Sunday, had been nothing but wish fulfillment.

He spread the paper on the bed and began to look through it. Underneath the dead horse item was a photograph of the marching band he'd seen in the park and a protracted interview with its trainer. "We have a good shot at being the best-drilled outfit in the entire area," the trainer was quoted as saying. He turned the page. A smiling bride in need of some bridgework and, in a separate item, the arrival of a new dentist in town. Very neat. Mayor LoBianco was still promising to keep taxes down. On page three the Chilton Samaritan Hospital announced the completion of its new maternity wing. Kenner flipped the remaining pages. More local news. High school sports. Want ads. An advertisement for MAC'S EXXON—FOR THE BEST SERVICE IN TOWN, and a picture of the gas station on Main Street. Up-to-date, too. Kenner recognized the black limo having its windshield shined, the Virginia plates hinting that folks who knew best were prepared to drive five hundred miles for a car wash at Mac's. An item concerning the proposed administration of the encephalitis vaccine to all the kids in Chilton, beginning the next day. And on the same page a single column headed WORLD NEWS, courtesy of a wire service. All you wanted to know about this great spinning globe you were riding reduced to four column inches.

The newspaper made him uneasy with its smugness, its sense of self-containment, as if it were nothing more than a commercial for Chilton—and the rest of the world reduced to the status of a rumor.

He put it down, catching the OBITUARY column on the back page. Somebody called Andy Clutter was dead. There was a photograph of Andy, smiling slightly. Underneath it, less prominently displayed, was another picture.

Kenner closed his eyes a moment.

Only the day before, only yesterday, the face in that picture had been alive; only yesterday that face had been arguing with a girl in the long grass of the dunes, arguing about marriage, about moving away. And now it was dead.

Kenner picked the newspaper up.

John Tobin, twenty-one, the victim of a sudden heart attack. A heart attack, Kenner thought. Twenty-one and the generator fails. The valves explode. Apocalypse. Christ, twenty-one. *John Tobin was engaged to be married to Dominique Lazarek, daughter of the Chilton High School principal. He is survived by . . .*

Kenner, suddenly depressed, put the newspaper down again. Chilton, the last place where you'd expect the stresses and strains that would lead to a coronary eclipse. The very last place. Poor bastard. A whole life to live, then snuffed out in one dark moment.

He opened the door of his cabin and looked out into the sunlight. He had an urge for movement, for action, something that would shake his mind. Something like Elaine Stromberg, maybe. Something filled with life and vitality.

He shut his door and went toward her cabin.

Another Sunday rebel, Elaine was wearing faded jeans and sneakers. Her hair, still damp from the shower, glistened on her shoulders. She was lovely, provocative, but no more than that until she got behind the wheel of the little white sports car, and then she was pure sex. It was like riding a roller coaster, fast and windy, all G-forces on the turns and in the sudden, squealing stops she made. She drove the way Katherine used to drive in Manhattan, but there her style had been unexceptional; in Chilton, Elaine's style was champagne on an empty stomach. Kenner could only shake his head at it, loving it.

"Incredible, isn't it?" Elaine yelled over the wind noise. "Capacity crowds in the churches."

"What do they have?" he shouted back. "Crap games in the vestry?"

Then the slipstream flicked some of her hair into his face. She laughed, but he made no move to brush it away. He could taste strands of it, clean and moist and sweet.

She made a two-wheel turn onto First, and with a fluid wrist shifted down to pass a family wagon creeping funereally to church. The Alfa's exhaust bubbled and Kenner glimpsed slick-haired children in the wagon, their faces pressed white against the back window, and the driver's startled face as they whipped past.

"Don't stop," Kenner shouted. "I want to see if it's true what they say."

"What do they say?"

"They say once you get beyond Chilton city limits you fall off the edge of the world. Want to check it out?"

"Not before breakfast, Christopher."

She pulled into the diner's parking lot and touched the throttle before she cut the motor so that it died with a full-throated sound.

The diner, predictably, was almost empty. Kenner wouldn't have been surprised to find it picketed, REPENT YE chalked on the door. They sat down and ordered from sticky menus, lit cigarettes and drank weak coffee.

Kenner was quiet a moment. Then he said, "Want to hear something really crazy?"

"You're getting to like it here."

"Crazy, not lunatic. A weird dream."

She groaned. "Me again?"

"Not just you. You were in it." She pulled a face and he said, "I guess you don't remember being in it."

"I apologize for my manners," she said. "I was asleep at the time."

"Want me to tell you what you missed."

"Could I stop you? No, go ahead."

"It was only a dream," Kenner said slowly. "I know that. I know it didn't happen, but it was more than that. I experienced it, Elaine. My mind was really there. Does that make any sense to you?"

"Sure," she said. "You're defining dreaming. That's

what it is, mental motion pictures. Your body stays in bed, your mind goes places. What's the weird part?"

"It wasn't like that. When you dream Paris, France, your mind doesn't cross the Atlantic, does it? You imagine Paris, sure, but your mind stays in Chilton, or Ithaca, wherever your head is. I'm talking about being there. I'm talking about a real place at a given time, the Chilton Country Club, tonight. That's where my dream was. I was seeing it last night, but it was happening tonight."

Elaine frowned. "You believe that?"

"I'm telling you what it felt like. That's how it felt."

"George," she said, "the only weird thing about any dream is if the dreamer doesn't recognize it for what it is, dramatized unconscious thinking. It doesn't relate to the external world. It relates to you."

"It bothers me," he said.

"Okay, tell me about it."

While they ate he gave her the outline. He found it easy to recall the events, difficult to communicate the atmosphere, the uncanny sense that he'd been somehow both observer and participant, himself yet not himself, in two different times, but at the same time. And though Elaine listened politely, attentively, Kenner had the feeling she was automatically discounting the dream, concentrating on the dreamer, worrying about his mental state. "Look," he told her, "I'm not claiming I saw the future. I'm just saying it must mean something."

She shrugged. "Dreams do mean something," she said. "Something about you, not about what's going to happen at the country club." She looked at him thoughtfully. "Have you had dreams like this before?"

"A few," he admitted.

"Do you always recall them so clearly?"

"I guess I do."

"That interests me," she said. "Most people forget their dreams within a few minutes of arousal. I do. That's why dream researchers wake their volunteers during REM sleep, while they're actually dreaming. You must have unusual RNA if you can recall your dreams hours later."

"Months," Kenner said. "There's a whole screwy pattern. The dreams are part of it." Elaine was looking expectantly at him, but he didn't want to tell her more. It made him feel weak and vulnerable. Telling her about the headaches and the flashes would be like confessing he was impotent or afraid of the dark. "I don't want to go into that right now," he said.

She smiled at him. "George, you seem pretty well-balanced to me. Trouble starts when well-balanced guys let their reason get overruled."

"I'm trying to keep an open mind," he said. "Look, you see some character walk through a wall. What do you say? 'Did you see what that guy just did?' And when the person you're talking to says, 'What guy?' you think: From now on, two martinis are enough. So how can you ever prove you saw somebody walk through a wall?"

"You can't," Elaine said. "Because it doesn't happen. There's always a preferable rational alternative, and if you can't find one you wait until one comes along. Magic manuals are getting thinner all the time. Science texts are getting fatter."

"What if I dream the Empire State Building will collapse next Tuesday? And what if next Tuesday it collapses?"

"Then I'd look for demolition tools in your apartment," she said. "No intelligent person has believed in precognitive dreaming since Joseph predicted that harvest. But there's such a thing as the self-fulfilling prophecy, which is when some yo-yo who believes in prophecy saws the edges off reality to make it fit. Is that the kind of person you are? Macbeth?

"I thought you weren't an analyst. You interest me. Do you know anything at all about neurochemistry, George?"

Kenner grinned. "I wouldn't know my brain if I saw it in a glass case."

"You surprise me," Elaine said. "Brain chemistry

was a required credit for Katherine. Didn't she ever
tell you what you have in there? It isn't ectoplasm. It's
a chemistry lab, full of test tubes of acetylcholine and
cholinesterase, amines like noradrenaline and serotonin
—they're pretty important in sleep. There's an enzyme
in there called monoamine oxidase, which breaks them
down, and there's an inhibitor we can synthesize that'll
prevent it from working. When we know enough there
won't be any mysteries left. It's all pure chemistry, not
ESP, not telepathy or telekinesis. Those words don't
explain a damn thing. The stuff that makes you function, makes you dream, think, learn, remember;
wouldn't fill that coffee spoon. You couldn't even . . .
Why are you looking at me like that?"

Kenner was suddenly very cold. "I dreamed it," he
said. "All of this. I dreamed this whole goddamn conversation."

5

KATHERINE came along in the station wagon, looking glossy and formal in a tailored gray suit and a wide-brimmed pink hat.

"David already went ahead with his parents," she said, stepping from the car. "They—" She stopped. "What's Elaine's car doing here?"

"I guess that's because Elaine is here," Kenner said.

"You asked her to come, didn't you?"

"Hold on," Kenner said, holding up his hand placatingly. "Don't get uptight. She was going to drive over anyway."

Katherine put her hands on her hips. "Then why didn't she come to the house or call me? She usually calls first. Daddy, I don't want to be worked on. I haven't committed any crime."

"Did you go to church?" he said.

"I went with David. I suppose you're going to nag now."

"You're incredible," Kenner said. "You never used to believe in all of that. God and Resurrection, all of that."

"Well, who do you think created the universe?" she said. "General Motors?"

"Hell, no. The sun would've burned out a day after the warranty expired. Some Jap company, maybe."

79

She said, "I don't find that kind of remark funny, Daddy."

"You used to," he said. "There was a time we'd have spent the rest of the morning guessing what kind of universe we'd have got from Sony or NASA, or General Electric, or Disney. We'd have had fun doing it, too. Do you ever have fun anymore, Kath?"

"We'll be late," she said. "Does Elaine want to come along?"

"She finds graveyards depressing. It's a healthy instinct."

They got in the car. Kenner strapped himself in the passenger seat at a slight angle, so that he could watch Katherine as she drove. She drove slowly, carefully; and for some reason that didn't surprise him at all. It seemed appropriate.

"You drive like David," he said. "You used to drive like you."

"Thank you. He's a very safe driver."

"I didn't mean it as a compliment."

"I didn't suppose for a second, knowing you, that you meant it as a compliment," she said. "But I take it as one. David has an accident-free driving record. Do you?"

"Okay," Kenner said. "Skip it."

They passed a church, disgorging its worshipers. A minister was standing in the doorway, smiling and shaking hands with people. Then, on the right, he saw the facade of the Chilton Samaritan Hospital. It was an elaborate place, constructed out of white brick, with a marble frieze over the entrance, narrow strips of windows.

"Impressive," Kenner said. "Ever been inside?"

"The hospital?" She glanced at him. "No, why?"

"I thought maybe you could tell me what it looks like inside."

"Are you really interested?"

"I guess not," he said.

Then there was silence in the car. He lit a cigarette but she didn't roll the window down, just reached over and pulled the ashtray open for him. He smoked for a time, noticing how Chilton gradually merged with the countryside. With the lake to the west and woods all around it was one hell of an isolated place.

Katherine was turning the car through an iron gateway and into the cemetery. She parked, then said, "You could have put on a tie. You could have done that much." Before he could say anything she was out of the car and walking across the lawn. Kenner shrugged, followed her.

A small group of people was gathered around the grave, standing in dark suits and ties under the hot sun, in the heavy air. Kenner recognized the Hensels, and there were a few other people who could have been friends or relatives of the dead boy.

"Good of you to come, George," Dick Hensel said. Kenner nodded. In the distance a low-flying plane, a Cessna, buzzed over the lakeshore, emitting clouds of spray which settled down through the trees like fog. They're afraid, Kenner thought. The town's afraid of an epidemic, or they wouldn't be spraying on a Sunday. They'd wait. And he wondered why, if equine encephalitis was that much of a problem, the hospital wasn't busier. There had been no signs of activity a few minutes ago when they'd gone past, and there had been no urgency in the switchboard girl's voice last night. But then maybe she'd taken so long to answer the phone precisely because they were so busy. Kenner watched the plane make an arc, glistening in the sun as it returned for another run over the lakeshore. Equine encephalitis. Inflammation of the brain. It mostly affected children and the town was terrified of it. Wouldn't any town be?

He realized that Dick Hensel had taken his hand and was drawing him gently toward the gravestone. Mrs. Hensel was holding the wreath close against her breast, as if reluctant to part with it. But her husband took it carefully from her and knelt with it in front of the stone. Kenner looked down at the inscription:

Edward Palmer Hensel
1950–1972
Died in the Service of his Country
Proudly Remembered

It was hard not to be moved by the tender scene
and the thought of other hometown Sundays, other
graves of kids mourned by their parents. It was an
unnatural kind of grief. Better to shoot yourself, Kenner thought, than to survive your own kid by even a
day. There was nothing here to mistrust. This wasn't
sentimentality. The grief was genuine, and it was prop-
er. He watched Dick Hensel lay the wreath, heard the
wretched, broken sound Mrs. Hensel made as she covered her face with a handkerchief, saw David put his
arm around her. Yet, despite all of it, despite the sym-
pathy he felt and his awareness of their sincerity, and
despite his own shame at the way he'd behaved yesterday at their house, he still had the feeling there was
something wrong with what he was witnessing.

He tried to think about the boy in the grave instead,
the twenty-two-year-old boy in the grave, and he wondered if, after all, General Motors couldn't design a
better universe than this one, if any smart eight-year-
old couldn't, given a set of encyclopedias and a well-
equipped garage.

The group was silent now. Kenner looked at Katherine, seeing how bound up she was in this family's
grief. She seemed to be mourning and missing a brother-
in-law she couldn't have known. He shifted his weight
uneasily, slightly dizzy in the sunlight. And again, he
had that sense of being an intruder. He'd felt it at the
Hensel house and in Katherine's moonlit bedroom; a
feeling of alienation at the deepest level; as if he could
talk to the Hensels but not communicate, eat their food
and witness their ceremonies but only in the role of a
privileged alien. It had been like that in his dream. And
it was like that with Katherine, too. As though she were
some kind of changeling, an insubstantial, holographic

figure; if he reached out to embrace her she might evaporate in his arms.

They were in the car, driving back toward town, when Kenner remembered that there was something he'd wanted to ask Katherine. He'd found some more of the other guy's baggage in his head, a spillage among the chemicals, stuff that shouldn't be there.

He knew a whole lot of new things that nobody had told him. Correction. Things he couldn't remember anyone telling him. The barman in Lombard's, for instance. He'd talked freely, and the Molson's had flowed pretty freely, too. It was possible he'd got what he knew from that source. Possible.

Edward Palmer Hensel, 1950–1972. He'd known that before seeing it on the gravestone.

That the boy was shot in the head by a Vietcong sniper. He knew that, knew it for a fact.

Other things, isolated bits of information. He couldn't think of any examples right now, but he sensed that he had them lodged somewhere in a remote corner of his mind. He hadn't dreamed them. He'd known them independently. They were somehow, impossibly, there.

"What are you thinking about?" Katherine said.

"Your brother-in-law," Kenner said. "I don't remember if anyone told me how he died."

"Eddie?" She looked at him briefly. "He died in Vietnam."

"I know," Kenner said. "How, exactly?"

She was quiet a moment. There seemed to be a faint movement of pain, of despair, even, across her face. She said, "He was shot. In the head."

Kenner was chilled again, all at once, despite the shafts of heat that blew in through the open car windows; as cold as he'd been an hour earlier in Jenny's diner, or, earlier still, in the night. But those had been responses to dreams. This was different. He wasn't responsible for his unconscious mind, didn't guard it against incursions as vigilantly as he guarded his waking, conscious mind. That was where he lived.

"Why?" Katherine asked.

Why? Why did it frighten him? Because it was unexplainable. No doubt Elaine would come up with some nice, safe, scientific explanation, like the one she'd given him for having dreamed their conversation. She'd talk about RNA and neurons and synapses, contextual transfer and reference error, soothingly, the way you explained away ghosts as shadows to a frightened child. A malfunctioning retrieval system was the answer to everything. Sure, Elaine, but convince me. I'm a primitive. I get scared when the moon crosses in front of the sun. When I see lightning strike somebody's house I assume they did something to make the sky spirits mad.

But why was it happening to *him?* Whatever weird thing the Hensels might have going, whatever they might have sucked Katherine into—why was it affecting *him?*

"Why, Daddy?" Katherine said again.

"I just wondered," he told her. "Look, I need a dose of caffeine right now, baby. Can we stop someplace?"

They stopped for coffee at a place called The Lake Shore Grill—all red plastic and muted Muzak, but smelling of freshly brewed coffee and overlooking the lake. The coffee, when it came, was better, too.

Katherine toyed with her spoon and looked down into her cup for a long time before she said anything. Kenner didn't push. It wasn't, he'd decided, the way to handle Katherine. He'd let her determine the pace and direction of their conversation, define their relationship in her own time and way. Harassment hadn't worked. Maybe if he alternated hard and soft approaches. . . . He pulled himself up. He was thinking like a cop again, treating his daughter like a suspect, dammit.

"How long are you thinking of staying?" she said after some time.

"I'm thinking of dying here," he said. "Then some weeks you can come and visit me and put flowers on my grave, and some weeks I'll visit you, and nobody'll notice the difference."

She stared at him in horror. Oh, Christ, he thought, you couldn't resist it, could you, Kenner? The cheap wisecrack. Like a sniper sitting in a tree. The image, relentless, came to him again: the dead, forlorn landscape and the patrol crossing a narrow strip of earth between forests; and the guy in the tree, slowly drawing his bead on Eddie Hensel's head.

"This is so sick, so horribly sick," Katherine was saying, and Kenner, nodding, was attempting to apologize, because she was right and it was time he showered her head on the inside.

"I'm sorry, Kath. Honestly. That was cheap."

"Okay," she said. "Let's just forget it."

"Tuesday. I plan on going home Tuesday."

"Okay," she said again. "Nobody's hurrying you."

He said, "Are you glad I came?"

"To the cemetery?"

"To Chilton. And to the cemetery."

"Of course," she said expressionlessly. "I just wish you'd worn a suit, that's all. People care about how other people look in small communities."

"You should have raised me better," Kenner said, smiling. "You taught me not to care if people don't like the way I dress."

"Well, the Hensels care," she said. "Respect's important to them. And Eddie was important to them." She stared into her cup, picked up her spoon, and chopped idly at the bottom of the cup with it. "He was a really kind person," she said.

"You sound as though you knew him."

"I feel as if I did. They talk about him so much it's like knowing him. Can you understand that?"

"I think so," Kenner said. "They kind of get inside you, don't they?"

She looked up. "That's exactly what it's like. You really do understand."

"Oh, I'm working on it. Don't give up on me."

A waitress was laying places at the next table, setting out knives and forks for the lunch trade. It wouldn't be long before Katherine said something like,

"It's time I was getting back," and then they'd part from each other without having communicated at all. Kenner remembered how they'd shared a shorthand of private jokes and allusions, so that often one word or a single phrase was all it took to encapsulate a feeling, a mood, a situation.

"David was very close to him," Katherine said. "He talks about him a lot."

Kenner could imagine it. Monday: "Eddie was nice." Tuesday: "He was some nice brother, that Eddie." Wednesday—what the hell would he find to say about Eddie on Wednesday? Kenner said, "He'd have been twenty-eight now, wouldn't he? So that makes David twenty-six, right?" She nodded. "When did he start teaching at the high school?"

"David? Year before I came, I think. Why?"

"Why anything?" Kenner said. "I'm practicing the art of conversation. Hey, remember that day on Fire Island when I said allowances were a boring subject? And you said there were no boring subjects, only bored fathers? Remember that? And we spent the whole afternoon trying to talk interestingly about the dullest damn subject we could think of. It was 'The Inside of a Tennis Ball,' remember?"

She said, "Daddy, I don't remember every little thing that ever happened in my life the way you do. In any case, I should be going. I have to cook David's lunch. Then I have dinner to prepare—"

"Screw dinner," he said. "Let me . . ."

"Let you what, Daddy?"

He hesitated. Then he said, "I guess I was going to ask you to let me take you out to dinner. But it just occurred to me David might have other plans. Look, it'd probably be a hassle. Forget it. We'll do it some other time."

"No," she said. "I'll ask David. I'll let you know what he thinks, okay?"

Sure, he thought. Call me as soon as the votes are counted. Go ahead and consult the oracle, examine the entrails, whatever it is he does. And maybe it will be okay to eat out tonight.

As they were going to the car he said, "Psst, little girl. Over here, in the shrubbery." It was the start of an old routine, but she didn't take up her part. She just looked at him. Kenner said, "How does it go after that, Kath? After I say, 'Over here, in the shrubbery.' What do you say?"

"I don't remember all those old gags of yours, Daddy." She seemed to be a long time opening the car door.

"You say, 'What do you want me for, mister?' Remember now?" She was shaking her head. "What's the payoff, Katherine? What do I say then?"

"Is it so important?"

"You bet it's important. It's important to me. So what's the damn line?"

"I don't know. I told you. I don't remember trivia."

"Think about it," Kenner said. "Take all the time you want. I'll stick around for as long as it takes."

Elaine was in the motel office and came out to meet them with a copy of *The Chilton Republic* tucked under her arm. Katherine left the station wagon on the forecourt, an indication that she didn't mean to stay long, but she got out of the car and gave Elaine a weak smile.

"You should have let me know you were coming," she said. "I'd have studied."

"No tests this time," Elaine said. "Just a social visit."

"Really?" she snapped. "Is that *all* it is?"

Elaine glanced at Kenner. "Aren't you overreacting, Katherine?"

"Maybe that's just another of my symptoms," Katherine said. "I do have symptoms, don't I? Of abnormality, I mean."

Elaine said quietly, "Not of psychosis, no."

"No," Katherine said, "of contentment. But I guess that's pretty abnormal these days, being a healthy, contented person. We can cut the analysis short, Elaine. You, too, Daddy. I confess. I'm a contented wife, and in forty weeks from now I intend to be a contented mother. Does that qualify as a psychotic symptom among women now, Elaine?"

Elaine smiled. "If it does, the human race is in trouble. If that's all you want out of life, fine."

"All? Is that how *you* see it, Daddy? As insignificant?"

Kenner wasn't sure how he saw it. There was something bizarre about the scene, and his reaction was too complex to be easily analyzed. He wanted to feel like a father again first before he got into grandfatherhood; and he guessed he'd want a notarized guarantee that there wouldn't be more than ten percent Hensel in the child, and none of that above the neck. "Christ," he said. "Why didn't you tell me before? When I was sitting down."

"We only knew today," she said, pouting. "I'm not actually pregnant. We were waiting for the new maternity wing. Now it's complete we can start our family."

Kenner stared at her. "Let me see if I can get this straight. You were waiting for the new wing to open *before* you had a baby? Is that it?"

"Yes," Katherine said. "Doesn't that make sense to you? Doesn't that make perfectly good sense?"

"It beats the hell out of spontaneity," Kenner said.

Elaine said, "Look, can't we go inside and talk about this? My newspaper's melting."

"I don't want to talk about it anymore," Katherine said.

"Well, can we go inside and not talk about it?"

Katherine turned toward the car. "I have to go home, Daddy," she said. "I'll call you later."

"Sure, baby. If I'm not here leave a message."

Elaine said, "It's okay, Katherine. I don't have to be hit over the head with a dirty diaper. I have to get back to class anyway."

"I'm sorry," Katherine said, looking appealingly at Elaine. "I didn't mean to be rude. It's just that I don't see any point in arguing about it. You're not going to make me change my mind."

Elaine laughed. "That's what I really like about you," she said. "Your perseverance. When you quit you really stick to it."

Touching Kenner's hand in valediction, Katherine got back into the car and started the motor. Through the open window she said, "Good-bye, Elaine. Anytime you want to visit, one friend to another, you'll be welcome. Truly."

When she'd driven off Elaine said, "Now you know how I got to be a psychology professor. It's the subtle way I handle people. God, how can somebody being so *nice* make you so mad?"

"I know," Kenner said. "I blew it, too. I put the thumbscrews on the poor kid because she forgot one of my old gags."

"We shouldn't feel too guilty, actually. She's pretty resilient, and I don't think either of us went very deep." She touched Kenner lightly on the arm. "See you in another two years."

"Hey," Kenner said. "You just chewed Katherine out for quitting."

"Who's quitting? I was fired."

"She didn't hire you." He pointed his finger at her. "You walk, and I'll sue."

Elaine looked hard at him. "Why do you really want me to stay?"

"I'm scared to death," he said. "I asked them out to dinner tonight, and something tells me I'm going to need you."

She shook her head. "I get the impression Katherine wouldn't want me in the party."

Kenner said quietly, "There were four of us in my dream."

"I wondered when that would come up. You're going to re-create it, aren't you?"

"I don't know what I'm going to do yet," he said. "I flunked brain chemistry in third grade, along with astrophysics."

"George, if I believed that, do you think I'd drive back to Ithaca? If Jesus Christ had dreamed the Last

Supper the night before, how many do you suppose would have been at table? In his dream. Thirteen?"

"You tell me."

"He'd have dreamed twelve," she said. "And then he'd have asked Judas Iscariot along to make up a safe number. If you accept precognition you will have to buy predestination along with it. Then what happens to free will?"

Kenner shrugged. "Jesus Christ wouldn't have had that problem in Chilton. I doubt if they even let Jews into the country club."

Later they went to the pool, a utilitarian concrete-lined rectangle full of slightly scummy blue-green water, ringed by notices with MUST and NO picked out in capital letters: proscriptions against swimming outside pool hours, poolside picnics, ball games, floats, immodest swimsuits, and unsupervised children; sun chairs were NOT to be removed and women MUST wear bathing caps.

He watched Elaine dive and swim, then emerge sparkling gold-and-tan where her white swimsuit didn't cover her. Nobody else was in the pool. A few adults and some children sat around in the sun, looking, Kenner thought, as if they were waiting for someone to come out and put up a notice to prove they were right, that the water was prohibited. A fat, tallow-colored guy was sitting on one of the tables. He looked up, caught Kenner's eye and waved. Kenner nodded, then looked away.

Elaine was playing dive-and-fetch with a baby girl. The infant would drop a cabin key into the pool and Elaine would dive for it, then return the key to the child, who would laugh and throw it straight back in. Kenner felt as if he were watching his own family, a close, laughing, communicating family, the kind he'd possessed for the first five or six years of Katherine's life. Elaine was teaching the child to ask for the key, holding the key out of reach until the little mouth formed an approximation of the word, then giving it

back for the little girl to throw into the pool once more.
Elaine was laughing and the child was bright-eyed with
excitement, chuckling and slapping her knees. Kenner
couldn't remember Barbara being that patient with
Katherine, or so gentle. He could have sat there for the
rest of his life, grown old right there in the sun by the
Lake Lodge pool in Chilton, New York.

He'd brought *The Chilton Republic* out to the pool
with him. Now he picked it up and looked through it
again, found and read the maternity-wing item. All it
told him was that the long-awaited wing was finally
completed and would open in a few days. Long-awaited.
That implied that everybody in town must have known
the wing was nearing completion. It made him wonder
why Katherine had waited until now to "start production," as she'd put it. As if she was working to some
strict, unalterable timetable. He closed the paper, and
the dead horse story on the front page caught his eye.
This time he read it.

It had to do with equine encephalitis. The horse had
apparently died of the disease (viral, transmitted by
mosquitoes), and a child, an eight-year-old girl named
Linda Ballinger, was in isolation at Chilton Samaritan
with symptoms of it. The child had complained yesterday of headaches and drowsiness, had vomited and run
a high fever, though according to the hospital it was
still too early to confirm the diagnosis. Meanwhile,
lakefront and riverside residents were urged to keep
their window and door screens closed and to avoid the
lake shore with its high mosquito concentrations.

As he read, Kenner became aware that somebody
was standing over him. He looked up and saw that it
was the fat guy.

"Leon Joyce," the man said, holding his hand out.
Kenner shook it briefly and said his own name. "Cabin
Ten. New York City, right?" Leon Joyce said.

"That's a good trick," Kenner said. "You some kind
of detective?"

Leon Joyce pulled up a chair and sat down, close

enough for Kenner to smell suntan lotion and see it glisten in the creases of the man's body. "Nah," Joyce said. "Saw your license-plate logo."

Kenner pointed to Joyce's body. "Hawaiian Tropic?"

"Body Bronze. Brand-new. Gonna wipe out the market next summer, pal. You'll see. I sell the stuff. We're still doing the trials. What's your line of work?"

"Insurance," Kenner said. "I sell insurance. You a family man?"

"Me? Sure. Four kids— Hey, I know where you're headed. Let's make a deal. I don't sell you suntan oil, you don't sell me insurance. What d'you say?"

"I say you need insurance more than I need a suntan."

Leon Joyce nodded reflectively. "You could be right," he said, rubbing the greasy lotion across his belly and hips. Then he shut his eyes and sat back for a time in silence. Kenner watched Elaine in the pool. She was still playing with the child, the same game with the key repeated over and over.

Leon Joyce said, "You come to Chilton often?"

Kenner shook his head. "First time. I hope the last."

Joyce opened his eyes and sat forward, his flesh hanging over his shorts in folds. "I know what you mean. It's the pits."

"You said it." Kenner listened to the laughter of the child, the sound of water breaking as Elaine dived.

"I don't know what it is about these hick towns," Joyce said. He whistled a few bars of a tune for a time, then he added, "I get the willies. I mean, it's so god-damn quiet and peaceful. It gets to me. I guess I need the city. Any big city'll do."

Kenner watched Elaine surface with the key in her hand. Christ, she looked good. Then Leon Joyce was whistling again. Kenner listened for a while, then he said, "I think you've been here too long already."

"How's that?" Joyce said.

Kenner stood up and began to move toward the edge of the pool. "When you start whistling the high-school-marching-band tune you should know it's time to leave," he said.

"Was I whistling that?" Joyce said. "Nah."

"Take my word for it," Kenner said.

"Guess it must be catchy, huh?"

"Or catching," Kenner said as he bent down to help Elaine out of the pool.

Katherine's call came just as they were going out to lunch. Kenner made phone signs through the open door to Elaine, who was waiting in her car, then said to Katherine, "Okay, what's the decision?"

"David would really like for us to have dinner together."

Kenner felt a sudden tightness in his chest, a fluttering somewhere deep inside, as if he'd drunkenly agreed to fight the champ and now, sober, found that the champ was taking him seriously. "Terrific," he said dully. There was a lengthy pause. He could hear a fly buzzing in the room. "Where can we eat?"

"Well, there are four pretty good restaurants in town," Katherine said. "There's the Lake Shore Grill, where we stopped this morning."

"Nice place," Kenner said. It was the kind of place where if you could taste the food you didn't recommend the ketchup. "But maybe something a little classier."

"How about the country club? David's a member."

"I don't get along with country clubs," Kenner said. "Keep going."

She named the other two restaurants. Both were on the road to Kanga Falls and one was closed Sundays. Kenner said, "The Burger Palace sounds fine."

"You don't like burgers, Daddy."

"It'll do fine. Why don't we use my car for a change? I'll pick you up at the house around eight."

There was another, longer pause. "I guess that'll be okay," she said then. "Daddy, is Elaine still there?"

"She's still here."

"I'm glad," Katherine said. "I was pretty rough on

her, wasn't I? Would it be all right if she came along, too?"

"I don't know, Kath. She's planning on driving back to Ithaca this afternoon."

"Will you ask her? Please."

"I'll ask her," he said tonelessly.

6

LUNCH at Jenny's Diner didn't appeal to Kenner or Elaine. So they bought food and drove out of town to eat it, in a spot that overlooked the lake but was far enough from it to be out of mosquito range. A slight breeze blew off the water, softening the heat a little, and the lake shimmered, silver-gray, cold, like a dead flatfish.

They talked about Katherine at first, but Kenner had the feeling it wasn't Katherine they were talking about; it was him.

"Maybe she needed the security of marriage," Elaine suggested. "How did she take it when your marriage broke up?"

Security, Kenner thought. Nothing so simple: he'd raised her with more love than anybody could ever know, and now there was a black hole where there should have been something shining and substantial, a hole that had sucked Katherine in so deeply there was nothing left of her. "I don't know," he said. "It never seemed to touch her. Our marriage didn't exactly break down. It just eroded away." He was silent for a moment, watching Elaine, seeing her pick up a blade of grass and place it between the palms of her hands and blow against it, creating a thin whistling sound.

"You thought it was love, right?" Elaine said. "But it turned out to be habit. Social cement."

"Cement sticks."

Elaine smiled at him suddenly. "Are you such a hard man to love?"

"I'd like to know the answer to that."

"I don't think you're as hard-boiled as you pretend."

"How would you know?" he said.

"I wouldn't be wasting my time if I thought that." She let the blade of grass fall from her hands. "Don't you think love's a myth anyway? You've got an intimate union that's supposed to depend on some mystical harmony of minds. Separate wills dovetailing. Isn't that a crazy paradox? I mean, the same ego drive that ought to make it *work* might actually make it impossible."

"I'm a simple guy," Kenner said. "I'll settle for sex and affection."

"They shouldn't be too difficult to find."

"You'd think so," he said. "They don't always come in a package, though. And sometimes I meet ladies preoccupied with other things."

She gave him a look of mock coyness. "Such as?"

"A bunch of rats maybe," Kenner said. "I don't know their names."

"A, B, and C," she said, looking down toward the lake. "And for the record, I don't find them the least bit sexy."

"I'm glad. I was thinking of growing whiskers."

Elaine laughed. She leaned forward and hugged her knees, then rested her face against them. "You don't have to do that," she said. "There's no competition. But I still have that class in the morning."

They sat in silence for a time, watching the lake, feeling the breeze blow moisture against their faces. Kenner said, "Morning's the best time of day for a drive in an open car."

She stood up. "Can we talk about that later?" she said.

"Later's the best offer I had since I got here."

* * *

After they'd driven back to Lake Lodge, Kenner put on his track suit and ran again; slowly at first to tune himself, then with gradually increasing speed, quickening his stride to match his excitement.

Now that he had the geography pat, the running was easy. He used shade where he could find it, moving in the shadows beneath trees, conserving his energy, training his body for difficult conditions. He started along the lakefront, but nothing was moving and there was nothing to see. He was there only because some nameless authority had told him not to be, and once he'd satisfied himself that he wasn't missing out on anything interesting he turned east onto Second Street. It was quiet there, too. Crossing Maple, he ran the block to Lombard's Tavern (closed), past a lemonade stand (different territory, different kids); Kenner waved and the kids waved back, but he didn't stop, had his stride now; beyond Main he went another block, past Mac's Exxon (closed), then finally took a left turn and began a long uphill block toward First, through what had to be the riotous end of town, where people were out in the gardens playing with their kids, cutting the grass, having cookouts. Nobody else was running, though, or even walking fast. Some stopped what they were doing to watch the jogger—and to them Kenner called out, "Am I right for Vermont?" Nobody laughed, though.

He planned to complete a two-mile circuit by heading back toward the lake on First, two miles being about the right distance after a meal and on a hot day. When he came at last to the end of the block, there was a tree-lined square and in the square a grandiose gray brick building with cupolas and wooden eaves. City Hall, doubling as police headquarters and courthouse. He'd passed it on the way into town Friday evening. Today three police cruisers were parked out front, two of them flanking a black Lincoln Continental, gleaming from its Mac's Exxon wax job. Mayor's limo, Kenner guessed, wheezing his way across the square. With out-of-state plates? Sure, would a smart mayor live in Chilton? Was Gracie Mansion in Harlem? No. . . . But

Virginia? Okay, okay, so it wasn't the Mayor's limo.
Who gives a damn? He was too exhausted to think
about it. All he wanted to do was sit on that bench in
the middle of the square and learn how to breathe
again.

While he sat there a young cop, his shirt dark with
sweat, came unhurriedly down the steps. He recognized
the cop—the same one who had pulled over to the
sidewalk Saturday night. He looked in Kenner's direction, then walked slowly over to the bench, hitching up
his gunbelt, playing cop.

"Enjoying your stay?" he asked Kenner.

Weary, Kenner made an indeterminate gesture with
his hand.

"Been running in this heat?" the cop said. "You
shouldn't run in this kind of weather."

"It was winter when I started out," Kenner said.

"Funny guy, huh?" The hand, thick and white, went
up to the scar over the eye and the fingertips traced its
ugly outline. A scar like that, Kenner thought. A man
would get self-conscious.

"I'm just kidding," Kenner said.

"Sure," the cop said, and smiled. "In heat like this,
though, you should check your life insurance policy
before you run." He walked over to one of the patrol
cars, climbed in, and backed the car slowly into the
street.

Kenner watched him go. It was easier to breathe
now, but his heart hadn't slowed much, and it seemed
that the sun was heating up, the town growing quieter.
So quiet, in fact, that when Kenner crushed out his
cigarette butt with his running shoe he could almost
hear the tobacco crumbling in the still air. He had the
sensation of being entirely alone on earth, as if everybody else had gone because they knew something Kenner didn't know. Something that hadn't happened yet
but was going to happen. The feeling of hot wax running
down his face made him think it had to be the heat,
melting his brain, making all the chemicals inside
bubble over and run into his eyes, from the inside.

Jesus, he felt crummy. Maybe the cop was right and
he shouldn't jog anymore, not in such heat anyway. He
decided to walk back to the motel.

He walked west on First, very slowly. Ahead of him,
the lake still shimmered, and the road shimmered, heat
rising from it like exhaust fumes, in unbreathable waves.
He crossed Main at the point where it became the
country road going north to the Interstate, and on the
far side of the street, where some buildings provided
shade, a kid was sitting, a kid about nineteen years old,
wearing jeans and a T-shirt that said KEEP ON THE
GRASS. A rolled sleeping bag was on the sidewalk next
to him. He grinned at Kenner, jerked his thumb.

Kenner sat down in the shade next to the kid. It
could have been the shade, or the sight of another
human being, but suddenly he felt a lot better. "I can't
even carry my own weight," he said to the kid. "How
long you been hitching?"

"Two, three hours," the kid said, sweeping his long
hair back from his face. "This a ghost town, or what?"

"Wait till you see it from the south end of a north-
bound truck," Kenner said. "It'll be a great sight."

The kid nodded and lit a homemade cigarette, offered
Kenner the tin box he kept them in.

"Regular tobacco?"

"Are you kidding? I don't travel with grass, man."
Kenner declined the cigarette. The kid said, "You live
in this town?"

"Do I look crazy?"

"I guess not. This place has to be Creation's asshole,
right?"

"Not enough activity," Kenner said, and the kid
laughed. "Where are you heading?"

"Montreal. Thought I'd visit with my sister a while,
check out the scene up there."

"You're about three hours from the border," Kenner
said. "How did you wind up in Chilton?"

"Stupidity. Some guy in a truck gave me a ride,
wanted to drop me off in Syracuse. I said I'd go as far
north as he was going, and this is where I wound up.

End of the line. I guess I really screwed up landing here on a Sunday, though. Nobody's going anyplace." He dropped the butt of his cigarette and crushed it with his hiking boot. "It's a real bummer," he added.

"What happened to the truck you came in?"

"Turned around and went back," the kid said. "Couple of hours ago. I should've hitched a ride back to Syracuse with him. I guess I'll have to crash on a bench and try again—Shit!"

The cruiser with the young cop in it was coming down Main Street, slowing for the intersection but already moving over toward the center of the road. Kenner didn't doubt that he was going to pull in where they were sitting. Neither did the kid. "Forget what I just said, man," he told Kenner. "About crashing on a bench. I'm about to make vagrant status."

"They do that?"

"Some places. Different degrees of heat. One day I'm going to try hitching in a blazer and crew-cut wig."

The cop car pulled over and stopped, and the young cop got out slowly. He walked over to where they were sitting and put his hands on his hips, the way belligerent cops do it in movies. Kenner studied the cop's stance. "Don't tell me. Rod Steiger, *In the Heat of the Night,* right?"

"You're a funny guy," the cop said. To the kid he said, "What's your story?"

The kid said, "Look, I'm just passing through. No sweat. You don't want me in town. I don't want to be here. Okay?"

"Who told you that?"

The kid looked puzzled. "Who told me what?"

"Smartmouth, huh? You want a ride out of town, that it?"

"That's all I want," the kid said. "No hassle."

The cop smiled. "Then how come you're on this side of the street? If you want a ride *out* of town."

"He's waiting for a break in the traffic," Kenner said.

The kid said, "It's shadier this side. I'll cross the street if a car comes by."

"I came by," the cop said. "You didn't cross the street."

"What?" the kid said.

"Why didn't you cross the street when you saw my car? Stick out your thumb? Do whatever you people do?"

"To a cop car?" The kid sounded incredulous.

"Why not? That's if you want to leave town."

"He does," Kenner put it. "How far can you take him?"

"City limits," the cop said. "Maybe further. Let's see some I.D. first, kid."

The kid pulled a wallet from his shirt pocket and gave it to the cop, who looked slowly through its various compartments, felt with his fingers under the lining. "Jerry F. Newstead," he said. "What's the F stand for?"

"Felix," the kid said dully. "It means 'lucky.' "

"What is that, Spanish?"

"No, it's Russian," Kenner said. "He landed from a submarine in the lake."

"Cut it out, will you," the kid told Kenner. "You want to get me jailed?"

"Why?" the cop said. "You do something to be jailed for?"

"Jesus," the kid said desperately. "What are you guys, a team?"

Kenner laughed. "Give the kid a break," he told the cop. "All he wants to do is get to Canada."

"Why do you want to get to Canada?" the cop said.

"I love an inquiring mind," Kenner said. "His sister lives in Canada. He wants to visit his sister. Ergo, he has to get to Canada."

"How come you know so much?" the cop asked. "You two know each other?"

"I read his mind," Kenner said. "Family trick. Maybe that's why Moscow sent him, to find out how it's done. Right, kid?"

"Please," the kid said to Kenner. "Don't say anything more."

"Why don't you want him to say anything more, Jerry? Something you don't want him to tell me?"

"Christ, he's paranoid," Newstead said despairingly.

"I'm what?" the cop said.

"Skip it."

"I'm what?"

"Paranoid."

"What's that? More Spanish?"

"It's a medical term, a psychiatry term. It means you keep thinking there's something wrong when there really isn't."

"Is that so?" the cop said. "You some kind of psychiatrist?"

"Help me out, will you?" Newstead appealed to Kenner.

Kenner spread his hands. "I'm supposed to keep quiet, remember?"

"Who said you're supposed to keep quiet?" drawled the cop.

"He did."

"You take orders from him?"

"You're right, kid. He is paranoid. No, I don't take orders from him. I don't take orders from anybody."

"Is that so?" the cop said. "Listen, everybody takes orders from somebody. That's how the world runs."

"Well, maybe running is bad for the world, too," Kenner said. "And if we're getting into philosophy, why don't we find a bar and talk over a cold beer?"

"We're not getting into anything," the cop said. "You're going wherever you're going and me and Jerry here are going to police headquarters. If he checks out okay I'll take him where he can get a ride."

"How come you're not interested in me?" Kenner asked. "I'm a stranger in town, too. Or is short hair some kind of guarantee of integrity?"

"You tell me," the cop said with a grin. "You're the mind reader."

Kenner said to the kid, "Look, my name is George Kenner. I'm at the Lake Lodge motel. Got that? If you need me for anything, that's where I'll be. Okay?"

"Sure," the kid said. "I understand. Thanks, Mr. Kenner. Lake Lodge. I've got that."

"This is going to sound a little paranoid, too," Kenner said, with a glance at the cop, "but if I wanted to call you in a couple of days, make sure you got to Montreal all right, how would I do it?"

"I know what you mean," the kid said. To the cop he said, "Could I have something out of my wallet, please?"

"What?" the cop said.

"Something to write on," the kid said wearily. "A piece of paper to write on."

"Write what?"

"My sister's phone number. In Montreal." The cop hesitated, then let the kid have his wallet. The kid searched through it until he found a scrap of blue paper torn from an airmail letter. He tore a smaller scrap from it, then said to the cop, "Could I use your pencil?" After a moment's thought the cop gave him a pencil and the kid copied what was on the scrap of letter onto the smaller fragment. Then the cop took the pencil back and copied into his notebook what the kid had written, before returning both little pieces of paper to Newstead, who kept one and handed the other to Kenner.

"Now everybody has one," Kenner said. "Isn't that nice?"

"Let's go," the cop said.

Kenner soaked in the tub for nearly an hour, half dozing in the tepid water while his skin shriveled and the swelling of his brain subsided. Afterward he put on a shirt with a collar, and a necktie, ready for the evening. He was watching auto racing on television when Elaine called room-to-room and asked him over for coffee.

It was the first time he'd been inside her cabin, which was slightly smaller and older-looking than his own, with worn places in the carpet and discolored patches on the walls, but he felt comfortable, perhaps because she occupied it carelessly, filling ashtrays and hanging her jeans over a chair (she was wearing the white pants again); it was warm and cluttered, in contrast to the sterile atmosphere of both Hensel houses.

Elaine handed Kenner his coffee, then removed the jeans from the chair and flung them on the bed so that he could sit down. "This place brings out the slob in me," she said.

Kenner said, "I like slobs."

They lapsed into silence and drank their coffee. A minute or two went by. Then Kenner said, "Okay, what is it you want to talk about?"

"You," she said, putting down her cup. "There's an inconsistency in you that bothers me. I'm still trying to work out why a hardhead like you, somebody as practical as you, could go for that ESP crap."

"We already did this bit."

"So let's do it again, okay? You said something this morning about your dreams being part of some screwy pattern. Remember?" Kenner nodded. She said, "Want to tell me about it now?"

He hesitated. "Okay, I get headaches sometimes."

"Keep going."

"It's going to sound lunatic." He looked at her for encouragement. She smiled. "Sometimes I feel like I'm somebody else," he said. "Like I'm not in control but the other guy is."

Elaine made a steeple of her fingers, touching them to her face like a child in prayer. "You get this when you get the headaches?"

Kenner nodded. "Different degrees, but every time. You can skip the next question. I had all the tests, and my head checks out."

"Physically, maybe. How about psychologically?"

"That's a private pool. The sign says NO SHRINKS."

"Does that include psychology professors?"

"I guess that depends how deep they want to go," Kenner said.

Elaine rubbed her lip. "Why do I have the feeling

Katherine hung up the same sign? I'm wondering if there's a connection."

"There isn't a connection," Kenner said, but even as he said it he knew she was right. He hadn't put the sign up. The other bastard had done that, the one who shared his head. "I don't know," he said. "Maybe there is. Maybe we're both afraid of what you'll find there."

"Start believing that and you'll wind up pouring gasoline over yourself." She reflected for a moment. "How do you know when you're dreaming?"

"What?"

"How do you know you're not dreaming right now?"

The question disturbed Kenner. "Come on," he said uneasily. "What are you trying to do?"

"I'm serious. What tests do you apply? Think about it."

"The quality's different," he said, thinking about it. "There's a logical sequence dreams don't have."

She said, "I know a math professor who solves chess problems in his sleep. You can't get more logical than that."

"I don't know," Kenner said. "Instinct, I guess."

"Isn't that a little untrustworthy? Nothing else?"

"You wake up. When the dream ends you know it was a dream. Most times."

"Okay," Elaine said, nodding. "So what you're saying is there's no way of telling, *in the dream,* that it's a dream. Next time try exercising your imagination, freely. Try dissociating your mind from the dream context. Imagine yourself somewhere else. Work out a math problem. Remember eating breakfast the day before. Reality-test. If you can do that, if you can control your environment, it's real. And as long as you can do that, George, you don't have a problem."

"Tell me that when I'm asleep," he said. "Tell me over dinner."

"You're really worried about this dinner, aren't you?"

"Wouldn't you be?"

"Let me tell you how dream language works, George," she said. "It's like a child's picture book. It can't cope with abstractions so it concretizes. To express a concept like 'dreamer worrying about daughter's mental degeneration' it has to give you a picture of Sigmund Freud talking about introversion, or your daughter's psychology professor discussing brain chemistry. Recognizable symbols. It's textbook."

"What does the textbook say about country clubs?" he asked.

"What do you say about them?"

Kenner snorted. "Show me one Richard Nixon couldn't join and Gandhi could."

"Neat. So you see them as hypocritical, stuffy, aloof, formal places, right? Cold. And you felt cold in your dream. A Freudian would equate that with fear of exposure. Dream interpretation's a heresy in behaviorist circles. All I can offer you is *Reader's Digest*—'How to Interpret Your Dreams' by a Psychologist. You want that?"

"Sure. Why not?"

She laughed. "Okay. I'd say that club symbolized Chilton for you. How does that sound?"

"*Reader's Digest*," Kenner said. "How come I woke up cold?"

"The dream environment's adaptive. Your body temperature falls, you dream Alaska. It can even work the other way round. What else?"

"Kath keeping her notes in a pigskin box. Where did I get that? Why not a folder?"

"Okay, I don't do too well on that," Elaine conceded. "I could have made something out of a binder; you know—in a bind. What does 'pigskin' suggest to you? Free associate."

Kenner associated and got: "Pigskin—football—hamstring—Hamlet—play—football— That doesn't make sense," he said. "I'm not even a fan."

"It means something," she said, spreading her hands. "Let's try another approach. Try 'books' instead of 'box.' Old, leatherbound books. Book burning—heresy —persecution. Do those connotations work for you?"

"The Spanish Inquisition? This doesn't sound like my mind, Elaine. I don't think that way."

"Everybody thinks that way in dreams. Actually, it makes a certain kind of Freudian sense. A psychoanalyst might say you dreamed a witch-hunt. Katherine the Heretic, burning her notes, challenging your values. He'd say you felt guilty for persecuting her, so you transferred the guilt to her by making her die in the dream. No guilt, no Katherine, no problem."

"It stinks," he said.

"I know," she said, and they both laughed.

Neither of them said anything for a while. Elaine lit a cigarette and puffed thoughtfully at it. "Do you happen to remember," she said at last, "what you were thinking about just before you fell asleep?"

"I don't even remember falling asleep. Why?"

"Something you said about the quality of the dream. It's been nagging at me."

"I was thinking about Eddie Hensel," Kenner said. "David's brother. I don't know if that was the last thing but I don't remember anything after that."

"Tell me about it."

Kenner ran his hands through his hair. "It was pretty weird. It was like I could see it happening. Remember that film somebody took in Dallas when Kennedy was shot? Like that. I could see the sniper drawing his bead on the kid, Eddie's head when the bullet hit, all of it, like watching a movie. Only I was still awake. I'd swear to that."

Elaine blew out a stream of smoke and said, "Hypnagogic experience, maybe."

"Is that good or bad?"

"It's an explanation," she said. She touched the back of his hand lightly. "Hypnagogic experience is a feature of threshold consciousness. People get it just as they're going to sleep. It isn't dreaming, more like semiconscious hallucination, and very vivid."

"You think that's what I had?"

She nodded. "I'd put money on it."

Kenner said, "I didn't know Eddie Hensel was shot

in the head, Elaine. I didn't *know* that until this morning. So where did my image come from? Last night."

"Somebody mentioned it, I guess. Does it matter?"

"Nobody mentioned it."

"Okay," she said, "so you can add cryptomnesia to
your problems. That's something we all suffer from occasionally. Writers, songwriters get it a lot, usually in
the middle of the night. Joe Soap writes a great new
song in the night, then in the morning he plays it to
his agent and the agent says, 'Great song, Joe; it's
called *Moon River.*' I once wrote a paper on nuclear
RNA in—"

Kenner didn't let her get any further. "Why *Moon
River?*" he said.

"What?"

"Why that particular song?"

"Any song," she said. "That was just an example."

"They were playing it in my dream," Kenner said.
"Moon River."

"Nobody was playing it in mine. It happened to be
the first song title that came into my head."

"Coincidence, right?"

"If that's the term you use. I'd say it was contingent."

"The hell it's coincidence," Kenner heard himself
say. Only it was as if somebody else had said it.

When, a little after eight o'clock, the Chevy drew
up outside the white frame house on Elm Street, Katherine and David were already waiting on the sidewalk;
the boy in the dark suit and wearing a green tie, Katherine in a long plum-colored dress with a wrap over
her shoulders. Kenner couldn't recall what she'd worn
in his dream, only that she'd seemed cold, had held
her coat collar closed (or had it been the ends of the
wrap?).

"Doesn't look as if we get invited in for cocktails,"
Elaine said as the car came to a stop.

"Maybe the coven's meeting in the house," Kenner
said. "Sunday night, Bible-burning night."

"Okay, interpret your own dreams."

The Hensels got in the back. "Wait long?" Kenner asked.

"Three minutes," David said. "It doesn't matter."

"I'm glad you're taking it so well. Which way do I go?"

The boy gave directions. "They hold the table five minutes," he said. "No hurry."

Automatically, Kenner made his right turn, thinking: Say something. Break the sequence. Remember breakfast. Wake up. Anything.

Jesus, it was happening.

"Take Main, Mr. Kenner," David was saying. "It's the next street. Then it's straight ahead, about two miles out of town."

Kenner tried to concentrate on his driving. A cop car was pulling out from in front of Jenny's Diner, and he had to brake to avoid colliding with it. A little farther on they crossed the intersection where Jerry Newstead had sat hitching earlier, and Kenner tried to think about the kid, almost expected to see him sitting there now; but he wasn't, was probably in a cell on a vagrancy charge, or else halfway to Canada. Check it out in the morning.

Then they passed the hospital and began to climb a long hill. It was the road that went to the cemetery.

"Go on about a mile past the cemetery," Katherine said. "It's right up on the hill."

"What is?" Elaine said, with a troubled glance at Kenner. But he knew the answer before David gave it, knew damn well what was on the hill.

7

"I SHOULD have told you," Katherine said as Kenner squeezed the Chevy between a new Thunderbird and an almost new Cutlass. "David wanted it to be a surprise."

"Our treat," the boy said, grinning. "It's a nice place. Food's good, and it won't be crowded on a Sunday."

Kenner shut off the motor and looked at Elaine, remembering as he did so that he hadn't told her every detail of his dream, hadn't mentioned this particular snatch of conversation. She looked back interrogatively, and he thought: Explain it, Elaine. Explain how I went through this last night.

David got out and held the car door open for Katherine, taking care to protect the Thunderbird's paint with his fingers. Then he started to walk around to Elaine's door. Kenner said quickly, "It's happening, Elaine. Word for goddamn word."

"Take it easy," she said softly. "I can explain it. I'd guess you're experiencing pseudopresentiment. There's nothing new or remarkable about it. Kraepelin described it in the nineteenth century."

"Terrific," Kenner said. "What does it mean?"

"It means you've got your wires crossed. You're backdating perceptual input, relating it to your dream. You're not really recalling the dream at all."

111

"Yeah?" Kenner said, pulling off his tie. "Let's see."

The club was housed in a low brick building, one wall of which was almost all glass. As he went inside Kenner looked to his left, forming a mental picture of the bar an instant before he saw it. The restaurant was to his right, a long, narrow room with about thirty tables, a dozen of them occupied, all of them covered by immaculate white linen cloths. David and Katherine were standing just inside the entrance, talking to a short, dark-haired waiter. Kenner didn't recognize the waiter, but the rest was familiar. Something else was familiar, too. He had to think for a moment to realize what it was. Then it struck him. It was cold in the restaurant, the cold of superefficient air-conditioning; he could hear the fans whining, working hard. He turned to Elaine and said quietly, "It is cold in here."

"Air-conditioning's up high," she said. "It's a warm night."

"You don't sound convinced," Kenner said, but before she could reply the waiter started explaining politely that neckties were required in the club. It was a club rule.

"Where's your tie, Daddy?" Katherine said. "Are you trying to prove something?"

"It doesn't prove anything," Elaine said. "Most clubs have dress rules, George. You may as well put it back on."

"I'm sorry, Mr. Hensel," the waiter was saying earnestly. "I have to enforce the club rules, sir."

And Kenner's head began to ache.

He put his tie on and followed the others to a window table ("Your usual table, Mr. Hensel"), where they seated themselves, as if by prearrangement, into the dream positions: Kenner opposite Elaine, David opposite Katherine. That made sense, though. Natural grouping. Yet it felt unnatural, as if the laws of nature were in suspension, as if solid objects might suddenly liquefy and a dropped fork might fall to the ceiling and stick in the pine cladding there. Crazy, illogical, impossible.

"Nice view, Mr. Kenner," David said.

Kenner looked. It had been dark in the dream, night outside the window. Now he saw a scene from the lid of a candy box: the club's golf course and part of the parking lot with the sun setting over them, layers of gold and green, window glass in the parked cars gilded, reflecting hundreds of clubhouses. A couple of figures, almost black against the skyline, were playing a late round in the distance.

But if it had been dark in the dream, how had he known the window overlooked the golf course? Then he remembered that it had grown light outside while they were eating. Time had been important for some reason, because he'd asked about the time, worried about time.

"What time is it?" he said.

"Half past eight," Elaine said, staring at him questioningly. "Is it important, George?"

"I like to know what time it is," Kenner said. "Right, Kath?"

Katherine, absorbed in the menu, said without looking up, "Daddy has this time hang-up."

And David Hensel said, "Pressure of city living, Mr. Kenner. You wouldn't have that problem here in Chilton."

He tried to dissociate himself from the restaurant, tried to imagine himself somewhere else; but there seemed to be something wrong with his concentration. As soon as he managed to shut out the country club it was replaced in his mind by the hospital, a place of long corridors and unlit rooms he wasn't supposed to enter. He ran from room to room, searching, knowing the answer was in one of them; running, running out of time, searching. Time was his problem, the future was his problem, and if he concentrated he could see a long way ahead, years ahead. But he also knew that the boy was wrong about the solution to his problem. Chilton wasn't the solution, rather the cause, though he couldn't quite see the connection. He had to con-

centrate, block out the present, their voices discussing
food and the whine of the air conditioner; if only he
could hear clearly what David was telling him from a
long way off. He could hear Elaine, just hear Elaine,
urgent, anxious, telling him to go deeper, to use dream
language, puns, symbols, to find a private code and
get below it, where it couldn't reach him. "Try, George,"
she was urging, but how could you in the crawlspace
between present and future, reality and dream, consciousness and unconsciousness? How could you think
at all where the moment froze and the mind froze and
all externals fused? Nothing was possible except passivity. You could only lie still and powerless while
events washed over your mind at will, printed themselves on your brain. . . .

"Are you feeling all right?"

"Mr. Kenner?"

It seemed that he came back a long way, like a diver
surfacing from the ocean floor; he could feel the pressure changes inside his head. He was in the restaurant
again, but no time had passed, apparently. Katherine
was still looking at the menu.

Elaine was looking intently at Kenner, her expression a compound of concern and disquiet. "You're
white," she said. "What happened?"

"Dizzy spell. I'd better lay off the jogging."

"Maybe he's just hungry," David said. "They do a
really good veal roast here. I'm having that. How
about you, Kathy?"

"Hmm," Katherine said, sucking her fingernail. "I
think I'll go for the crab."

Kenner stared at her. It had to be some kind of act,
the whole thing some kind of performance they were
putting on for his benefit. Nothing else made sense.
He searched Katherine's face for a sign, a hint of
self-awareness, but she seemed perfectly natural. Then
he glanced across at Elaine, who shook her head very
slightly to indicate puzzlement. What else? Kenner
asked himself. Christ, what else could it be? He'd
dreamed all this, and now it was taking place exactly as

he'd dreamed it. Yet if the dinner was somehow being stage-managed, how could anybody fix a dream?

"Why?" he said aloud. "Why the crab, Kath?"

Katherine frowned. "I like crab," she said.

"Sure you do. But why here? Tonight?"

"What?" Katherine said, looking around for support.

"Why tonight?" Kenner persisted. "What's wrong with the veal? The veal's good here, didn't you hear that?"

"Daddy," Katherine said, "I know what I want. I don't have to order veal just because my husband recommends it."

"She's entitled to make her own choice, sir," David said.

Elaine said, "I was once at a symposium that was decimated by crab. An associate professor from Harvard nearly died."

Katherine's expression turned sulky. "Nobody has to eat it."

"I don't want you to eat it," Kenner said.

"Why?"

"I just don't."

"That isn't good enough."

"Okay, I had a dream about it. I dreamed you ate crab and got sick. So will you indulge me and choose something else? Please?"

"You *dreamed* it? You? Daddy, you're the least superstitious person I ever met."

He attempted a smile. "Maybe I'm getting senile," he said. "Humor me."

"A dream," she said again. "Is that supposed to be a reason?" She exchanged glances with her husband, then shrugged. "I don't want to make a federal case out of it," she said. "Is it all right if I order veal roast? Is that permitted or did you dream veal roast, too?"

"Veal roast is fine. I'll have that myself."

Then Elaine said veal roast was fine with her, too, and Kenner relaxed a little, not knowing what any of it meant, but pleased that they'd all chosen the same dish. It seemed to him that he'd won some kind of victory.

And there was trouble with the wine waiter, a stupid argument over New York Chablis, which Kenner said couldn't be Chablis if it wasn't from France and which the waiter, on his dignity, insisted was Chablis because that was what the growers called it, and they ought to know what they produced. Kenner didn't try to stop himself. The script called for a hassle with the wine waiter, and that was what he'd provide. Why disappoint anybody? "Okay," he said finally, "the hell with it. Bring a French Chablis."

But it seemed the waiter couldn't do that. The club served only New York wines. "You don't say," Kenner told the waiter. "Club rule, huh?"

"I don't make the rules," the waiter said.

"You got your line wrong," Kenner said triumphantly. "Your line is: 'I can't *change* the rules,' not 'I don't make the rules.' Dumb mistake."

The waiter looked appealingly at David, who must have made some gesture that Kenner missed, because the waiter shrugged and went away without saying anything more.

There was an embarrassed silence at the table. "How did I do?" Kenner asked.

"Daddy, why are you behaving like this?"

"I thought this was how I was supposed to behave. Did I make a mistake?"

Elaine said, "Cut it out, George. You're sawing off the edges. You're trying to make it fit."

"Make what fit?" Katherine said, looking from Kenner to Elaine. "What's going on here? I don't understand any of this."

"Me neither," Kenner said. "You understand what's going on here, David?"

"No, sir. Is it some kind of game?"

"That's what I think," Kenner said. "I think it's some kind of game. Only what I haven't figured out is why we're playing it or whose game it is. Anybody want to come clean before it gets out of hand?"

Nobody came clean, though. The boy just sat looking at Kenner. Everybody just sat looking at Kenner.

The food came, and the New York Chablis. Conversation was minimal. David sniffed the veal roast and said, "That smells great, doesn't it?" Then he ate a mouthful and said, "Mm," and Katherine ate some of her veal and said, "Mmm, yes."

"You two should write a good food guide," Kenner said, then tried to remember if he'd said that in the dream, and couldn't.

It was crazy. Elaine was right, he was sawing off the edges to make reality conform to his dream.

He picked at the veal, sipped the raw wine, wondering what the people at the next table were talking about. Him, probably. They were leaning toward each other, speaking in low tones. Why not? he thought. There was a name for it, for people who thought everybody was talking about them, plotting against them. Paranoid schizophrenia. He was schizo, that was all it was. No problem. They had drugs that could clear it up in six months. No sweat.

Then he thought: Okay, a little test. The big scene's coming up, the sequence where I badger Kath about her notes. Suppose I don't play. Suppose I don't say a damn thing about these notes, don't even respond if somebody else brings up the subject. What then? He considered the notion for a moment, decided it was a good test. So good that if, somehow, they made him participate, made him have the conversation about Katherine's notes and the pigskin box (books?), he'd accept that as proof that he'd dreamed the future.

He smiled to himself, waited.

"What are you looking so pleased about, Daddy?" Katherine said.

"Private joke."

David said, "He's not going to tell us, are you, Mr. Kenner?" Then he grinned.

"What might that be, David? What is it I'm not going to tell you?"

David shrugged. "I don't know, sir. I'd have to read your mind to know that, wouldn't I?" He laughed.

"Why don't you?" Kenner said.

"Why don't I what, sir?"

"Read my mind."

The boy caricatured surprise. "Are you serious, Mr. Kenner?"

"Why not? It's a simple question."

David scratched his ear. "Nobody can do that, can they?"

Katherine said, "Will you stop this, please? Daddy has this thing about ESP, David. ESP and dreams. I don't know what else. What do you believe, Daddy?"

"Crazy things," Kenner said. "You really want to go into it?" Elaine was signaling for him to stop, but he didn't want to stop. He had the feeling he was finally about to get somewhere.

Katherine put down her knife and fork. "All right," she said, "let's get it out in the open. What is it you and Elaine think is going on? Once and for all, what do you two think is supposed to have happened to me?"

"Don't involve me," Elaine said, holding up her hand. "I'm keeping out of this."

"Daddy?"

"I don't know what's going on, Kath. I'm waiting for you to tell me."

"Does it have to do with what you think I got into two years ago?"

"It could," he said carefully. "What did you get into two years ago?"

"You seem to think some pretty weird things," she said. "Like that David can read your mind and I'm some kind of ventriloquist's doll. ESP is something you dug up out of your own imagination, Daddy. Elaine will tell you I could never have gotten into that stuff."

Elaine said, "I'd have said so, once. How about all those periodicals you were borrowing just before you quit school?"

Katherine frowned. "What about them?"

"You were sending for a lot of papers that had nothing to do with your research."

"Such as? I didn't read anything that wasn't strictly scientific, strictly orthodox. Whatever you and Daddy are cooking up between you, you're wasting your time. If you want you can check my bibliography. It's all regular psychology. No ESP, nothing weirdo."

"How do we do that?" Kenner said. "How do we check your bibliography?"

"I'd like to see it, too," Elaine said. "Very much."

Katherine looked pensive. She said, "I think I still have it someplace. I don't think I burned that."

Elaine glanced quickly at Kenner. "Why didn't you burn it, Katherine?" she said. "Why not burn that along with your other notes?"

"I don't know. I guess I wanted to see it."

David said, "She doesn't want to go back to school, Professor Stromberg. She sold all her books and she burned all her notes. She's going to be a mother. Right, honey?"

"Why did you want me to see your bibliography, Katherine?" Elaine asked softly.

Katherine began to pout, like a child being interrogated about a lost glove. "I don't know," she said. "I'm not even sure I still have it. I probably don't have it anymore."

"You're upsetting her," David said. "Can we please drop it now? She's through with psychology, aren't you, Kathy?"

She nodded.

"Why drop it now?" Kenner said. "We haven't come to the part about the old books yet. The ones she burned."

"She sold her books, Mr. Kenner. I told you."

"Old books, with leather bindings. Remember those, Kath?"

"I don't know what you're talking about," Katherine said. But she looked agitated, looked at Kenner as if she knew precisely what he was talking about. "I never burned a book in my life."

"Katherine, did you keep any of your notes in a box?" Elaine asked.

"What? What is everybody talking about?"

"A pigskin box," Kenner said. "Is that where your bibliography is? In a pigskin box?"

"A pigskin box?" She looked at David, touched her hand to her forehead. "I'm sorry," she said, "but I have a headache. Would anybody mind if we went home now?"

It had all been there, but with differences; subtle differences, few exact correspondences. He concentrated on that, detached himself from what was happening by concentrating on the little, subtle changes, kept his mind from wandering ahead.

Fact—nothing *had* to be the way it was in the dream.

Similar; uncannily, disturbingly similar, but not exactly the same. So it didn't have to end the same way.

They were in the car now, driving fast down the long hill into Chilton. I'm driving, Kenner thought. David isn't driving. I'm driving fast, he drove slow—difference. And we didn't stay for coffee. That's another difference.

So it didn't have to be the way it was in the dream. It could be altered. *He* could alter it.

"Will you please stop the car, Mr. Kenner? I think Kathy's going to throw up."

Kenner pulled over and cut the motor. Then he got out of the car and helped Katherine to climb out. The night was warm and still, but she was shivering violently and was clammy to the touch. Kenner supported her head while she vomited, and afterward put his arm around her shoulders and walked her a few yards into the darkness. Behind them mosquitoes swam in the headlight beams, as if the car was spraying them out into the night. Elaine's door opened. She came around the front of the car, through the double spray of insects. "How is she?"

"I'm okay," Katherine said. "It's just a stress reaction. It happens sometimes when I get uptight."

"Sure," Elaine told her. "That's probably what it is. You ought to get back in the car, though. You're shivering."

Katherine nodded and stared unsteadily back, while Elaine gripped Kenner's arm to keep him from following. When Katherine was out of hearing she said, "Did you tell her she got sick in your dream?"

"Christ, no. Why would I do that?"

"I don't know," Elaine said. "There's something odd about the way she suddenly came up with those symptoms."

"My dream's bothering you, isn't it?"

"You know better than that, George. Actually, I think Katherine's closer to the truth than she realizes. It could be a hysterical reaction, but she is sick."

"You think we touched a nerve?"

Elaine sucked her lip contemplatively. "Could be. Let's talk about it later. Right now I want to check out the somatic side."

"Not the hospital," Kenner said. "We're not taking her to the hospital, Elaine?"

"Okay, we can take her to the house and call her own doctor. I just want somebody to take a look at her."

"In my dream it was food poisoning," he said. "It can't be that, can it? We all ate the veal roast, right?"

Kenner thought about the hospital as he drove down the long hill. In the dream he'd left Katherine alone, gone back to the motel. But it didn't have to be like that, he reminded himself. He could wait with her at the hospital, insist if he had to. Then he'd know if anything was going wrong. And hospitals were set up to handle emergencies in a way that some hick general practitioner, dragged from in front of his favorite TV show on a Sunday night, wouldn't be. What if it wasn't hysterical? What if it was physical, some serious physical illness? Time could be an important factor if she was really sick.

He glanced in the rearview mirror, saw that Katherine was resting her head on David's shoulder. It was too dark to tell if her eyes were open.

"How is she back there?"

"Still kind of feverish," David said. "We'd better stop by the hospital, Mr. Kenner."

Katherine mumbled something, but Kenner couldn't make out what it was. Right then, as the Chevy rounded a curve at the bottom of the hill, a low, brightly lit building came into view on the left. Chilton Samaritan Hospital—white brick, he remembered, with a marble frieze over the doorway—a modern, well-equipped hospital, and he was thinking of driving right past it, with his daughter sick in the back of the car. It didn't make any kind of sense. That was modern medicine in there, and he was passing it up in favor of what? Superstition; presentiment. Balancing penicillin against a rabbit's foot talisman. In the most advanced industrial-technological complex in the world he was acting like a guy with a bone through his nose.

He swung the wheel over.

Although Katherine was conscious and able to walk to the entrance lightly supported by Kenner, she babbled like a child, denying she was sick, begging to be taken home, waving her arms about to demonstrate how fit she was. "See? I can move my arms."

There was something about her delirium and the suddenness of it that unnerved Kenner. Yet all he seemed able to do was make soothing sounds and stroke her cheek. He felt powerless, without knowing why. And when Katherine balked at the hospital entrance, tried to turn back, pleaded, promised to be good if he'd take her home, Kenner led her inside with meaningless reassurances. "Nothing bad's going to happen, baby," he promised. "I won't let anything bad happen."

The interior was spacious and bright. Nurses moved briskly around in soap-commercial whites, carrying IV trays, smelling of medication and know-how. Somehow everything was recognizable but nonidentical, like a color remake of an old black-and-white movie. He couldn't pin it down, though. It had to do largely with atmosphere. But if it was no more than the difference between dream and reality, why hadn't he felt the same way in the country club?

They waited on green plastic chairs, Katherine sitting stiffly, her hands in her lap, staring straight ahead. "I'm not in shock," she said quietly when Elaine bent to look into her face. "I know where I am. I know why I'm here."

"Where are you, Katherine?" Elaine asked.

"Hospital. I'm sick."

"They'll make you well, Kathy," David said, patting her hand. Kenner noticed sweat on the boy's forehead, intense concentration on his face. He felt he ought to know what it signified, too, but for some reason he couldn't put it into words. A vital part of himself appeared to be missing, in another place; its absence bothered him, like an empty hand that ought to have been carrying something.

Elaine was touching Katherine gently on the shoulder, speaking softly to her and turning slightly toward Kenner. "Who's that, Katherine?" he heard her ask.

"Daddy. That's Daddy."

"Good," Elaine said. "And who's that on the other chair?"

Katherine seemed to be having difficulty answering. Her lips moved but no sound emerged. Then, without turning her head to look, she said, "That isn't Eddie."

"I'm David, hon," the boy said, with a nervous laugh. "I guess she's thinking of this morning. The wreath-laying."

Kenner leaned forward. "Why Eddie, Kath?"

"Poor Eddie," she said, her eyes filling with tears. "Take me home. I don't want to be dead. I don't want to be like Eddie."

Kenner saw Elaine start, turn sharply, questioningly in his direction. There was bewilderment, disbelief in her face. He knew the feeling, recognized the signs. He felt a strange excitement, too, as if he'd held all his life

to an unpopular theory and was about to be vindicated,
though he couldn't say what the theory was or how its
truth might be established by his daughter babbling
about a dead man she never knew. There was something he had to ask her, a single question that would
clear it up, if he could only think for a moment.

But Elaine was already asking her if she'd dreamed
about Eddie. "Did you dream you were dead, like
Eddie?"

Katherine nodded emphatically, spilling tears onto
her face.

"Tell us about your dream," Elaine prompted. "What
happened in your dream, Katherine?"

She didn't answer. She stared straight ahead and said
nothing.

Elaine stood up and drew Kenner aside. "She needs
psychiatric help, George. I don't think there's anything
physically wrong with her. She's shutting something
out."

"Eddie Hensel," Kenner said. "Eddie's the connection, Elaine. Why did we both dream about Eddie
Hensel?"

"When was he killed?" she said.

"1972. The year Kath started college. It doesn't make
sense."

Elaine rubbed her chin. "A lot of things don't make
sense. She's regressing. I don't understand why she's
regressing." She thought for a few seconds, then
crouched in front of Katherine once more.

"Katherine, what day is it today?"

The answer was a long time coming. "Sunday," she
said faintly.

"Good," Elaine said. "What year is it?"

"Year?"

"How old are you, Katherine?"

Katherine closed her eyes. She seemed agitated.
"Now?"

"That's right, now. How old are you now?"

Another long pause. Then, "Twenty-three. I'm twenty-three now." Now, Kenner thought. When, exactly,

is now? It was suddenly a meaningless monosyllable. He couldn't even recall what month it was. Now was nothing. There was no now.

He put his arm around Katherine, who was sobbing uncontrollably, and pretended she was little again, rocking her protectively while she repeated, "I don't want to be dead, I don't want to be dead," over and over, as if it were a lesson she had to commit to memory. David came and stood by Katherine's chair. He reached out and touched her, tentatively; as if she'd been a dead bird that he feared might suddenly flutter back to life in his face.

Now.

Now the doctor from Kenner's dream was trying to coax Katherine away. He was young—about David Hensel's age—with a pink face and light brown hair. He wore blue-tinted glasses. Same doctor.

Katherine didn't want to go with him. She resisted by clutching at Kenner's shirt, buried her face in his neck.

"Hey, am I that ugly?" the doctor was saying. "Want some candy?"

Now. It was happening now, here, in the hospital, in Chilton. But that wasn't how it felt. He wasn't here, taking part in it. He was someplace else, observing. Not living it. If he spoke nobody would hear him. It wasn't real.

"There's nothing wrong with her," he said. "I didn't let her eat the crab. She's fine."

He could feel Elaine squeezing his arm, hear her telling him to take it easy.

"It's okay," the doctor was saying pleasantly. "I get this all the time. You're on Anxiety Row here."

Katherine was real. Kenner could feel her arms around his neck, gripping him with a strength he didn't know she possessed, her body rigid, trembling, warm. Real. And all he had to do was stand up and carry her out to the car, drive her home, home to Manhattan. He could do that anytime and it would all be over. But it seemed to require too much effort, too much energy. It was like dying of thirst and not having the energy to pour yourself a drink.

"Ten minutes is all it'll take," the doctor was telling him. "See that little door right there?" He pointed along the corridor and Kenner looked, saw the door. "It's through there, okay?"

Elaine saying, "I don't think it's physical. What kind of tests?"

"Blood, couple of others. What is it with you people? Don't you believe I'm a doctor? Look, it'll only take ten minutes. You can wait right here."

And Kenner began pulling at Katherine's fingers, prying her loose, whispering reassurances in her ear. He couldn't help himself.

Half an hour later they still hadn't come back.

8

THE door didn't lead to an examining room; it led to an emergency stairway. Fire instructions were posted on the wall.

"Take it easy," Elaine said, following Kenner through the door. "He probably took her for an EEG or something. We'll find her."

But Kenner knew they wouldn't. Not here, not now. She was in some inaccessible place, dead or as good as dead. He'd known all along that he couldn't alter the future. He could fight it, win a few small victories, maybe, but in the end it made no difference. All you had left, finally, was anger; and the anger consumed you until nothing at all was left.

"George?"

"It's a ritual," Kenner said. "A fucking ritual."

"What? What is?"

He couldn't answer that. But he was certain suddenly that there was a way to beat it, to lick the future, screw up the ritual. He had to keep looking. Determination was a factor. And so was time. The time factor was part of the ritual.

Then he was taking the stairs, two, three at a time, Elaine just managing to keep pace; and after that he was running along a corridor, memorizing the layout as he went so he'd know it again.

It was classic dream stuff: the route through the maze, right turns and wrong turns, right doors, wrong doors, unending corridors, empty rooms, himself searching for Katherine and never finding her. Like his dreams, it was somehow both image and reality: analogue, model, paradigm. It meant something. It had to be interpreted.

A ward. Rows of beds, rows of faces watching television, a hard-faced nurse remonstrating with a fat guy in pajamas. But no Katherine. Wrong door, no reward. Keep going.

He ran on. Elaine, breathless, ran after him, calling for him to slow down.

No way. He had a time factor to beat.

Some of the rooms he passed were locked, empty, dark behind the glass. The new maternity unit was closed, dark. He pressed his face against the window, made out the shapes of complicated electronic machines, monitoring equipment with dials and display screens, something that looked like an old-fashioned dentist's drill, a couch with straps. None of it in use. Nothing connected yet.

"Isn't it a little early to be looking in there, George?" Elaine put her face to the window. "Christ," she said, "where do they get their money from? There's a million dollars' worth of equipment in there."

Kenner was already running on.

Up a floor now, and there was the pathology lab, locked dark. How could they be doing a goddamn blood test if the lab was closed? That was where they did the tests, wasn't it? So why wasn't Kath in there?

Elaine found him staring at the door.

"Why isn't she in there?" Kenner said.

"Why should she be?"

"The tests," Kenner said. "That's where they do the tests."

"On the samples, George. Not on the patients."

But it didn't satisfy him. He just knew he wanted to break the door down and smash everything inside. He even raised his foot and kicked the door a couple of times. It was only a gesture, though. Katherine wasn't in there.

Elaine pulled him gently away, saying, "Where now?"

"ICU," Kenner said. Something was telling him to look in ICU.

"Why the hell would she be in there?"

She won't be, he told himself.

Look anyway.

She won't be there, dammit.

How do you know?

"I just know," he said aloud. "I'm not even sure she's in this hospital."

"What?"

"I don't think this is the right hospital."

"You're not making sense."

He couldn't afford the time to argue.

A little farther on there was another stairway. He went down a floor, then along another identical corridor. And that meant something, too. An absence of landmarks; streets and corridors all looking the same. He felt like Theseus in the labyrinth, Theseus without a ball of string. In his dreams he used dream language as string: puns, private symbols, private codes. You marked your route with words and pictures in a dream. But this wasn't a dream. And in any case you still had the problem of locating your own markers. Right now he had to concentrate on locating Katherine.

This corridor forked. Fire doors to the left led to another wing of the hospital. He went to the right, memorizing the route. Two lefts, and there it was, ahead. There were the cushioned, no-admittance double doors to ICU; beyond was the humming, green-glowing interior veined with blood and saline lines, pulsing electronically, the inner temple of life-support.

He pushed his way in.

All the beds were empty except one, and that had a screen around it. A doctor and a nurse were in attendance. They turned as he came in, startled, wary.

Then the nurse began walking toward him, making pushing gestures with her hands, shooing him out as if he'd been some animal. But he brushed her aside, went on until he got to the bed, pulled the screen away, and looked.

A body, wired to a machine, tubes sticking out from its arm, from its nose, electrodes taped to its chest. The chest rising and falling slowly, almost imperceptibly. Heartbeat traced in pulses on a screen, cartoon images of life, vital signs he didn't know how to interpret.

Not Katherine.

The old drunk who'd asked for a ride. Who'd followed him through the dark.

The poor bastard.

Then the doctor was yelling for the nurse to call security, grabbing at Kenner's clothing to hold on. Bad mistake, Doc. Payoff time.

A couple of leisurely hours went by before Kenner heard Elaine shout for him to stop. "For God's sake, stop it," she was shouting, and trying to pull him away from the doctor, who was pinned against the wall, his face all bloody, repeating over and over, "I swear I don't know where your daughter is."

Kenner didn't want to stop. This was the best part, the part where he got some satisfaction at last, wielded a little power for once. What did that signify, Elaine? That he was a repressed megalomaniac? That he was a sadist? Because it didn't even matter that he was beating up the wrong guy. What Kenner couldn't understand was why the doctor was being so stubborn. What difference could it make if he said where they'd taken Katherine? If she was dead he had a right to claim her body, didn't he? He wasn't asking the bastards to bring her back.

"All I want to know is where she is," Kenner said. "Maybe it won't do me any good to know, but that's what I want. So why not save yourself some pain?"

The bloody lips parted, seemed ready to form words. But before the words came out Kenner was jumped from behind, tackled by a couple of linebackers in hospital whites, held powerless.

Which wasn't how it was supposed to happen.

After that nothing was the way it was supposed to be.

Suddenly the doctor's face wasn't a mess anymore. There was just a slight trickle of blood from a split lip which he dabbed with a handkerchief, shaking his head in mild rebuke as if at a troublesome child. And when he said, "Okay, let him go," the linebackers let Kenner go.

Just like that.

Then Elaine was leading him out of ICU and down the stairway, asking what had got into him, and all Kenner could think of to say was, "I don't know. I honestly don't know."

He was reminded of the comic-strip universe, where there were no consequences, where cause and effect didn't have to interrelate and a character shot full of holes merely leaked water when he drank. He'd just made hamburgers out of a guy's face and there was the guy a few seconds later dabbing at a split lip with a handkerchief and shaking his head.

"Well, you lucked out," Elaine was saying. "I'd have sued you."

"How many times did I hit him, Elaine?" Kenner said.

"You keep score?"

"Come on."

"I don't know. Twice, I think. The orderlies were right outside."

"It took seconds, right? The whole thing was over in seconds?"

She stopped on the stair. "Why, George?"

"Because it felt like a lot longer. Because I think I'm going crazy."

She descended two stairs and opened the door that led back to the waiting area. "Subjective time distortion isn't psychotic," she said. "Holding conversations with a light bulb is psychotic."

"How about acting out dreams?" he said, but Elaine went through the doorway without answering.

Katherine was waiting on the other side, a cartoon Katherine, resurrected; emerging happily, after a fall from a cliff, out of a Katherine-shaped hole in the ground.

Kenner didn't want to question it or puzzle it; it seemed too fragile, reality seemed too tenuous. He went to her and put his arms around her, just wanting to start over, wanting Friday night again, the joy of seeing her after two years. She hugged him back, laughing.

"Are you okay now, Kath? How do you feel?"

"I'm fine," she said. "Doctor Diamond took me to see the new maternity unit."

"Is that where you were?" Elaine said, glancing at Kenner. "In maternity?"

"We didn't go inside," Katherine said. "It isn't officially open yet. We looked in through the window."

"They did some tests," David said. "That's what took so long."

Katherine nodded. "He did an EEG, but the trace was normal. I can go home now."

"Did he show you the trace?" Elaine asked. "What was it—alpha?"

"I didn't have to see it. He said it was normal. I had a stress reaction, that's all."

Kenner said, "You had us worried for a while, Kath. We were wondering if he gave you anything, any treatment."

"Why should he? There's nothing wrong with me." She touched her finger to her head. "You mean because I panicked? I guess I was just being a big baby."

"I told you they'd make her better," David said, standing up. "You did the right thing bringing Kathy here, Mr. Kenner."

Sure I did, Kenner thought. I put two years back on

her life. Katherine's twenty-five, not twenty-three, dummy. She was twenty-three when she first came to Chilton.

"Regression," Elaine said. "Maybe she wants to cut the whole Chilton experience out of her mind. She can do that if she makes herself two years younger. Those two years never happened."

They were in the car, driving back to the motel after dropping Katherine and David at their house. It wasn't eleven o'clock yet, suppertime on Broadway, but too late, according to David Hensel, to ask them in for coffee. Kenner didn't mind that ("Sanka keeps me awake anyway," he'd told David). What he minded was the invitation he did get, minded because it was too much of a damned coincidence, because the boy had casually offered him what he most wanted, tossing it through the open car window like fish to a performing seal. "Why don't you stop by the school tomorrow, Mr. Kenner? We're kind of proud of it. If you don't have anything else to do, that is." Come and see me work, Mr. Kenner. Catch my act, Mr. Kenner. See if you can figure out what's going on, Mr. Kenner.

The way Katherine did? Two years ago?

"That stuff about Eddie Hensel," Kenner said, "about not wanting to be dead like Eddie—how does that tie in with 1976? Eddie died four years before that."

"Who says it ties in? She thinks about death, dreams about Eddie. Eddie died young. David was probably right about that. The wreath-laying could have been on her mind last night. It was certainly on yours, or you wouldn't have been thinking about Eddie Hensel either."

"Something tells me we had the same dream," Kenner said. "Is that common? When two people are close, a lot like each other?"

"There's no good evidence for it. Tell me something. Is death a family preoccupation?"

"Sure," Kenner said. "All my ancestors tried it out."

"Any of them die young? Say, in a hospital?"

Kenner laughed. "Psychology, huh?"

"I like it when you laugh," Elaine said. "Morbid introspection just isn't your style."

"It isn't Katherine's either."

She nodded. "I know. You're very like each other."

He said, "That's why I thought it might be some sympathetic reaction. She stubs her toe, I say 'Ouch.' "

Elaine clicked her tongue. "I'm a scientist," she said. "When a student tells me one of his rats showed anxiety symptoms and then another rat showed exactly the same, I don't say 'Hey, maybe they're buddies.' I say, 'What are the environmental factors in common?' "

"Okay. What are they?"

"The family relationship could be relevant. Or there may be some other factors we haven't identified yet. You're the investigator, George. You investigate. You find it, I'll analyze it."

Kenner swung the Chevy into the forecourt of the Lake Lodge, drove around the back, and parked outside his cabin. Then he shut off the motor, switched off the lights, and sat listening to the ticking of cooling metal for a while. It was pleasant and peaceful. He wanted to sit there and listen to the night sounds a little longer, and then go inside, to bed, maybe with Elaine. He really didn't want to think anymore.

"Something in Chilton," he said eventually. "Affecting both of us. Right?"

"We haven't established that yet. It's a hypothesis."

"Something to do with David, and Eddie, and dreams. We dream the future, and it doesn't work out exactly the way we dreamed it."

"Nobody played *Moon River*," Elaine said. "Katherine didn't eat crab, and she didn't die. Isn't it about time we closed the book on ESP?"

Kenner shook his head. "I came damn close. I got it almost right, didn't I?"

"You made it conform," she said wearily. "You acted it out. I explained that already."

"I changed it," Kenner said. "I changed it by an act of will, Elaine."

"Your own future, sure. You can determine that to some extent by will."

"More," Kenner said. "Much more."

"What?"

"That's the message I'm getting." He turned and looked at her. "I can change the objective further. If my will is strong enough. I can do it."

"You're sounding like Hitler," Elaine said. "Cut it out, George."

"I'm telling you how it feels," he said. "I guess it's a metaphor. Part of me knows it isn't literally true, that it's irrational, but right now, at this moment, that's what I honestly believe."

"I think I'd be happier if you were talking to the light bulb," Elaine said.

"Are you going back tonight?" Kenner asked as they were getting out of the car.

"If I don't," she answered, "you'll think you willed me to stay."

"You believe in that?"

She smiled.

"How about your Monday morning class?"

She closed the car door softly. "I can call and cancel it," she said. "That much future I can manage."

"I told you it was easy."

"Only because I want to," she said. She touched the side of his face.

"Tell me why you want to."

"Out here?"

"Not out here. In my cabin. Tell me in bed."

At first it was urgent, wordless coupling. Clouds obscured the moon, and in the darkness they touched each other for comfort and reassurance. Nothing here to remember or analyze, nothing to question or doubt. No need to think. This was the old, blind ritual; primal, instinctual, unlearned. All he wanted was to bury himself deep for as long as he could, to be mindless, totally dependent, unborn. The old, old seduction. And her body told him: Sure, stay as long as you want, stay forever if you want, where it's warm and you never have to think. He didn't want to argue with that. Not right now.

Then the moon came out from behind the clouds and Elaine propped herself up on her elbows and looked at him. "How was that?" she said.

"They have a word for it in Chilton. Nice."

"That good, huh?"

"Know what I'd like to do now?"

"Tell me."

"Sleep."

"Sleep? Like regular married people?" She laughed quietly. "Why not?"

An image came to him of the moonlit room in the Hensel house, where the old, blind ritual was unpracticed, replaced by something remote and alien that he didn't understand. "Married people watch TV. I'm talking about what lovers do. Put your arm under my neck. Now turn on your side."

"Is this something you dreamed?" she said, doing it.

"This is something I do," he said. "Now go to sleep."

She slept, her breath soft on his shoulder, her hair touching his face. For a while it was calm, untroubled sleep. Then she began to grow restless. She started to mumble, tried to turn away. Kenner put out his hand and touched her face, placed his fingertips on her eyelids. There was tension in her facial muscles, movement under the eyelids, the movement of REM sleep, dream sleep. He wasn't sure if Elaine had told him about it or if he'd read about it someplace, in one of Katherine's textbooks, but he knew what to do. There was a moment of arousal to be judged, a point of optimum recall between REM and non-REM stages. Too early and the recall was incomplete; too late and it was erased altogether. And an abrupt arousal stimulated recall better than a gentle one.

He brought his hands together sharply, jolting her awake with the sound and violence of the movement. She sat up with a little cry, startled, disoriented.

"What was that?"

"I woke you," Kenner said. "You were dreaming."

"Why? Why did you wake up?"

"I'm investigating, remember? What did you dream?"

"You scared the hell out of me."

"What do I need?" Kenner said. "A license?"

"Go to hell."

She reached for the light, groping to find the switch in the darkness. Kenner said, "You have them, too, don't you? Weird dreams, dreams about the future, about Eddie Hensel. What was this one about, Elaine? Tomorrow? Next week?"

She located the light switch and turned it, shielding her eyes from the glare with her other hand. Then she lit two cigarettes from the pack on the bedside table and drew deeply on one, giving the other to Kenner. "I dreamed you were in jail," she said.

"Is this for real?"

She nodded. "I don't know what your crime was, but you were dressed like an Old Testament prophet. Prophesying doom, maybe. Anyway, you must have been a three-time loser. A whole bunch of judges passed the death sentence on you. It was okay, though, because I asked for a retrial and got the sentence commuted to life. Now can I go back to sleep?"

"Is that it?"

Elaine drew hard on the cigarette. Her hand shook slightly. "No," she said. "I tried to help you, but you wouldn't listen. You kept looking up the wrong books in the prison library, the thin books instead of the fat books. Then I tried to help you break jail and wound up in there with you. We were both in there for life."

"Cozy," Kenner said.

"Terrific," she said. "We were in the prison hospital. In the psycho ward."

She crushed out her cigarette in the ashtray.
Then the phone rang.

"Daddy?" Katherine's anxious whisper.

"What is it, Kath? What's wrong?"

"Are you all right, Daddy?"

"I'm fine," Kenner said. "Why shouldn't I be?"

"I had a feeling," she said. "I'm sorry if I woke you. I guess it was silly."

"That's okay. What kind of feeling?"

Pause. Eventually, "I just wanted to check you were all right?"

"Did you have a dream, Kath? Is that it? Did you have a bad dream?"

"Just a feeling," she said. "You're not smoking in bed, are you?"

"What?"

"That's how fires start."

"I know. I know all about how fires start."

"Daddy?"

"I'm still here, baby."

"Wanna buy some insurance?"

"I don't understand," he said.

"I remembered the punch line. That old gag of yours. After I say, 'What do you want me for, mister?' you say, 'Wanna buy some insurance?' Did I get it right?"

"You got it right," Kenner said. "That's how the story ends."

9

WHILE Elaine was in the shower, Kenner went out to
buy breakfast, out to a heavily overcast, humid day
that immediately saturated and depressed him. Driving
as far as Main, he parked, then walked the two blocks
to Jenny's Diner.

In the feeble grayish light, trucks were making deliveries to the stores on Main Street, and garbage was
being collected. The collectors came in immaculate
denim coveralls, the garbage in plastic sacks two-thirds
filled and neatly wired at the neck, spill-proof, secure;
so clean it was being taken away in an open truck. The
days were gone, Kenner thought, when you could study
people by picking over their garbage—if you'd known
how to look, how to interpret what you found. He and
Phil Marlowe and the Golden Age of Garbage-Grub-
bers. But it wasn't only garbage. You could still learn
a lot from other things.

Like the mailman. The mailman was working his
way along the east side of Main, whistling, waving to
people, smiling a lot. Kenner watched the man stop
briefly outside Macnamara's Funeral Home ("Digni-
fied Funerals With Homelike Atmosphere—Serving All
Faiths"), check rapidly through his pile of letters, then
move on. No mail for the funeral home. Low-literacy

zone. Or maybe it was just a healthy town without a mortality problem.

Kenner walked on, past the A&P, which was just opening its doors. He had to wait while a truck pulled out from behind the store and joined the traffic on Main. PASKIN WHOLESALE DISTRIBUTING CO. it said on the side of the truck in red letters. Paskin. The name rang a bell. Paskin. It sounded like an Americanized European name, a shortened form of Paskinsky or Paskinowicz. So what was he thinking of? Paskin's Kosher Deli? Paskin's Bakery? But it wasn't Manhattan he associated it with; it was something more immediate.

Then he caught sight through the store window of a stack of unopened cartons, all marked with the red lettering: PASKIN WHOLESALE DISTRIBUTING CO. One of the big cartons was open, though, being unpacked by a store assistant who was pulling smaller cartons from it; small, flat boxes with the Paskin name on them. And suddenly the answer was obvious. A Paskin box.

Not pigskin books; old, leatherbound books.

Not even a pigskin box.

Kath had kept her notes, the supposedly burned notes, the notes she claimed she didn't have anymore, in a Paskin box.

Kenner didn't go as far as Jenny's Diner. He stopped at a little donut shop and bought coffee and donuts, then drove back to Lake Lodge.

Elaine, wearing a bright orange and white dress belted with a gold chain, was drying her hair on a towel. "I canceled my class," she said when Kenner came in. "They want me back tomorrow, though. Which leaves us where we were, with one day."

Kenner said, "Ever hear of a company called Paskin? They're distributors, wholesale distributors."

"Vaguely. Why?"

"P-A-S-K-I-N, that's why. They deliver in boxes. Paskin boxes."

"So?"

"So," Kenner said triumphantly, "Katherine's pigskin box is probably a Paskin box. Somewhere in that house is a little cardboard box with answers inside."

She tore open the donut sack. "Look, I don't like to spoil your fun, George, but that only came up in your dream. Katherine didn't say anything last night about any kind of box, Paskin or Bonwit Teller. All she said was she might still have her biblio someplace. Might. Seven, eight sheets of paper tacked together. For that you don't need a box." She smiled. "But even skeptics look inside boxes. If I come across one I'll check it out."

They worked on a program for the day over breakfast, debated whether to double up on tasks, and decided, finally, to save time by dividing the labor.

"That doesn't apply to the school," Elaine said. "I want to join you on that trip. I want to see those kids again, the ones from my '67 study."

"The unexceptional six-year-olds?"

"It could be interesting to see how they turned out."

They considered other approaches, tried to define an area of relevance, but there wasn't one; there was just isolated phenomena, singularities; everything was relevant and nothing was; it was like trying to look at air through a magnifying glass.

"Something I'd like to do," Kenner said, "is take a look through some back numbers of *The Chilton Republic*, say for the last ten years. Trouble is, if I do that, there goes the day."

"Make that the year," Elaine said, prizing the lid off her coffee. "And count me out. I read yesterday's."

"Okay," he said. "I'll take care of that if you'll help Kath find her bibliography. Box or no box, I wouldn't know it from a laundry list."

Two more items were added. Elaine was to try, somehow, to gain access to hospital records at Chilton Samaritan, and Kenner was going to check out the Macnamara Funeral Home.

"How the hell can I get at those hospital records, George? What do I say? 'Hi, I'm Elaine, and you've been selected as a candidate for our Silver Bedpan Clean Records Award'?"

"Just say you're Doctor Stromberg."

"I don't even know what I'm looking *for*."

Kenner shrugged. "That place smells bad. This whole town does. Look for anything that feels irregular, inconsistent. You'll know it when you see it. And go back as far as 1967 if you can."

"Oh, sure," she said. "While you do what? Why the funeral home anyway?"

"Edward Palmer Hensel," Kenner said. "That kid figures in all of this somehow. Maybe Macnamara knows where the bodies are buried."

Kenner called police headquarters. A thick, nasal voice said over the phone, "Not that one, lunkhead, the CP-Twelve. Yeah? Chilton Police Department, Chief Stratton."

"My name's George Kenner. I'm inquiring about a Jerry F. Newstead." He covered the phone with his hand. "That kid I told you about, the hitchhiker." Elaine, licking her fingers, nodded.

"What about Newstead?" said Stratton.

"Are you still holding him?"

"Who wants to know?"

"His lawyer," Kenner said. "Are you still holding him?"

"Lawyer, huh?" the cop said. "Where's your practice, lawyer?"

"Montreal. Where's Newstead?"

Chief Stratton laughed. "I guess he's in Montreal by now. And here you are in Chilton, Mr. Kenner."

"Yeah," Kenner said. "I guess I wanted a trip."

"Why waste it?" Stratton said, laughing again. "Why don't you in-vest-i-gate something while you're here? That's what you do, isn't it?"

Then he hung up.

"I don't think I want to be Nancy Drew anymore," Elaine said when Kenner told her.

"He was just trying to be smart," Kenner said. "He

probably collects Bertha's registration forms, then runs routine checks on the strangers in town. Sounds like he's into forms. Hell, that's all any small-town cop has to do with his time. They don't have any crime here."

"Are you convincing yourself, or what?"

"Listen," Kenner said, "if I was a Kleenex salesman from Passaic he'd be telling me to keep my nose clean. He probably warned that character from the pool to stay out of the sun."

But on the way to pick up Katherine half an hour later, Kenner thought about his reading of Chief Stratton, and it didn't fit the facts. The cop should have been throwing his weight around, making himself important, warning Kenner against playing detective in his town, saying things like: "This ain't Manhattan, Kenner. In-vest-i-gating's what *I* get paid for in Chilton." Instead of which he'd issued what sounded like an invitation, a come-on.

Why don't you investigate something while you're here?

Why don't you stop by the school?

Challenges.

The school was east of town, not far from where David's parents lived. As the streets thinned out the Chevy began to climb, complaining, too old for hills, and Kenner thought: you and me both, pal. Below, the town had a hazy appearance in the sunless half-light. Looking down across South Main, Kenner could see the park and, beyond it, the lake, impossibly placid, like a backdrop, unreal. It made him think of Coleridge's "painted ocean."

"It's really worth the climb," Katherine was saying. "It's something of a showplace in Chilton."

Kenner glanced at her as he drove, wondering where she'd picked up the Intourist manner, wondering how much sleep she'd managed to get last night. She looked haggard, like a convalescent back on the job too soon after serious illness. He'd already asked her how she was feeling, and she'd said she felt fine, and was he okay? "Fireproof," Kenner had answered, and Katherine, sighing, had said, "I know, I was being silly."

Now he said, "Did you get a chance to look for that book list, Kath?" She stared blankly at him and he thought: Oh, Christ, don't let's start that who-said-what-when? crap again.

But Elaine, from the back seat, said, "Your college biblio. You told us you still had it someplace."

"Oh, that. I burned a lot of my school stuff. I'm not sure I still have it."

"Do you have any cardboard boxes in the house?" Kenner asked.

"Cardboard boxes?"

"Boxes made out of cardboard. Like the ones food gets delivered in to stores. Cartons. With lettering on the outside."

Katherine looked appealingly at Elaine. Save me from this lunatic, my father. "I don't know," she said. "I guess so."

"Will you look and see if you have any Paskin boxes?" Kenner said. "As a favor to me, will you do that?"

"Paskin?"

"It's a wholesale company," Elaine explained. "They distribute to stores."

Katherine made a puzzled face. Two lunatics, the face said. "Is it supposed to be important or something?"

"Will you just look, Kath?"

She smoothed her hair. "Oh," she said, pointing, "that's the Chilton antenna. It's a hundred seventy-two feet, second highest in—"

"Will you *look,* dammit?"

"Why are you always yelling at me these days, Daddy?" She said it quietly, her voice shaky, and Kenner didn't trust himself to answer.

Elaine said, "He's worried about you, Katherine. We both are."

"And that's the school, over there," Katherine said.

Kenner looked and saw a white brick hexagonal building surrounded by lawns. A low-pressure fountain stood in the center of one lawn; then there was a paved walkway and then another lawn whose center was occupied by a piece of sculpture, a shiny, two-dimensional-looking figure with a crooked protrusion linking top to middle. It might have been made out of flattened tin cans. Katherine was smiling now, the tourist guide revealing the pièce de résistance, the breathtaker; there was also something proprietary about the smile, as if she'd helped build the place with her own hands. "What do you think of it?" she asked eagerly.

"Nice," Kenner said flatly. He couldn't understand her enthusiasm. The school looked like what it was: a modern, neat, institutional, functional high school. What was he expected to say about it?

"Any idea what that shiny metal thing is?" Elaine said.

" 'Looking Forward.' It's a sculpture. The figure's looking west, across the lake, shading its eyes with its hand."

Kenner said, "Why 'Looking Forward,' Kath? Why not 'Looking West'?"

" 'Looking Forward' is the school motto," Katherine said.

There was a parking lot for senior students and a separate lot for faculty and visitors. Kenner parked in a space marked out with green lines, two cars away from the Hensel station wagon ("Oh, look, David's car"), then walked behind Katherine toward the building. The sound of a baseball game in progress came from somewhere behind the building, and just audible in the distance was the marching band going through its paces. Same tune, too. Didn't they ever march to anything else?

Elaine, walking alongside him, said, "Your theory just went out the window." Kenner looked at her. "According to you," Elaine said, "Katherine made some portentous discovery here that scared hell out of her. Right? Look at her, George. She's crazy about this place."

They followed Katherine through glass doors into an open, gray-carpeted area. Somehow, though there were no books, it had the atmosphere of a library; Kenner got the feeling that he had to be quiet, that if he wanted to say anything it would have to be in a whisper. Overhead, the fluorescent lightstrips were inordinately bright, as if burning at maximum power. There were no walls between classrooms.

"Open-class concept," Katherine explained, stopping, deciding where to take them first. "Counters compartmentalization."

"What happens to concentration?" Kenner said, half-listening to a teacher's voice in a neighboring classroom. The teacher was saying something about responsible citizenship, giving a spiel about community loyalty and service and the use of special talents, individual gifts to further the interests of all. "What if the guy who invented the wheel had taken out a patent?" Kenner heard. The next couple of sentences were in French, from a class along the hall, repeating a lesson in unison. Christ, Kenner thought, how do they keep their minds on what they're learning? "They get used to it," Katherine said. "Nobody ever complains." "Sure," the civics teacher was saying, "if there's the right motivation, they do." And a kid's voice saying, "Profit." Then Kenner was aware of someone walking behind them, and Katherine turned and said, "Principal Lazarek. This is my father."

Kenner found himself shaking the hand of a sturdy middle-aged man with prematurely gray hair but bright-eyed as a child.

"Good to know you, Mr. Kenner," He pumped away at Kenner's hand. "Delighted you could come. Feel free to look around all you want."

"And this is Professor Stromberg," Katherine said.

Lazarek shook Elaine's hand warmly. "A special pleasure, Professor. Katherine used to talk about you a lot when she was working here. You did the study down the hill, didn't you? When was that?"

"Sixty-seven," Elaine said. "I guess they're seniors here now."

"Indeed, indeed they are. I came here in 1968. I expect you're finding Chilton's changed a deal since your day."

"Nobody was looking forward in my day," Elaine said.

Lazarek laughed. "Guilty," he said. "The school motto under Principal Kay was 'Perseverance and Integrity.' Now, while I have nothing against those qualities, they seemed to me a little abstract, a touch pious even. Students know how to look forward, though, even if it's only as far as the next vacation." He laughed again, then excused himself and disappeared into a side office, closing the door behind him. He has a door to close, Kenner thought. He turned and caught up with Katherine and Elaine, who'd started along the corridor.

They passed the citizenship class, freshmen, now busily writing. Kenner stood a while, looking at their faces. The French class was still going on in the next area, but it didn't seem to be disturbing any of these kids. Maybe they were taking a test; nobody was looking up. They weren't even aware of him standing there. Like Katherine and David that night, Friday night, when he'd stood in the open doorway. Here was the same superconcentration, the same sense of inner life; and again he had the uncomfortable feeling that he was watching people who operated on a totally different plane of reality, where externals were irrelevant and a different kind of truth prevailed.

Katherine, at his shoulder, whispered, "You want to go in?"

Kenner shook his head. And he found himself remembering the day she'd told him about her decision to go to Chilton, to do a field study in Chilton. "Where the hell is Chilton?" he'd said, and she'd said, "East of Eden someplace. Elaine said she spit ice in the winter, so I'll go in the spring, I guess." Then, when he'd asked her why Chilton, she'd told him it was a representative small community, a nineteenth-century holdout, anthropologist-bait, according to Elaine, who wanted her to stay home and stimulate rat brains instead. "Rat brains," Katherine had said with distaste. "That's what everybody else is doing." "And you want to be different, right?" he'd said, and she'd said, "You bet I want to be different." And now she was different. It reminded him of *The Monkey's Paw,* where the couple lost their only son in an accident and used the paw to wish him alive again; only he came back the way the accident had left him, all chewed up by machinery, a living corpse.

He was about to turn away when he noticed that one of the freshmen in the class was the kid who'd given him back his dime, the freckle-faced boy from the lemonade stand. Katherine was pulling at Kenner's sleeve, anxious to move on, to get to where David taught, he guessed. Elaine was shaking her head slightly, as if she was trying to make some connection, figure out something that was eluding her. "This way," Katherine was saying. "I don't see what's so fascinating here."

"Do you know these kids?" Kenner asked her. "Know their names?"

"Mostly," she said. "It's a small town. David teaches some of these students."

Kenner said, "Who's that kid in the end row? Blue shirt, red hair, and freckles."

"That's Marty Ballinger."

"Has a kid sister, right?"

Katherine nodded. "Linda."

Linda. Linda Ballinger. He knew that name from somewhere. The realization sickened him; more unaccounted-for knowledge, another intrusion. Jesus, how long was it going on?

Then Katherine said, "Did you read about her in the

Republic? Linda's the suspected encephalitis case. Poor little kid."

They entered a wide area given over to students' work: models, maps, paintings. Chilton predominated as a theme. The familiar parochial obsession, Kenner thought, glancing at scenes of Chilton from every angle, Chilton from every direction, Chilton in every season.

Elaine was beside him. "Imaginative bunch, aren't they? Anything strike you yet?"

Kenner took a step closer to a pen drawing, a competent but lifeless interpretation of woodland in the fall. A label identified the drawing as the work of a sophomore named Margaret Loomis. She'd entitled the work "Margaret Grieving."

"I haven't figured it out yet," Kenner said.

Elaine said, "Gerard Manley Hopkins. 'Margaret, are you grieving/Over Goldengrove unleaving?' It's a lament for lost innocence."

"Right," Kenner said. "Saturday morning I happened to buy a cup of lemonade from a little girl near the park. Next day I read she's in Chilton Samaritan with suspected equine encephalitis. Saturday she was fine, nothing wrong with her. I want to know about that."

Elaine nodded. "I'll tell you something else that's odd. Have you been taking a good look at this school? They're using some pretty sophisticated equipment here; expensive, too. Katherine told me they have a computer. I mean, I'm getting the impression this town has a budget the size of New York City. And that open-class concept of Lazarek's? I've seen it elsewhere, but never working the way it does here. The fact he's getting away with it here at all is interesting. This is a conservative community. It's a sociological model of hysteresis—or it was when I was here in '67. Now I'm not so sure."

"What the hell is that?"

"Hysteresis? It's a concept used in the physical

sciences mostly, for when a physical effect lags behind its cause. California's ten, fifteen years out in front? Socially. Chilton used to be maybe twenty, thirty years behind. I have the feeling that in a lot of ways that isn't true anymore."

Kenner said, "Maybe it just caught up. It's been a revolutionary decade. Television came in, they discovered the outside world, got to be like every other place." Elaine looked hard at him. "Okay," he admitted. "I'm the devil's advocate." He turned toward a social science display on another wall. It was mostly maps and graphs. There was a map of New York State (Chilton prominently marked) and a large outline map of the United States with large and small dots on it (he looked, and there, predictably, was Chilton, one of the tinier dots, pierced by a white pin); but all the remaining maps, graphs, and tables were of Chilton exclusively. One graph showed the town's ethnic mix (regular), another its climate (goddamn cold in winter, goddamn hot in summer, Kenner summarized); a third graph indicated the population growth of Chilton since 1900. He looked at that one more closely and noticed that a dotted line continued the population curve to the edge of the graph. Neatly printed alongside the dotted line was the word "Projection."

Kenner ran his finger along the time axis, saw that it extended to the year 2000, then checked the other graphs and tables. They all had dotted continuation lines or unshaded blocks, all had projections as far as 2000. Almost every area of social data he could think of was covered: ethnic mix, population distribution, industrial growth, social mobility, life expectancy, marriage and divorce rate, crime rate, educational attainment. Some of the curves continued steadily into the future, while others showed a sharp rise or decline in the projection zone. He looked quickly from one to the other, confused, excited, apprehensive. He turned and beckoned to Elaine.

"Look at this," he said when she came over. "Looking forward, right? See all those projections? They're predicting crime, marriage, birth, death—everything."

Elaine studied the graphs. "Projection's standard in social science these days. I know what you're getting at, but this is a different kind of prediction. This stuff is statistically based."

"Death rate? Look at the decline, Elaine. It peaked a couple of years ago, and it's already declining, fast."

"Chilton Samaritan probably accounts for that," she said. "Modern health facilities, intensive care, and everything. But then, why the peak in 1976/77? They've had that hospital three or four years." She ran her finger over the graph. "Looks like birthrate's projected to rise," she said. "Then they expect it to even out, so they'll have a stable population by the late nineties."

"The new maternity wing," Kenner said. "It ties in. Jesus, how do they know that? Look, do you have a pencil?"

Elaine looked in her purse, found a pen and a notebook and handed them to Kenner. He began to make notes, writing rapidly, afraid he was going to be interrupted, afraid that any moment somebody was going to stop him. He looked around to see where Katherine was, saw that she was talking to the school nurse on the far side of the display area, where a line of kids with bared arms was waiting for booster shots, and guessed that he had maybe five minutes before the nurse would be through, before she'd find something else to do and Katherine would be coming over to fetch him. It seemed important to finish making his notes before that happened. Take your time, Kath, he thought, noting that since 1967 Chilton's population had increased by ten percent. He showed the figure to Elaine.

"That's about the state average," she said. "Maybe a little high for Chilton, but not exceptionally."

Kenner went on writing. Elaine was reading the information to him now, and he was writing it down, trying not to think about what he was writing, trying not to work out what it signified, saving that for later. Just write, he told himself. Crime. Crime was way down, marriage on the increase, motor-vehicle deaths almost nonexistent. Don't think about it. Write. Analyze it later. But he found himself remembering Katherine's smug phrase: "It'll swing back," and David saying whatever it was he'd said about the pendulum, and Jesus, he thought, how did they know? Was it the graphs, the tables? Did they get it from the graphs? Or did the students who drew the graphs get it from David Hensel? Or was it all coming from some other source? He forced himself to concentrate on writing the notes, determined to get down as much as he could before somebody stopped him. Because somebody was going to stop him. He knew that.

Elaine fed him some more data. Then she said, suddenly, "You're right. This is more than straight stat-based projection. Either it's irresponsible guesswork or this stuff has to be predicated on some other kind of data."

"They aren't projecting on any kind of basis," Kenner said, without looking up. "They *know* it's going to happen."

Nobody stopped him. It was as if Katherine was letting him write everything down, waiting politely for him to finish. The moment he closed the notebook she seemed to be there, at his side, smiling at him.

"I could see you were absorbed," she said. "I didn't want to hurry you. Ready to see David's class now?"

They went past other teaching areas on the way, past a windowless room divided into small cubicles, a set of earphones in each cubicle.

"Want to look in on the language lab?" Katherine said. "Nobody's using it. It's the best time."

"Sure. Why not?"

"I can't play you a tape," Katherine said. "I don't like to fool around with their equipment. But you can get the feel of it."

They sat in the soundproof cubicles, one behind the

other, and put on the earphones. No sound came through. No sound reached Kenner from outside. It didn't take him long to get the feel of it.

It gave him an eerie feeling to be sitting in a totally silent world listening to his own thoughts, an uncomfortable, disquieting feeling. He suddenly found himself wondering what it would be like in there with the lights out, with the earphones on, in that windowless room, in total darkness; along with maybe twenty other people all plugged into silence, all getting the feel of it, involved, immersed in the inner life at the same time, in the same place. He wondered but he didn't really want to know. The thought of contemplating the inside of his own head in a totally silent, dark space spooked him. Yet he was tempted just to try it, just for a minute or two; he was tempted to get out of his seat and turn out the light, get the feel of it.

Why not?

Because it wouldn't prove anything. Because nobody did it that way. The light was supposed to stay on. Sound was supposed to come out of the earphones, not silence. That was why not. Sound, not silence. Light, not dark.

So why no windows?

Acoustics. It was a language laboratory, wasn't it? Where the students learned foreign languages. Wasn't it?

Was it?

What else?

Think about it.

What the hell else?

Think about it. Think hard about it. Think very hard, concentrate.

No, it's too damn hard, I don't want to, don't want to think, want to get out of here, now, get out now, get out . . .

And in front of him, Elaine, standing up, tearing off the earphones, turning, her eyes full of torment.

* * *

"Do you remember me?" Elaine asked.

The boy, a dark-haired senior in a red sweatshirt, shook his head. He looked at Principal Lazarek, who was in the room, then at David Hensel and finally back at Elaine. "I guess I ought to," he said with a grin, and one or two of the other seniors laughed. "Did you teach me when I was a kid?"

"Not exactly," Elaine said. "We did some tests. Learning tests, memory tests, that kind of thing."

The boy grinned again. "I guess I wasn't very good at it."

"Average. You were all above average." She looked around the class, as if she expected somehow to recognize her study group after eleven years, the four that were in the room, four out of thirty-two, after eleven years. "Okay, I give up," she said.

Kenner saw David glance at Lazarek. "Alison Devine," David said, and a pretty chestnut-haired girl stood up.

Elaine said, "You're *Alison?*" The girl laughed, showing even, gleaming teeth. Miss Average Small-Town Coed, Kenner thought. Not Wonder Woman. Not Bridey Murphy.

"I had my teeth fixed," the girl said. "If you knew me when I was six you'll remember me with buck teeth."

"You don't remember me, though, right?"

The girl gave an apologetic shrug, then sat down again.

David said, "That's about how good they are at remembering history. Try them on the Saratoga Campaign sometime."

"Maybe they're all looking forward," Kenner said, but nobody laughed.

Principal Lazarek gave a brief smile, then said, "Want to try for the other two, Professor?"

"I have the feeling I'll strike out," Elaine said. "Okay, who are they?"

Lazarek named the other two, both boys. They stood

up and looked at Elaine and Elaine looked back at them. "Which one's Gary Andrews?" she said.

One of the boys raised his hand. He was husky, with short-cropped blond hair and the look of a football player. "Did I have to read something about rabbits?" he said. "I remember reading some piece about rabbits having a picnic once."

There was some laughter among the students at that. Elaine shook her head. "These weren't reading tests," she said. "You had pictures to study, series of numbers to memorize. I used a buzzer. Do you remember a buzzer? Any of you?"

Nobody remembered a buzzer. Nobody remembered Elaine.

"I hope you found your visit interesting," Principal Lazarek said, opening the door. "Did you see the computer?"

"We didn't get around to it," Katherine said.

"Next time," Lazarek said. "You bring them again, Katherine. Anytime they want to come."

Kenner stared at the principal a moment. Then he held out his hand, which Lazarek took in a grip that was warm and slack.

"I read about your tragedy," he said to Lazarek. "I'm sorry."

Lazarek said nothing for a time. He took his hand away from Kenner's. Kenner thought: He doesn't look like a guy who's suffered a loss; he doesn't look like somebody who's just lost his future son-in-law.

"It was unexpected," Lazarek said. "I don't think it's really hit us yet."

Kenner glanced at Katherine, who was staring at the floor. Then at Elaine, whose eyes were turned toward Lazarek's face. He had the feeling he'd committed some social blunder, fallen out of grace, mentioned the unmentionable. Maybe it was something else: maybe Lazarek hadn't approved of his daughter's engagement.

"Only twenty-one," Kenner said, and shook his head.

Lazarek clasped his hands in front of his body and said, "Given time, my daughter will get over it."

Kenner thought: It doesn't ring true. It sounds hollow. Okay, maybe Lazarek hadn't liked Tobin, but the kid was dead after all, and hypocrisy didn't have any place in that hard fact. There was a protracted silence now and Kenner had a flash of the kid in the dunes, a quick memory. Only now, strangely, he couldn't bring the face to mind. It was gone, a complete blank.

Lazarek said, "I hope you find the time to visit with us again, Mr. Kenner. Anytime. Anytime at all."

Outside, dazzling after the interior's subdued light, the sun had broken its cloud cover, unpleasantly hot now, brash and brassy. Kenner stood, shielding his eyes for a moment, as Katherine went on ahead. His lips were dry, the roof of his mouth parched.

"What was all that about?" Elaine asked.

"You don't read your obituaries," Kenner said, and looked longingly at the fountain.

"I make an effort not to read *The Chilton Republic*," Elaine said.

"His daughter's fiancé died suddenly," Kenner said. "Look, I could use a cold drink. You?"

"I don't know what I could use," she said. "Maybe some psychology classes after today."

"Enroll me, too," Kenner said.

They started to cross the lawn toward the parking lot, following Katherine like a couple of adults keeping up with an energetic child, or a couple of kids lagging behind their teacher. It wasn't clear to Kenner anymore what the relationship was. He just felt tired, ready to go home. Tomorrow, he thought. Tomorrow for sure.

The sound of the marching band came to him across the lawns, still distant, filtered by the thick air, but now he could hear singing, too. If he strained he could even make out the words being sung to that tune the band never seemed to tire of playing.

Chilton High, keep looking forward,
Cherish hopes that never die,
Put the past behind you always—
Forth to glory, Chilton High

"Looking forward to what?" Elaine said.

Kenner didn't answer. Across the lawns, close to where the band was playing, something glassy, something metallic, glinted in the sunlight, and it took him a moment before he realized it was a man with a movie camera set up on a tripod, and the camera was panning the lawns, turning slowly from the white brick building, the fountain, the strange sculpture, panning in a 360-degree shot that lingered momentarily on Kenner and Elaine before coming back to its original position. Against the sun, his head bent, the cameraman was a shadow, a dark shape. Another home movie, Kenner thought, remembering the guy who'd been filming the evening he'd arrived in Chilton. What was it this time? A commercial for the Chilton Board of Education?

He didn't like it. He didn't like the idea of being in somebody's movie, any kind of movie. It was as if the capture of his image had some other significance—more than just a celluloid representation, something of himself, of the person he was.

He put his hand on Elaine's arm.

"Looking forward to what?" Elaine said again.

"I don't know," Kenner said. And he was afraid—here, in all this glaring sunlight, he was afraid.

10

KENNER was driving too fast. They were going north on Main, heading back to Katherine's house for lunch. Katherine had suggested an early meal, so that they'd have a long afternoon in which to see the rest of Chilton. "You haven't seen everything yet," she'd said, "and it's your last day."

His last day. Elaine's last day.

But when Kenner asked Katherine how she knew it was their last day she said, "Elaine has a faculty meeting Tuesdays." He looked in the rearview mirror and Elaine, catching his eye, nodded.

"How do you know I'm planning to go home tomorrow?" Kenner said, and Katherine, sounding surprised, said, "You told me, Daddy. You told me yesterday."

So he drove fast, urgently, not certain why; sure only that he had to clear it up today, whatever it was that was going on in this creepy little bastard of a town.

"You're driving too fast," Katherine said.

"I checked the graph," Kenner said. "There isn't an auto accident planned for today."

"You frighten me, Daddy. You frighten me when you talk like that."

"I know," Kenner said. "I frighten me, too."

A police car, traveling south on Main, flashed its lights as it passed the speeding Chevy. Kenner waited for it to swing around and come after him, watched in his mirror for it to slow and turn, but it kept on going. Maybe it was answering a call, racing to the scene of a crime, to arrest some kid for stealing apples off a tree, some one-legged vet for jaywalking. Kenner cut his speed, though, and by the time he reached Elm Street he was driving almost sedately.

He pulled into the driveway of the Hensel house, then got out of the car and went up the porch steps behind Katherine and Elaine through the screen door and into the dull, tasteless Hensel living room, as he'd done Friday evening; and it felt different, looked the same but felt unaccountably different, as if Friday belonged to another time, another life, another world.

Katherine went straight through into the kitchen and re-emerged moments later wearing a pink apron with frilly edges. "Eggs be okay? I haven't been to the market yet."

"Fine," Kenner said, but when Elaine asked if she could just have cheese and crackers instead, Katherine looked hurt and bit her lip.

"I can cook eggs four different ways," she said.

"I'm sure you do great eggs," Elaine said. "It isn't a slight, Katherine; it's a preference, that's all." Katherine turned and went back into the kitchen without saying a word. "God, she's touchy," Elaine said. "Or is it me rubbing her the wrong way?"

"Both of us," Kenner said. "We don't take it as it comes. We're rocking the boat somehow. Don't you get that impression? That everything we say and do around here rocks the boat?"

"What boat?"

"It feels like the fucking *Marie Celeste*."

He could hear voices in the kitchen now. And suddenly he had the crazy feeling that if he were to go in there he wouldn't find anybody. The eggs would be cooking all by themselves, but nobody would be in there, not even Katherine. With that feeling came another, a certainty that he was seeing his daughter for the last time, had already seen her for the last time. Remember her, he seemed to be telling himself. Remember what she looked like, how she talked, how she laughed, how she moved. Live on it. Forever.

He hesitated, afraid to move. It was as if he'd heard a rattler somewhere in the room and knew he'd tread on it if he moved, if he took a step in any direction. It didn't matter which direction. Wherever he put his foot, there the rattler would be.

Then, as suddenly as it had come, the feeling went away; and like a character on film that has been stopped, then run on, Kenner unfroze. He crossed the room and went into the kitchen.

The voices were coming from a portable TV set, the earnest voices of daytime soap opera: *Love of Life* or *As the World Turns*. Katherine was at the stove, breaking eggs into a pan. Her back was toward him and she didn't seem to hear him come in. He stood and watched her, thinking how vulnerable, how pathetic she looked, trying so hard to please all the time, like a child absorbed in playing house. He felt a great surge of tenderness, a powerful impulse to protect her, to pick her up and carry her somewhere safe. He wanted to weep. He wanted to hold her and say her name over and over. Poor Kath, poor lost baby.

She must have sensed his presence because she turned suddenly, smiled, pushed her hair back from her face with her sleeve. "Five minutes," she said. "Hungry?"

A guy on the TV screen said, "I guess I've always loved you," and the music started to get loud. "You watch that garbage?" Kenner said.

"Why is everything you don't like garbage, Daddy? Do you happen to know the ratings for that show?"

"I know the argument," Kenner said. "Fifty million people can't be wrong. Here's a flash, Kath. Eighty million Germans kept Hitler in power for twelve years. Most of the people are probably wrong most of the time. Good taste usually keeps select company."

She turned back to the stove. "I thought you were a Democrat, George Kenner."

"Sure I'm a Democrat," Kenner said, and a hearty voice across the kitchen said, "Okay, here's the answer, right here in the new blue pack." Kenner said, "Democracy isn't about most of the people being right. It's about most of the people electing a handful of guys to make the decisions and hoping to hell *they'll* be right most of the time. I guess it comes down to judgment. You have to know once in a while if the right decisions got made. Like every four years."

"I really don't want to talk politics," Katherine said, picking up a spatula. "I vote, and that's it."

"What do you train your judgment on, Kath? *As the World Turns?* Or doesn't it matter because you already know who's going to get elected?"

"How do you like your eggs?" Katherine said.

"You know how I like my eggs."

"Over easy, right?"

"Medium."

"David likes his over easy," she said, turning one of the eggs with the spatula.

"Jesus Christ," Kenner said. "How do I get through to you?" She shrugged, and the shrug meant what it always meant these days: I don't know what you're talking about. It was the only one of her gestures he understood anymore. Once, he'd understood them all, every expression, every tone of voice. Now, now he knew nothing. "Look," he said, "I didn't come in here to fight. I came in to ask you something."

"Will you ask Elaine if she wants Saltines or Ryvita?"

"Kath, will you come back to New York with me tomorrow? Return the visit? Just for a few days."

Katherine turned another egg. "I can't."

"Why not? Can't David unfreeze a TV dinner?"

"I can't," she repeated.

Kenner breathed out heavily. "I must be picking up the technique," he said. "That wasn't hard to predict at all."

*　　*　　*

But when, after lunch, they started looking for Katherine's college book list, she surprised him by making a thorough search. Instead of the half-hearted affair he'd anticipated, he got a top-to-bottom sweep of the house, Katherine emptying drawers and closets and letting Kenner and Elaine look downstairs while she searched the bedrooms. There were no forbidden areas either, as far as he could tell, no locked rooms, no Gothic attic or basement with a permanently locked door and the key around David's neck. She even let them into David's den, a room the size of a large closet with an old rolltop desk and a swivel chair. It had a neat, sanitized look that reminded Kenner of those museum reconstructions of famous studies; he felt there should have been a wax model of David Hensel sitting at the desk. Katherine gave the room a reverent, perfunctory search, the kind that would turn up anything that hadn't been deliberately concealed; the other kind would have involved taking the furniture apart and pulling up the carpet. Nobody was going to do that to hide a college bibliography, or to find one, Kenner reasoned. If it existed at all, if it had been hidden instead of burned, Katherine must have done the hiding; and it followed that she was best qualified to do the finding.

She didn't find it, though. And there were no Paskin boxes in the house either.

Once, on the pretext of using the bathroom, Kenner wandered upstairs and found Katherine rummaging through a closet in the little pink-and-blue guest room. The closet was full of toys, baby clothes, crib blankets, and new, neatly folded diapers.

"You're pretty sure about that baby, aren't you?" he said from the doorway.

Katherine looked up and smiled. "We still haven't decided if it's going to be President or State Governor."

"Or even Mayor of Chilton," Kenner said. "Why the two colors?"

A puzzled look now. "Babies only come in two varieties."

"Yeah, Republican and Democrat."

He returned downstairs, to the living room. Elaine was looking at a small shelf of books in the alcove, picking volumes at random and leafing through them. There were about a dozen books on the shelf, mostly paperbacks; he'd noticed them Friday night, had intended then to see what titles the Hensels had, but they'd hustled him off to bed early and he hadn't got around to it.

"Have you seen their library?" Elaine said, putting back one book and taking down another. She opened it, flipped its pages. *"The Living Bible. The Friendship Book. Better Homes and Gardens Home Canning Cookbook.* Four years of college and she reads Motherhood Book Club choices."

Kenner pulled out *The American Heritage Dictionary,* flipped the pages. There were no inserts; no book list was tucked among the leaves. He was about to put the book back when he noticed, through the gap on the shelf, that there were more books, smaller volumes, behind. He pulled out another volume, and then Elaine saw what he was doing and helped him clear the shelf.

"Tapes," she said. "They're tapes."

Eight cassette tapes lay on the shelf behind the books. Kenner picked one up and looked at it. It was a sixty-minute tape in a plastic box. A label on the box, neatly typed, read: *Funtime Greats.*

"What do you have?" Elaine said, looking at another cassette.

"Funtime Greats. You?"

"Andy Williams Sings Old Favorites." She pulled a face, turned the cassette in her hand, held it up to get the light on it. "They've stuck the label over something," she said. "There's another label underneath."

Kenner checked his cassette and it was the same. An edge of the old label protruded, gray-white, from under the new one. "Kath used to tape her notes sometimes," Kenner said, and Katherine, coming into the room, said, "Oh, you found my tapes. Where were they?"

"Hiding behind the books," Kenner said, "with new ID's. Who's after them, Kath? The Mafia?"

"I don't know what they're doing there," she said. "It's only music. David recorded over my notes."

They played samples of most of the tapes, got *Moonlight Bay* and *Che Sera, Sera,* a lot of barbershop singing ("David likes barbershop"), some ersatz Glenn Miller, snatches of Perry Como, Crosby, Sinatra, and Dinah Shore. No notes, only musical notes. No psychology. No book list.

"Can I borrow these?" Kenner said. "And the machine? I'll let you have them back tonight."

"Why?" Katherine said.

Ah, why? It was always "why?" Because our relationship is all fouled up, Kath, that's why. Because I can only stand your company in small doses, but I'm afraid for you, want to keep coming back all the time to check on you, and the tapes are an excuse to do that. Okay? Is that why enough? Or do you want the other reason, too?

"I'm a *Funtime Greats* freak," he said, gathering the cassettes, covering them with his hands so that she couldn't count them. Eight cassettes. She wouldn't remember how many she had. People only remembered the future in Chilton. He'd take eight and return seven. The other one he'd take back to Manhattan, see if he could find some electronics genius who could get at what was under the music. Maybe. If it could be done. If it was worth doing. If David didn't ask where the eighth tape was.

Then Katherine was handing him the cassette player, and after that they were crossing the living room and going through the screen door into the sun, talking about maybe having supper together later to round off the visit, Elaine saying, "I'm not sure I'll be able to make it, Katherine. I have to go back tonight."

And Kenner, on the porch, watching the way his daughter's hair glinted in the sunlight, saying something meaningless like, "Sure, why don't we? That'd be nice," thought: Why do we go on kidding ourselves? Why are we always acting out roles? It isn't going to be like that, dammit. It isn't going to work out that way at all.

"Why the tapes?" Elaine asked as they were driving back to the motel. "He's erased whatever was on them."

Kenner said, "We didn't play any right through. Maybe the barbers hiccuped."

"It'll take eight hours to find that out," she said. "Good luck."

"Good luck yourself. It's Samaritan time."

He pulled onto the Lake Lodge forecourt and they sat in the car, smoking, while Kenner reminded her what he wanted from the hospital. "And see what you can turn up on that kid," he added. "The encephalitis case. Linda Ballinger." He spelled the name and Elaine wrote it down in her notebook. "Admission record, where they're keeping her, whatever."

"Whatever," she said.

She got out and walked toward the white Alfa. A minute later, tires spinning, the car screeched past him and out into the night. Elaine blew him a kiss.

In his cabin Kenner picked up the phone and dialed the motel. Bertha answered almost immediately.

"Haven't seen you today, Mr. Kenner," she said. "Hope you enjoyed your stay."

"Home from home," Kenner said. "How do I make a call to Canada?"

Bertha hesitated. Then she said, "Oh, that's too bad, I already made up your bill."

"You did what?"

"Tuesday tomorrow," she said. "You're checking out, remember?"

"Who said?"

"You did. You said Tuesday. I made up your bill."

Kenner tried to remember. He remembered Bertha asking how long he'd be staying, and he remembered some joke he'd made about wanting to stay forever, and something about a weekly rate. But he hadn't said anything about Tuesday. He was sure he hadn't said anything about Tuesday.

"That's my trouble," he said. "I'm unpredictable. Throws people all the time."

"I guess I can add the phone charge," Bertha said. "Where did you want to call?"

"Canada. It's a country north of Chilton."

She laughed. "That'll be an international call. You dial 8, then 0."

"Maybe you can save me the trouble," Kenner said. "Did Newstead get to Montreal okay?"

"I don't get that one, Mr. Kenner," Bertha said, laughing, and Kenner told her to skip it, pressed the cradle down, then dialed.

"I want to call a Montreal number," Kenner said when the operator answered.

"Are you calling from a hotel?"

"Why?"

"Do you want the call charged to your room?"

"Is there another way?"

"Not really."

"Then why are we discussing it?"

He gave his cabin number, and the motel's number, and the number in Montreal that he wanted to call, and then he waited. He waited a long time. At first the line seemed dead, and he wondered if he should hang up and try again, but before he could make up his mind the line came back to life with a series of clicks and buzzes. Then there were a lot of electronic tones and finally, very faintly, very far away, a ringing tone.

The ringing stopped, and for a moment or two there was nothing but crackle on the line. Then a woman's voice, barely audible, said, "I can't hear you. Can you speak up?"

"Is Jerry Newstead there?" Kenner shouted. "Jerry Newstead."

He didn't hear her reply, if there was one, but the connection wasn't broken. Kenner waited. The static seemed to fluctuate, sometimes uncomfortably loud, sometimes a mere background hiss. It was during one of the quieter periods that he heard the kid's voice.

"Jesus," the kid was saying, "it sounds like they're calling from the moon."

"Jerry?" Kenner yelled. "It's George Kenner. Chilton, remember?"

". . . Kenner . . . calling."

"How did the cops treat you?"

The kid's reply was inaudible.

"You okay?" Kenner shouted into the phone, debating with himself whether to try for a better line. But something told him he wouldn't get a better line. Not from Chilton. Not today.

". . . okay," the kid said. "Thanks for taking . . . call."

"No trouble," Kenner said in one of the spaces between noise. That's it, he thought. I can hang up now. He made it to Montreal, he's okay, nobody beat him with rubber hoses. No further business. But there was something else, something he'd wanted to ask the kid.

". . . weird town," the kid was saying. Then, as the hissing hit a trough, he heard, ". . . one Sunday I'm not going to forget."

Kenner said, "Jerry? Can you hear me?"

"Just," came back faintly.

"Question," Kenner yelled. "The truck. The truck you came in."

"Truck. Right."

"Why was it in Chilton?" He spaced the words carefully, giving each word equal stress. It was like trying to ask directions in an Arctic blizzard. From an Eskimo. An Eskimo-speaking Eskimo.

". . . delivery," Newstead said. But he was learning, too. He waited for a space in the noise, then said, "Special delivery. Some medical stuff."

Kenner waited, rode the static like a surfer riding waves, waiting for the next trough. When it came, he yelled, "What exactly? What were they delivering?"

The static was getting worse, though. The waves

were longer, the troughs further apart. ". . . equipment . . ." was all he heard.

"Where? Where was the equipment going?"

Crackle.

"Was it the hospital? Jerry? Were they taking it to the hospital?"

He could hardly hear the kid at all now. Something about a name. The kid was trying to remember a name.

"Samaritan?" Kenner tried. "Was it the Samaritan Hospital?"

All that came back was noise, continuous crackle, occasionally a hiss. Then, just for a fraction of a second, just before the line went dead, Kenner thought he heard Newstead's voice once more, from very far away, saying a word, or part of a word, from farther away than the moon, from another world, another time.

The word sounded like "hope."

He didn't want to drive to Macnamara's Funeral Home. He didn't even want to walk there. What he wanted to do was put on his track suit and jog along the lakeshore, jog and think. And that was crazy, because he didn't have the time to think, didn't even have a theory to think about, just a lot of pieces that seemed to come from a lot of different puzzles. If he put them together he'd get a picture a spaced-out chimp might have painted with a brush between its toes. Bits of reality and snatches of dream. Gobbets of the future and visions of dead people. And he had until tomorrow to find the way out.

So why was he sitting on his bed? Why wasn't he out there finding the answers?

Because it didn't matter. Because it wouldn't make any difference.

Say that again.

Because he couldn't change anything. Because even if he found all the answers he couldn't alter a damned thing. Like, *che sera, sera*.

Are you for real, Kenner? I'm talking about answers

and you're giving me Doris Day. You're giving me *Funtime Greats*.

Che sera, sera, George. So jog. Don't waste your time with Macnamara. Forget *The Chilton Republic*. Jog instead.

But he didn't listen. The bastard was trying to sidetrack him, or worse. He'd had some bad experiences jogging on hot days. Something to do with the supply of oxygen to the brain, he thought: too much or too little. You could kill yourself staying in shape.

What are you trying to do, Kenner? Drum up business for Macnamara?

He got in the Chevy and drove to Main Street.

A short man in a dark suit opened the door, then stood in the shadow of the doorway, his head inclined slightly forward. Bela Lugosi, Kenner thought. The handshake would be soft, the voice sepulchral, practiced in condolence. He'd have a Webster-size lexicon of pious, consolatory clichés. For some reason he made Kenner think of Dick Hensel.

"Mr. Macnamara?" Kenner asked, and the man nodded, a measured nod, the ten-dollar nod. "My name's George Kenner."

"Why don't you step inside, Mr. Kenner?" He had a surprisingly thin voice, not at all sepulchral. And Kenner's name came easily off his tongue, as if he was familiar with it, as if the visit was by appointment.

Kenner went through into the hallway. To the left, apparently, were the living quarters; through a half-open doorway he could see the flickering blue light of a television, hear Popeye's voice. "Take that," Popeye was saying. It was strangely incongruous.

Macnamara said, "What can I do for you, Mr. Kenner? Is there a loved one?"

Kenner found the phrase disquieting. He shook his head, looking at the same time to the right of the hallway. There were two doors, both closed. "No, there's no loved one," he said. He felt an urge to say, conversationally, "How's business, Mac? I see death's on the slide in Chilton these days. Tough. Any particular reason for that? Somebody find an antidote?" He said, "I need some information, that's all."

"What kind of information?" Macnamara said evenly.

"It concerns Edward Hensel," Kenner said.

"Edward Palmer Hensel," Macnamara said, nodding again. "Yes."

"You took care of the burial arrangements?"

"I'm the only one in town, Mr. Kenner. I remember the funeral well."

"You actually remember it?"

"Why not?"

Because there wasn't supposed to be two-way traffic, was there? Maybe he'd got it wrong. Maybe there was two-way traffic, access to past and future, but not for everyone, for the privileged few only. Maybe it was like one of those pictures you turned in the light, and each way you turned it you saw a different picture. If it was like that—Death, Time, whatever—if it was like that, how would you know which picture you were in?

"This was back in 1973, right?"

"1972," Macnamara said.

"You did the embalming?"

Macnamara hesitated, appeared uncertain: "Embalming? Did I?"

Kenner waited.

"No, I remember now," Macnamara said, with a faint smile. "It was a closed-coffin affair."

"Closed coffin?"

An image came to him of Katherine in the hospital, delirious, saying, "I don't want to be dead." Why that phrasing? Why not, "I don't want to die?" Why: "I don't want to be *dead?*"

"His remains were shipped home ready for burial," Macnamara said. "It's the usual procedure when there's a time lapse or the injuries are . . ." He left the sentence unfinished, gestured instead.

Kenner's attention was caught by a movement at the top of the stairs. A child, ducking out of sight.

That explained Popeye, at least. The kid had been sent upstairs, out of the way, and was waiting for him to leave so he could come back down.

"I won't keep you any longer," Kenner said. "I guess you're busy."

Macnamara didn't answer. Now, in one of the upper rooms of the house, the child was singing in a high, tuneless voice, the phrases squeezed together. Kenner tried to make out the words. It was more like chanting than singing, like a single phrase being repeated over and over.

"I hope I've been of some help," Macnamara was saying.

"You've been very helpful," Kenner said. "Thanks a lot."

Sure, he thought, the world is full of holes, full of spaces. Spaces between atoms, spaces within the atom. More space than matter. What if they were using the spaces between reality? Somehow.

As Macnamara held the door open Kenner listened again to the child's chanting. It sounded like a commercial jingle for some patent medicine, but he didn't recognize the brand name. *"Kennedy's your remedy,"* the kid seemed to be singing, and there was a second line, something equally brutal, something about energy.

"Anytime," Macnamara said.

He stopped at Lombard's Tavern for a cold beer. The place was dark and cool, empty except for the barman and one customer. The barman looked up from polishing a beer glass and gave Kenner a grin of recognition. Then the customer looked up and Kenner saw who it was, but it was too late to turn around and go back out.

"Kenner," Leon Joyce said. "Hey, let me buy you a drink."

Kenner slid on to a stool, trying to think of an excuse for not staying; but lying took too much effort and the barman was already looking at him expectantly.

"Give me a beer," Kenner said. He saw the barman reach for the Sentry tap and tilt a glass under it.

"Local pisswater," Joyce said, scooping a handful of salted peanuts out of a bowl on the counter. "Still in town, huh?"

"They're giving me till tomorrow," Kenner said. He raised the beer, sipped, then put the glass down.

"Beats me why they send us to these fucking places," Joyce said, watching Kenner push the glass gently away. "Didn't I warn you about that beer? Town sewer runs right under the factory. That's their water supply."

"I can believe it," Kenner said. "How long you in town for?"

"This is it, pal. Last farewell drink. Then I'm off to Lingfield, Connecticut. Your people ever send you there?"

"What's in Lingfield?"

"Chilton without mosquitoes. It's another stinking town like this one." He glanced at the barman. "No offense, pal. But I could be in Miami, Palm Beach maybe, someplace like that."

"Why aren't you?" Kenner said. He sipped some more of the beer. What the hell. It was cold and wet and his throat was burning.

"I go where they send me," Joyce said. "These god-damn test markets."

"Test markets?"

"Sure," Joyce said.

"I don't get it. Tell me about test markets."

Joyce laughed. "It's a load of garbage. Miami's where you test a suntan, right? These one-horse places might be okay for regular junk. But what makes them think a bunch of hayseeds know anything about sun-tan? What makes them think a town of hicks knows what you and me are gonna buy? They got crystal balls or something?"

Something was moving inside Kenner's skull, moving very slowly; something left for dead, a brain-shot ani-mal starting to crawl slowly and with a lot of pain.

"Where else?" Kenner said. "Where are the other test markets?"

"They got a whole bunch of them," Joyce said. "They keep adding places all the time. Jesus, I don't know how many they got right now. Thirty, forty. All in different states."

"Lingfield, Connecticut," Kenner said slowly.

"Yeah, that's one of them. Then someplace in Massachusetts." Joyce turned to the barman. "What's that place in Massachusetts? Little place, begins with a P."

"Search me," the barman said.

The animal was on its feet now, shot to hell, trailing its brains in its tracks, impossibly still alive, still functioning, moving by pure instinct. Keep going, you dumb bastard. Keep going.

"How about Pennsylvania?" Kenner said. "Is there one in Pennsylvania?"

Joyce nodded. "Yeah. Some funny name. Indian name."

"Taquanna," Kenner said. It wasn't a question.

"That's the one," Joyce said. "Hey, they've sent you there, too?"

Kenner was halfway to the door, to the sun, to the light, when he heard Joyce say to the barman, "I can't figure out what makes them think you small-town people know what the whole goddamn country's gonna be buying."

11

HE didn't want to think. He didn't want to investigate. He wanted to go home; climb back in his car and get away.

Because now, finally, he could start putting it together. Now he had the framework. Now he could be in trouble.

He started walking. It didn't matter which direction he took, as long as he stayed in the open, in the sunlight.

Test markets. That was the framework.

Go home, Kenner. Don't try and work it out. Go home.

"Test markets." Thirty or forty little one-horse towns across the nation. Jesus. Crystal balls, Joyce had said. Joyce was right. And pretty soon, Kenner guessed, there would be fifty of them, one in every state: fifty little psychic communities, fifty little windows on America's future.

And they weren't there to test suntan lotion either.

The pain in his head was making him nauseous. Get it amputated, he told himself. Get the sonofabitch surgically removed; replace it with a plastic one. Hygienic, pain-free, antistatic plastic.

He was walking the two blocks to where *The Chilton Republic* had its offices, at Fourth and Main. Was that

his decision? Or was somebody else deciding he should
go there? Test it? Turn around. See if you can.

I don't want to turn around. I like the view.

He kept going. It was the middle of the afternoon,
hot and sleepy, with not much traffic on the street and
few people on the sidewalk. A small town on a hot
afternoon. Normal. Average. Representative.

Like hell.

It had to be federal. Even a guy with his head in a
car-crusher could figure that out. The spread of the
communities said federal. The funding involved—all
those expensively equipped hospitals and schools—
said federal. And the black limo with the Virginia
plates whispered it.

A federal program. A psychic program. ESP. Precognition, telepathy, everything the psychologists, the
hardheads, the skeptics said didn't exist. It existed. It
existed here and now, in this town, in a lot of other
towns. It was being developed.

Hey, that didn't even hurt.

Keep going, Kenner. It doesn't hurt anymore.

He understood a lot of things now. They'd have a
security blanket over the whole operation, which explained why the phones were so bad, and how Chief
Stratton knew who he was, and why Kath's tapes had
been erased. Test marketing was only the cover.
Though they could also be running a test program on
consumer products. Today: suntan lotion and cigarettes; tomorrow: Kremlin foreign policy, Soviet weap-
ons technology, and domestic trends—political, social,
economic, whatever. Predict the next energy crisis,
then avoid the conditions necessary for it. He didn't
even want to think about what else accurate, reliable
prediction could be used for.

He stopped at the corner of Third and Main, waited
for the light to change. As he stood there a police
cruiser turned the corner, but it kept going, and Kenner didn't recognize the cop driving the car.

That, too, he thought. That was part of it. Surveil-
lance. Me, Leon Joyce, Elaine, Jerry Newstead.

Strangers. Security headaches. But they couldn't keep strangers away, not entirely, not away from a supposedly ordinary little community, not without putting up security perimeters and blowing their cover. So the perimeters had to be invisible. They had to keep tabs on strangers, know who they were, what they were doing. Which meant suspicious cops, hidden cameras (maybe), bugged hotel rooms (maybe), phone taps. No "maybe" about the phone taps.

But they'd let Jerry Newstead go. The cops had questioned him for a while, then they'd released him. Why would they do that?

Because Newstead hadn't found out anything.

The light changed and Kenner crossed the street.

Because the kid wasn't a threat. He didn't know what was going on in Chilton.

Kenner knew, though.

Don't even think about it.

Katherine knew. Katherine had known for two whole years.

And she was still in Chilton.

A small bell tinkled overhead as he pushed open the door of the newspaper office. It was a gloomy, old-fashioned-looking place with four desks and a heavy wooden balustrade around each desk. Only two of the desks were occupied; one by a severe-faced woman of about sixty with her hair in a tight knot and a lace-trimmed blouse buttoned to the neck; the other by a man, a young guy with neatly parted hair, white shirt-sleeves rolled tidily at the elbows. A typewriter was clattering somewhere in back and a sign on the wall said: IF IT HAPPENED YESTERDAY IT'S HISTORY. IF IT'S HAPPENING TODAY IT'S NEWS. IF IT'S HAPPENING TOMORROW IT'S ADVERTISING. Below that was a list of the newspaper's advertising rates: advertising in Chilton came cheap, Kenner noticed.

The woman ignored Kenner. She seemed to be correcting proofs. The young guy smiled at him, picked up a pencil and made a note on a scratch pad, then leaned back in his chair and waited.

Kenner automatically checked his watch, sensing that he was late. His watch said 3:36. Did it mean something? Were they expecting him at 3:30, or what? Was this guy making a note of the time, logging him in?

Come on, that was crazy. He didn't have an appointment here. He hadn't known himself exactly when he was going to arrive, even *if* he was going to arrive here. How were they supposed to know he'd stop for a beer at Lombard's?

The barman could have told them. The barman could have picked up the phone and said, "He's on his way."

Did he believe that? Did he really believe that?

"Maybe you can help me," Kenner said.

"Sure. If I can."

"I'm doing some research. I'd like to take a look through your back issues, if that's possible."

"It isn't," the young guy said, smiling again. "Don't have any. Don't have the space."

Kenner pointed at the sign on the wall. "History is junk, right?"

"History is bulk," the young guy said. "We keep the back issues on microfilm. How far back do you want to go?"

"How far back can I go?"

"We keep ten years here. They have forty more years over at the library, though."

"Ten ought to do it," Kenner said. "How was 1968 around here?"

"Terrific. First year we got to see the Super Bowl game in color."

"Memorable," Kenner said. "Remember who won?"

"Packers won. Chandler played a great game," the young guy said. "Miss Lewis'll show you how to work the viewer."

The woman, hearing her name, stood up and beckoned to Kenner. He followed her through a door and along a passageway, then into a room with one small, high window. A photocopier stood against one

wall, and there were some gray metal cabinets, metal
shelving, and, in the center of the room, a small table
with the microfilm viewer on it. The room smelled
dusty, stale. There was thick dust on the shelves, but
none on the viewing table, Kenner noticed.

"Know how to work one of these?"

"I've used them before," Kenner said.

"I expect you have," she said. "Fiches are in the
cabinet there. Office closes at five. That's five sharp."

She went out, closing the door behind her. Games,
Kenner thought, carrying a stack of microfiches to the
table. Everybody's playing games. They know who I
am, what I do, why I'm here; maybe they even know
what I'm looking for, which is more than I know.
What the hell am I looking for? PSYCHIC RESEARCH
COMES TO CHILTON? TOWN WITH A FUTURE, PREDICTS
MAYOR?

He slid the first 1968 fiche into the viewer and
started to read.

By 3:58 Kenner had worked his way through two
weeks of 1968. Mayor Reynolds had fêted Senator
Harcourt on one of the senator's upstate swings, a lost
dog had been found floating in the Chilton River, some
high school seniors had cut classes in protest against
the bombing of North Vietnam, and a seventy-two-
year-old widow had remarried. Kenner made a rapid
calculation. At this rate he'd need about an hour to
get as far as 1969. He had a decade to cover.

He decided to restrict himself to the front page of
each edition. If nothing significant showed up on Page
One, too bad.

He slid a fresh microfiche into the viewer, adjusted
the focus, and looked at January 14—CHILTON VIEWS
SUPERBOWL IN COLOR. Check. That much local history
he already knew. The guy in the front office probably
came back here on slow days and read the back numbers. He probably didn't remember watching the game
at all; he remembered reading the files. Skip. January
10—CITY JUDGE FINES CYCLE GANG. Judge Milton

Safferman had fined some local punks two hundred dollars in total for terrorizing Chilton. "We are not going to tolerate this kind of behavior," he was quoted as saying. Kenner skipped. January 25—Heavy snowfalls were blocking the roads. A kid had been busted for smoking—no, possession of pot. Somebody from the Health Services Department had resigned for health reasons (what else?). The time was 4:07. Kenner moved quickly on.

Then, January 30—POLICE CHIEF RESIGNS. He read that item carefully. It seemed the kid busted for possession was Senator Harcourt's nephew, which must have added weight to his claim that Chief Meeker had planted the stuff under the seat of his motorcycle. Meeker temporarily replaced by Vernon S. Stratton. Kenner didn't stop to analyze it. Suddenly he had the feeling there were going to be a lot more resignations before he was through with 1968. Ignoring a NO SMOKING sign, he lit a cigarette and read on.

February 1968—HOW DOES IT FEEL TO BE TYPICAL? A newly revised NSSRF list, based on the latest demographic data, had confirmed Chilton's status as a "Representative American Community." Kenner went back and read the item through again. NSSRF stood for National Social Science Research Foundation. Their exact function wasn't stated, just the fact that they published the list. A final paragraph anticipated a fresh influx of marketing analysts and a fresh flow of test products into Chilton's stores. "It has to be good for Chilton," commented Albert LeFarge of the Junior Chamber of Commerce.

February 1968—High school Principal David L. Kay had accepted a post in Maine. Chilton wished him well and welcomed Joseph Lazarek in his place. Kenner glanced at his watch. 4:15. He didn't stop to read about Lazarek's credentials. He put a new fiche in the viewer and read instead about Herbert Reynolds, Mayor of Chilton, who, after twelve years of service to the community, had resigned from office on February 27. Reason: ill health. There was a photograph of Acting

Mayor Anthony LoBianco, smiling, fresh-faced Lo-
Bianco. Still acting in 1978. The guy who predicted
that there weren't going to be any tax raises.

March and April were full of new city ordinances,
changes in the zoning laws to allow for industrial
development by the lake. A hot local issue that spring
was a project to construct an electronics factory near
the site of historic Fort LaSalle (wherever that was).
A preservationist faction opposed the plans and seemed
concerned, too, about pollution. It wasn't clear what
kind of pollution they worried about. And the Health
Department got a budget increase.

May 1968—*The Chilton Republic* got itself a new
editor, Irving D. Rees. Rees took two front pages to
express his editorial policy, but what it boiled down
to was "Screw the rest of the world."

And then it was all births, marriages, and deaths
in what seemed like the right proportions, and high
school basketball and summer fairs, and after that it
was the apple harvest and the retirement of Judge
Safferman, and taxes, and highway improvement
schemes, and some new arrivals in town. A couple
of new doctors set up practice in November, getting a
long-paragraph item and a lot of free advertising. Both
doctors were from Texas, though the article didn't say
from where in Texas.

And that was 1968. The year in which Robert Kennedy and Martin Luther King had been assassinated,
and Richard M. Nixon had been elected President, and
Borman, Anders, and Lovell had orbited the moon.

It was 4:25, and he wasn't going to make it. There
wasn't time to do it all. He'd have to skip whole years.
So which years did he want to cover? 1972: the year
of Eddie Hensel's death. He wanted to read *The Republic's* coverage of that. And 1976, the year Katherine
had come to Chilton. That most of all. Maybe glances
at some other years along the way. First, 1972, though.
When in 1972?

Without having to think, without consciously having
to remember the date, Kenner looked through the

microfiche holders and pulled out the little pack for November 1972. Then he sorted through them until he found the one for November 19, slipped it into the viewer, and scanned the front page for that day.

And there it was, Eddie Hensel's picture, Eddie in his uniform, earnest, serious Eddie. Below the picture was the obituary, headed: THE SUPREME SACRIFICE. Kenner read the piece through. It was mostly a summary of the boy's high school achievements (brilliant, apparently), a lament for lost promise, a character testimonial (with quotes from classmates: "Eddie was a terrific guy" and "We are all going to miss him a lot"); the item ended with a brief, factual account of "the fatal patrol": Edward Hensel had been shot near the Cambodian border.

Kenner stared at the picture, then at the words. Something didn't quite fit, but he couldn't think what it was. It was the right face, the face in the photograph on the Hensel mantelpiece (same photograph); and the prose was standard obit. So what was nagging at him? Something. It didn't look right.

But there wasn't time to worry at it. He removed the fiche and replaced it with one taken at random from the middle of 1973. It happened to be July 12. Christ, he remembered that year well enough. Watergate year. The nation traumatized by the Senate hearings, and what had *The Chilton Republic* found to write about? Sewage? A modernization program for the sewage treatment plant at Blanchette.

1974 was a fascinating year, too. Kenner's sample for that year was April 8, the day of the Great Chilton Power Blackout. Homes without electricity for eight hours and an entire edition filled with what-did-you-do-in-the-blackout? stories. Some cub reporter trying to win himself a Pulitzer Prize.

September 2, 1975—The second tract of Lakeview Homes was nearing completion, atmospheric disturbance was affecting TV reception, the A&P market was to stay open later two nights a week, and a New

Hampshire-born biochemistry professor was retiring to Chilton after twenty years in southern California ("I guess I missed green grass most of all"). Kenner was about to remove the fiche when he noticed something odd. There was a wide border around the A&P item, and a large photograph of the store's exterior. No picture of the professor or of Lakeview Homes, but a picture of a store on Main Street that everybody in Chilton probably saw at least twice a week.

Something. Some thing.

He moved on to 1976. It was 4:41.

In July 1976 Chilton staged its Bicentennial pageant, reenacted the capture of Fort LaSalle, waved the flag along with the rest of the nation, and lost eight kids and three adults to equine encephalitis. Kenner looked at the names. Joey Dumas was among them, but he recognized none of the other names. It gave him a strange feeling of relief to find that he recognized none of the adults' names, as if, irrationally, he'd expected to see a face he knew among the small, sad photographs of the dead, find a life he knew among the tidy little obituaries. Katherine's face. Katherine's life.

Crazy.

He scanned the next few pages, confirmed that there had been no further deaths, then moved to August. August was harvest and vacationers, a new cabin for Lake Lodge (check), a couple moving to Lakeview from Cutler, Montana (Montana!), and talk of drought.

He skipped to February 1977; to February 5, 1977. Page One was given over to flu, which seemed to have hit Chilton hard that winter, and the weather got a lot of coverage. Katherine's wedding wasn't mentioned. He tried Page Two. More flu—a mass immunization program was underway—but still no wedding. Somebody from Kanga Falls, a plumber named Frank Paston, had died of flu. DEATH TOLL CLIMBS TO 27, Kenner read.

Flu?

What the hell kind of flu was that?

He checked his watch (4:50) and quickly scanned Page Three, and there it was: BRIDE AND GROOM SMILE AWAY THE GLOOM. Katherine Kenner, a student teacher (why that?) from New York City, had married David Baxter Hensel, son of Richard and Louisa Hensel. The couple were pictured, smiling, on the church steps, surrounded by guests. Kenner recognized Principal Lazarek and Dick Hensel. The other faces were unfamiliar to him. He quickly read the text, something about love among the chalk dust and Katherine saying, "I'm really looking forward to living here in Chilton."

Then, suddenly, Kenner was afraid to put the next fiche in the viewer.

The door opened and Miss Lewis came in. She stood sniffing the air for a moment, then said, "Have you been smoking in here?"

"I make it four minutes to go yet," Kenner said, looking at his watch.

"Smoking isn't permitted in here."

"Four minutes," Kenner said.

"Did you hear what I said?"

"Give me a break," Kenner said. "Give me three minutes."

"I'm going to fetch Mr. Elliott," she said.

She turned and hurried from the room.

Kenner looked at the viewer. Then, slowly, he slid the next fiche under the glass and brought it into focus.

Sunday, February 13, 1977.

He was afraid to look, afraid to see what it said.

He knew what it would say.

The headline would be: FLU CLAIMS 28TH VICTIM. Underneath would be a photograph, a smiling face, and under the smiling face it would say: *"Katherine Hensel as Chilton will remember her."*

He turned, hearing footsteps along the passageway. The young guy from the front office, Elliott, came into the room. He smiled at Kenner.

"We're closing now. Why not come back tomorrow?"

"It's right here," Kenner said. "On this page."

"Oh? What is?"

Telepathic dreams, Kenner thought. My dead daughter. My dead-and-now-alive-again child. Survival. Life after Chilton, Mr. Elliott, that is what's here on this page, in this town, in this creepy little morgue of a town, where people die but nobody dies. And maybe tomorrow won't do, because tomorrow maybe I'll be here, on a microfiche, on the front page; and the headline will read: CITY MAN KILLED IN AUTO ACCIDENT. But there won't be anybody to dream about me, will there? How is it done, Elliott? Is she really there, or am I seeing some electronic miracle of holographic projection when I look at my daughter? And what happened that night in Taquanna, Elliott? That rainy night in Taquanna, Pennsylvania. Am I really here now, or am I still in that hospital bed in Taquanna, and is this whole visit some kind of vision, some kind of mirage? Is this like the dream I had about the country club? Am I going to have to live through it again next year, Elliott, when 1978 really comes around?

Or did I die in that wreck, Elliott? Tell me if I'm dead. Because I'd like to know. Because I'm ready to believe anything right now. Any damn thing at all. Just lay it on me. I'll buy it.

"I don't know," Kenner said. "I didn't look yet."

"Take a look," Elliott said.

Kenner took a look.

BIG FREEZE CONTINUES, the headline said. The entire front page, except for one small paragraph, was taken up by weather reports and pictures of cars stuck in snowdrifts. The one small paragraph was headed: FLU CLAIMS 28TH VICTIM.

Kenner looked up. Elliott was standing in the doorway now, a bunch of keys dangling from his finger. "Take a look," he said again.

Kenner read the paragraph. It said that Dr. Benjamin Goodhart was to replace Dr. Kenneth Frazer as Medical Director of Our Lady of Hope Clinic. Dr. Frazer had been the twenty-eighth flu victim.

"Bad winter," Elliott said conversationally from the doorway.

And Kenner, hurrying back to his car, thought: There's still time. Stay cool. They want to spook you. Don't let it happen. Fight it. Fight the madness, use your reason, think it out. Second sight doesn't exist, can't exist. Nobody can tell the future. Nobody can read minds. The dead stay dead, and now is now: June 19, 1978.

Figure it out, Kenner. Figure out how they're conning you.

Sure, but what if they're not?

They are.

What if they're not, dammit? What if I'm right?

Then you're in bad trouble. But you're not right. Elaine's right. That psychic stuff is garbage. Everything that's happened here is scientifically explainable, rationally explainable. Believe it. Find Elaine. Elaine can explain it. Go back to the motel, see if she's there yet.

Kenner reached his car, climbed in, and started the motor. The sound of the motor calmed him a little. It was a reassuring sound, real, physical, familiar. There was that goddamn car hiss where the gasket was worn, the tappet noise when he raced the motor, that squeak the mechanic in Binghamton said was mice.

He pulled out and drove north on Main, past Third Street, past Macnamara's and the Exxon station, past Lombard's and Jenny's Diner.

Take a left, Kenner. The motel's that way.

He checked his mirror, and that was when he saw the cruiser, four car lengths behind, matching the Chevy's speed as if attached by a tow line. The young cop was driving, the cop who'd advised him not to jog in the heat, the cop who'd questioned Newstead, the paranoid cop. Tailing him, four car lengths behind.

Kenner glanced at his speedometer. He was doing twenty-four; the limit on Main Street was twenty-five. He checked his mirror again, and this time caught the young cop's eye. The cop smiled. Then he winked.

The intersection with First was coming up. A left turn would take him to Maple and the motel; a right turn, a right turn would take him home. Six hours and he'd be back in New York City: crazy, violent, sane, safe, understandable New York.

Why not? Why not make that right turn and keep on going?

Forget Chilton. Forget Elaine. Forget Katherine. Forget NSSRF and Eddie Hensel, and the hospital and the school. Forget everything.

Go home, George. Take a right.

He took a left.

The cop followed him west on First, matching his speed exactly. As Kenner approached Maple, touched the brake, slowed, ready to turn, the cop slowed behind him.

Sonofabitch.

Two blocks ahead the lake sparkled. Lakeshore ran north-south, another route out of town. Kenner thought for a moment.

Then, instead of turning, he drove the two blocks to Lakeshore, swung the wheel to the right, and floored the gas pedal. The Chevy rumbled sluggishly forward, pickup like a Sherman tank, all noise and no action.

Thirty-eight . . . thirty-nine . . . forty . . .

The cop stayed four lengths behind, grinning.

Forty-one . . . forty-two . . .

Move, you bastard.

The limit along Lakeshore was thirty. Kenner wasn't intending to outrun the cruiser. He just wanted to see how far over the speed limit he'd have to go before the cop would do something about it.

He passed the entrance to the clinic, Our Lady of Hope Clinic; Director: Dr. Benjamin Goodhart. Our Lady of Hope Clinic, where, maybe, they made special Sunday deliveries of special medical equipment. Maybe. And where on Saturday night, maybe, the light-

colored station wagon, maybe an ambulance, had
turned in.

And he was doing fifty-two miles an hour.

And still the cop was four lengths behind, no lights
flashing, no siren wailing, no attempt to pass. Just the
young cop's face set in a confident grin.

For a couple of miles the road ran straight, bordered
on one side by woods, on the other by the lake,
darkened by metal barrier fencing. Kenner kept his
foot down hard, taking the Chevy to a screaming,
vibrating sixty-five on the straight. The cruiser had
dropped back a little, but that was safety distance,
Kenner knew, stopping distance. Kenner had the picture now. He could light the afterburners and fly the
Chevy at Mach speeds, and still the cop's supercharged
Le Sabre would be there on his tail, until they reached
city limits; and then . . .

Try him.

Kenner eased off the gas, brought his speed down
to a comfortable fifty-five, and then they were into
curves, and the road was tree-lined both sides, and the
Chevy rolled sickeningly like a small boat in a swell,
using a full width of the road, tires shrieking. Once,
coming out of a right-hand curve, Kenner glanced in
his mirror. The cop was framed there, close enough
to touch, riding in Kenner's trunk, it seemed. And the
bastard waved. The tailgating, lawbreaking, joy-riding
sonofabitch waved.

Then the signs flashed past, one after another.

YOU ARE NOW LEAVING CHILTON—A GREAT LITTLE
PLACE TO LIVE.

SPEED LIMIT 55 M.P.H. DRIVE WITH CARE.

The cop made no attempt to pass. And Kenner
thought: He'll stop me at the Interstate. And then he
thought: No, he won't. He'll wait for some quiet stretch
of road, some lonely tree-shaded stretch, and he'll make
sure no other traffic is around, and that's where it ends,
Kenner, where it's all been leading, all your life. . . .

No way. No goddamn way.

He began to pump the brakes, slowing in spurts, backing the cop off with his tail lights, weaving at the same time to throw him, confuse him. And once in a while Kenner would floor the gas pedal again, gaining a few yards before the cop realized what the new tactic was.

It wasn't going to change the outcome, though. When the cop was ready he'd make his move, go for the kill.

There was something up ahead. Kenner glimpsed it the second before it was obscured by foliage, before the Chevy barreled into a long, curving tree tunnel. A sign, a gas station sign. Kenner was going to stop for gas. And the cop was going to stop, too. What happened after that depended on a lot of things.

The cop was tailgating again, but Kenner didn't mind that. He'd have to back off before he could pass, and if he tried to pass here, in the tunnel, Kenner was going to flick his tail and send the bastard sideways into a tree, explain it later. The cop made no attempt to pass, though, just sat on Kenner's tail through the tree tunnel, slowing when Kenner slowed on the other side.

It was a Shell station, open. A guy in coveralls was working on a jacked-up Ford.

Kenner sounded his horn, stood on the brakes, and swung the wheel over, wrestling the Chevy onto the forecourt, scattering a stack of oil cans and sliding to a rubber-scorching stop inches from the jacked-up Ford.

The cruiser screeched to a halt a foot behind him.

The mechanic pushed himself out from under the Ford and stood up. He had a wrench in his hand.

Kenner got out of the Chevy slowly, and the cop got out of his car at exactly the same time, as if the maneuver was the result of long practice, much rehearsal.

Then the mechanic said, "Need any help, Larry?"

And the cop said, "Gas her up and check the oil, will you?" He hooked his thumbs into his gunbelt and walked over to the Chevy, kicked its rear tire. "Wheel's out of true," he said. "Been trying to tell you for the last eight miles."

There was a phone booth on the far side of the fore-court. Kenner sipped a Coke and stood looking at the phone booth while his car was being gassed up. The cop was by the pump, talking to the mechanic.

Call Masterson, Kenner was telling himself.

Call Andy Masterson in Washington and ask him what the hell is going on here. Ask him about NSSRF and Eddie Hensel's service record; and while you're at it, ask him what day it is. Masterson's a bird colonel. He must have some clout. Maybe he can help. Call him, if they'll let you.

"Sure, George," Masterson would say, "it's June 19, 1978. My calendar says so. And you sound as if you could use some help, old buddy. I know this analyst who's terrific. . . ."

Call him anyway.

Kenner walked over to the booth expecting to hear his name called, expecting to hear the cop say, "Hey, where do you think you're going?" The cop didn't say anything, though. And when Kenner was inside the booth he looked through the glass and saw that the cop was still over by the pump talking to the gas station guy.

He picked up the phone. Only then did it occur to him that he was still in the Chilton area, that they might have a tap on all Chilton phones. He replaced the phone and thought about it. Quicker, safer to dial station-to-station. But for that he'd need a lot of change. He didn't have a lot of change. He had two quarters and a dime.

He looked in the directory to see how much change he was going to need. It was after five P.M., so he'd need thirty-three cents for the first minute, twenty-three for each additional minute. Say five, six minutes and then Masterson could call him back.

Somebody was tapping on the glass. Kenner turned, saw that it was the gas station guy. He opened the door and the gas station guy said, "You calling local or long-distance?"

"Why?" Kenner said.

"Need change?"

"I could use some change."

The gas station guy reached into the pocket of his coveralls and pulled out a handful of dimes and quarters. "Always carry change," he said. "How much you need?"

"Guess," Kenner said.

"I'm trying to oblige, pal."

"Sure," Kenner said. "It's a friendly town. Dollar should do it."

He gave the gas station guy a bill and got two quarters and five dimes back.

Then he placed the call to Masterson.

He didn't have any trouble getting through. There was a clear ringing tone, and then the phone was picked up and a woman's voice said, "Colonel Masterson's office." Loud and clear.

"My name is George Kenner," he said distinctly. "Put me through to the Colonel, will you?"

"One moment, Mr. Kenner."

There was a pause. It's too easy, Kenner thought. Too clear, too quick, too damn straightforward.

And then Andy Masterson was on the line, his voice a little tired-sounding, but recognizably Andy Masterson. Masterson was an old friend. He and Kenner went back twenty-seven years. Now Kenner didn't know how to start telling him, didn't know what to say to him.

"You just caught me, George," Masterson was saying. "Two more minutes and I'd have been out the door."

"How are things in D.C., you old bastard?" Kenner said.

"Fine," Masterson said. "We'd better make this quick, though, George. Ann's giving a dinner party."

Three years, Kenner thought. I call him after three years and he wants me to make it quick. I'm in trouble to my hair roots and he's worrying about a goddamn dinner party.

"I need some help," Kenner said. "I'm going to talk fast. Record the conversation, will you, Andy? Do you have a tape recorder?"

"No. What kind of help?"

"Information, for openers. You're an Information Officer. I need to know about a couple of things, okay?"

"Shoot," Masterson said.

"Wait a minute," Kenner said. "Let me give you my number first. It's a pay phone in Chilton, New York. If I'm cut off, call me back right away. Okay, Andy?"

"Okay," Masterson said. "Let's not make it too long, huh?"

"As long as it takes," Kenner said. Then he gave Masterson the number of the phone booth.

"I've got that," Masterson said. "What's your problem there?"

Kenner thought: Don't overload him. Not too many questions. Just the most important items. But what were the most important items? Harcourt? NSSRF? Eddie Hensel? The limo? Goodhart?

"Try and get back to me tonight if you can, Andy," he said, to buy time. He wasn't prepared, didn't have his notes, wasn't ready to call Masterson. And here he was calling him. "It's pretty urgent. You can reach me at the Lake Lodge Motel, Chilton. Got that?"

"Just say what it is you want, George."

Kenner licked his lips. "Okay," he said. "One: I want the service record of a guy called Edward Palmer Hensel. That's H-E-N-S-E-L. Served in Vietnam."

"Second?" Masterson said.

"Second," Kenner said, thinking hard. "Second is a car, a black Lincoln Continental with Virginia plates. I think the license number is PZ-nine, six, four, zero."

"You think?"

"I didn't write it down. I guess I memorized it."

"Okay," Masterson said. "That it?"

"One more thing," Kenner said. "There's something

called NSSRF. That's National Social Science Research Foundation. It published lists, but I have a feeling it does a whole lot more, like funding hospitals, schools, clinics. See what you can dig up on it, will you, Andy?"

"Any particularization on that?"

"Yeah, since you mention it. Anything here in Chilton or in a place called Taquanna, in Pennsylvania."

"Check," Masterson said. There was a slight pause, the sound of papers being shuffled. Then Masterson said, "Okay. First, Edward Palmer Hensel. Record shows he went out to 'Nam with an infantry outfit in 1970, POW January 14, 1971 until December 8 of same year—"

Kenner said, "Hold it. What is this, Andy?"

"He seems to have had a tough time as a POW," Masterson was saying. "They must really have worked him over, got him to sign the so-called confession of war crimes. Seems he rejoined his outfit in December, killed on patrol November 18, 1972."

"What kind of shit is this, Andy?" Kenner said. "How the hell do you just happen to have all that in front of you?"

"The car," Masterson said, "is a rental; leased to Eileen Hennessy, administrative assistant to former U.S. Senator James F. Harcourt . . ."

Kenner said, "Oh, Jesus, Andy. Why? Why you?"

". . . retired late 1969 as junior Senator for New York, joined Presidential Special Commission on National Security, then dropped out of public life. All this, George, is a matter of public record. I'm giving away no secrets."

"Andy? Please." Kenner's head had begun to pulse; he could feel it pulsing, the skull soft, like the skull of a newborn infant; soft and vulnerable.

"NSSRF," Masterson was saying, "funds research and study-indicated program development in the social sciences. It's an independent, apolitical foundation, and confines its activities to the Representative American Communities on its published lists. Chilton and Taquanna are both RAC's. That's it, George. I have to go now. Nice talking with you again, old buddy. Give my love to Katherine, will you?"

"You sonofabitch," Kenner said. "Okay, helpful old buddy, while you're on the line, while you have it all there on your desk, while we're playing these fucking games, Masterson—tell me about Goodhart and Our Lady of Hope. Tell me what the fuck's going on here, old buddy."

"No secondary questions," Masterson said. "I'm not authorized to answer your secondary questions."

Then the line went dead.

12

KENNER drove back to town slowly, keeping the Chevy below thirty all the way, thinking about Masterson, about Korea twenty-seven years ago, where they'd shared the same cubic yard of latrine ditch for eight months. So he'd never saved Masterson's life, had never carried the guy on his back through a minefield, nothing dramatic; but being a guy's latrine buddy was a whole lot more intimate. And he thought about the years since, the reunions, the drunken parties, the favors done on both sides, and about what it meant to know somebody all those years and still know nothing, not a damned thing.

Katherine for twenty-five years. And Masterson for twenty-seven.

Not a damned thing about either one.

But Masterson knew about him, where he was, what he wanted.

Masterson knew everything.

Why don't you stop by the school, Mr. Kenner?

Why don't you investigate something, Kenner?

I'm not authorized to answer your secondary questions, George.

They were testing him, testing their security, using him the way they used dogs to trigger mines.

Something. His head was thick, fuzzy. It was all he

could do to stay on the road. Something he should have figured out by now, would have figured out if his goddamn head wasn't filled with cotton, packed full of cotton and hurting like a gaping wound.

The cop followed Kenner all the way into Chilton; then when Kenner turned left onto First, the cop kept on going, and just for a moment Kenner was tempted to swing around and head out of town again. But, cop or no cop, he didn't think he'd be able to make it. He turned right instead, onto Maple, then pulled into the motel entrance.

Elaine's car was in its space outside her cabin. As Kenner drove up she came out of the cabin, looking anxious, fearful, angry, all at the same time, like a worried wife. If he hadn't felt so drained, he'd have found her expression endearing.

"Where the hell have you been?" she said. "Didn't it occur to you to call and tell me where you were?"

"Let's not fight," Kenner said wearily. "A lot of things occurred to me today, and that wasn't one of them."

"George," she said, "I'm going."

"Going where?"

"I want to drive back to Ithaca while it's still light."

"Hold it," Kenner said. "Let's talk first, okay? I'm sorry if I was inconsiderate, but I've had a lot on my mind."

"I'm packing," Elaine said. "We can talk while I pack."

They went into her cabin. The ashtray was full of butts. He guessed from the number of butts that she'd been waiting a couple of hours. Her clothes were all laid out on the bed next to an open suitcase.

"Thanks for waiting," he said. "But why the rush?"

"I guess it looks like I'm running out on you," she said. She folded the sleeves of a dress, unfolded them, then folded them again. "I could tell you I'll come back tomorrow, after the faculty meeting, but it wouldn't be true, George. I'm not coming back here. This town gives me the creeps if you want to know."

"Hey," Kenner said. "What spooked you?"

"I hate night driving," she said.

"What did you find at the hospital?"

She closed the empty suitcase and sat down on the bed. "It's what I didn't find. No cadavers in closets, or in the files."

"You looked in the files?"

"They let me look," she said.

"So?"

"They were glad to let me look," she said with emphasis. "Confidential hospital records, George, and I just walked in, said I was Doctor Stromberg from Ithaca and I wanted to check a former patient's file. And they said, 'Sure, Doctor. Which patient?' "

"What did you find?"

"You're not seeing it, are you? That was how you jokingly told me to get access to the files. You didn't really expect it to work, did you? But it did. It worked as if the whole thing had clearance, as if they expected me to turn up and ask to see the records. You really want to know what spooked me? I had the feeling they were letting me look in the files because it didn't matter what I found there. It didn't matter because there was nothing I could do about it. Do you know how that feels?"

"I know," Kenner said. "Believe me, I know. What did you find?"

"Nothing. Nothing that means anything. Their records are color-coded. Four colors. Pink, yellow, blue, and green. But there's no apparent correlation with patient's age, sex, or disease-type. I checked that."

"Did you see Kath's file?"

Elaine shook her head. She opened her suitcase again and began putting clothes into it. "It wasn't there. They had a space for it, with her name on a pink label, but no file. Maybe they're bringing it up-to-date after Saturday night. I don't know. And when I asked, everybody acted surprised. 'Oh, isn't it there?' "

"Pink," Kenner said. "Why pink?"

"It isn't because she's a girl. David's file is blue with

a green stripe, a diagonal green stripe. Like something
from heraldry."

"What's in his file?"

"Standard stuff. Flu immunization record, allergic
reactions, that kind of thing. The detailed medical history would be in his general practitioner's records."

"Flu. They had a flu epidemic here in '76 and '77."

"Here and everywhere else," Elaine said, folding her
jeans and putting them in the suitcase.

"Let me take another look at those school projections," Kenner said.

She searched among the things on the bed, found
her notebook and gave it to him.

"How about the little girl?" Kenner said.

"Linda Ballinger? Nothing. No file, not even a space
for one. She doesn't exist."

"Christ."

"Right. And that's it for me. I don't know what's
going on in this town and I don't want to know. I just
want out."

Kenner looked at the notes he'd made in the school,
some of them barely decipherable. There were so many
damned factors, so many variables, no way of knowing how many of them were relevant. Yet he had the
feeling there was a clear, simple pattern somewhere,
obvious once it could be extracted from among all the
extraneous detail. 1968 was the key year. The new
guard, the NSSRF boys, had taken over the town like
a bunch of bad guys in a western. Then crime and
divorce had decreased and the school had started
looking forward, and utopia seemed to be on its way.
Then the peak in deaths during the winter of 1976–77;
flu, according to the *Republic*. It wasn't flu. It was
mistakes, accidents, malfunctions. Something in the
psychic development technique malfunctioning. Those
were program-related deaths. Some kind of brain inflammation, maybe? Something that produced the same
symptoms as equine encephalitis?

But in spite of all the deaths the population hadn't
declined. It had increased. And he remembered the

steady flow of newcomers reported in the *Republic;* people from Texas, California, Montana. Doctors, a biochemistry professor. Okay, that fit. They were technicians. And the flip side, the fact that nobody was leaving Chilton, then or now: that was because they were being prevented from leaving. But how? And how did Masterson tie in? And Katherine? And how did George Kenner tie in? Masterson was an Information Officer, not a goddamn spook. Kenner was certain he'd have known if Masterson had some intelligence function. He'd have *known,* dammit. And why Taquanna? How did Taquanna come into it? That was eleven months ago. The dreams, the flashes, the intrusions— they'd all been occurring for a lot longer than eleven months. So why Taquanna?

He said, "Ever hear of the National Social Science Research Foundation?"

"Sure," Elaine said, without looking up from her packing. "They funded my research here in '67. Why?"

"They did what?"

Now she looked up. "Well, why do you think I did my study in Chilton? Because of its famous nightlife? I thought we went into all that this morning, at the school. Chilton was a stable, isolated, homogeneous community. Representative of America, but old America, pre-global-village values. Not now, though. Not anymore."

"How long has NSSRF been around?" Kenner said. "When did it start publishing lists?"

"I'm not sure," she said. "Mid-fifties, I think. Why?"

"Because I got it the wrong way around," Kenner said. "The chicken came before the egg. They didn't designate Chilton a test town so they could check out their program; they chose this place *because* it was already a representative community."

"Who chose it? What are you talking about?"

"I'm talking about spooks," Kenner said. "The intelligence kind, the scary kind. The kind that likes to bug motel rooms."

Elaine looked around, as if trying to spot hidden

microphones, concealed cameras. "You mean bugged as in Watergate?"

"I'd bet against it," Kenner said. "In this town I'd take bets the only bugs are mosquitoes."

"Listen," she said, "shouldn't we be discussing this in the bathroom, with the shower running or something? My God, this is lunatic, you know that?"

"It gets worse," Kenner said. "They don't use bugs because here they don't need bugs. Elaine, this town is part of a federal program in psychic research and development. The whole town is involved. The whole goddamn town and every other town on the NSSRF list. They're developing the sixth sense, second sight, whatever number you want to call it by. Systematically. Scientifically. That's what is going on here."

Elaine stared at him. Then a flash of anger crossed her face. "That is bullshit," she said. "How can you believe that? That has to be the most fatuous idea I ever heard in my life."

Kenner said, "Did I ever mention the name Masterson to you at any time in the last two days? Andy Masterson?"

"Who's he? Merlin the Magician? Or just a plain, ordinary medium?"

"I'm trying to give you evidence," Kenner said. "Masterson's a guy I served with in Korea, a Pentagon Information Officer. Until this afternoon, until five minutes before I called him on the phone, I hadn't thought about Andy Masterson in I don't know how long. But he knew I was going to call. He was waiting for my call. *I* didn't even know I was going to call him, but he knew it. And he knew what questions I was going to ask, Elaine. He had the answers ready on his desk. So you tell me how that's possible. How does science account for a thing like that?"

"I can't explain that," she said. "But that doesn't mean it can't *be* explained. That doesn't sell me telepathy. I'll believe UFO's before I'll believe telepathy and precognition."

"What *would* convince you?" Kenner asked. "If I suddenly disappeared up my pants leg?"

She closed the suitcase, sat on it, and clicked the clasps into place. "Why don't we both just get the hell out of here right now?" she said. "I mean it."

"Is that with or without Katherine?"

"With. If she wants to come."

"What if she doesn't have a choice? I mean what if *they* don't give her the choice? Or us, for that matter."

"Who? The spooks? The little green psychic people?"

"They're using kids," Kenner said. "Developing the faculty in kids, newborn babies. They may even have a breeding program. What else is the maternity unit for? The language lab? Young minds are more responsive. You want to walk out on that?"

"Stop trying to make me feel like I'm letting you down, George. I'm not walking out. I just don't want to stay in the front line. I can check out NSSRF better from Ithaca anyway."

"I guess you were the one who taught Kath quitter psychology," Kenner said.

"Foul blow, George. The difference between what I'm doing and what she did is that she quit school to stay in this creepy little town, and I'm quitting this creepy little town to stay in school. What do you want me to find out about NSSRF? I'll call you tonight."

"I need a list of the towns, the RAC's," he said. "And I want to know what they fund besides research."

"Okay," she said, making a note.

"There's a clinic here," he said then. "Our Lady of Hope. It's on Lakeshore. See if you can find anything on Dr. Benjamin Goodhart. He's the medical director."

"Anything else?"

"Yeah. Take it easy on the way. A cop followed me eight miles out of town this afternoon. I don't think they like people to leave town suddenly."

"You've seen the way I drive," Elaine said, smiling

for the first time. "He'll have to catch me before he can stop me."

"Call me from Ithaca, will you?"

"Don't worry," she said, touching his face. "I never wrecked a car in my life."

She kissed him, then said, "When you go home, go through Ithaca. Look me up."

"If I get that far," he said.

If either of us gets that far.

When Elaine had gone, Kenner went into his own cabin and sat in a chair, smoking, thinking. It was a little after six-thirty. He wouldn't know for another two hours whether she made it to Ithaca, if she called as soon as she arrived. Yet, illogically, he found himself anticipating the phone's ring, the panic of her voice at the other end of the line. He wanted to sleep. It had been a hard weekend.

Maybe I'll watch some TV, he thought. Catch the news. Then he thought: Maybe I'll listen to some music. Kath's *Funtime Greats*. Eight hours of ballads and barbershop; music to hide by.

He looked through the cassettes. For no particular reason he picked up the one labeled *Andy Williams Sings Old Favorites*. He turned it over. Andy Williams was on Side One and Side Two. Kenner fed Side One into the player, punched the play button, then lay back on the bed to listen.

It wasn't a prerecorded tape, he remembered. David Hensel had erased Katherine's notes, systematically, painstakingly erased them. He'd probably taped individual tracks from an album or from a TV concert, because the tape started with hiss, white noise, then joined the first song after the intro. The first song was called *Where Do I Begin?*

Kenner smiled. You and me both, he thought. The song was about love.

"Give my love to Katherine," Andy Masterson had said. He'd said it right at the end, out of context, and he'd also said, "I have to go now." Kenner wondered if that meant anything. And at the beginning, something about Ann giving a dinner party. Some kind of coded message? Andy trying to tell him something? If the guy was really a spook he'd be into codes. Kenner wasn't. Too bad. The remark about Ann giving a dinner party could just mean his wife, Ann, was giving a dinner party.

Andy Williams was singing *The Way We Were,* and Kenner thought: What do you know? Another mind reader. The world was suddenly full of mind readers. The way we were. Check. B.C. Before Chilton. What have you got lined up for me next, Andy?

Moon River was next.

Something stirred inside Kenner's brain. What was that old adage about once being accidental, twice coincidental, three times intentional? Nobody had played *Moon River* at the country club. He'd dreamed it but nobody had played it. Until now. Now somebody was playing it. *He* was playing it.

". . . wherever you're going, I'm going your way. . . ."

Somebody was playing games.

David Hensel was playing games. Kenner sat up, waited for the next song, anger building inside him. Don't make me mad, David. You won't like me when I'm mad. I'm a mean sonofabitch when I'm angry.

The next song was *Days of Wine and Roses.* Kenner listened to the lyrics attentively, reminded of those wartime BBC messages that told the French Resistance when to expect a supply drop, messages in a prearranged code like, "Aunt Mabel has toothache and cannot go out tomorrow." Was it like that? The same kind of correspondence? If it was, the bastard ought to be telling him what the goddamn code was. The song's lyrics meant nothing to Kenner. All he could think of was the Jack Lemmon movie about alcoholics.

The side ended with *Both Sides Now,* and that was when Kenner was sure. David Hensel had chosen those songs deliberately, recorded them in a precise order. Dumb hick David wasn't so dumb. It was Kenner who was too fucking dumb to understand the game.

He turned the cassette over and played Side Two.

Side Two was mostly hiss.

For fifteen minutes the tape unwound and nothing came out but white noise, the "nothing" sound of erasure.

Then Andy Williams was back, singing *Almost There*. After that there was more hiss, more blankness. It disconcerted Kenner.

Finally, right at the end of the tape, the hiss suddenly stopped and he heard Katherine's voice, faint, breathless-sounding, sibilant; as if she'd held the mike close to her lips and had whispered into it. Soft and sibilant. He turned up the volume, rewound the tape a little way, played the section again.

She was saying names. Names and dates. There was a desperate quality to her voice, and something else, a strangeness he couldn't quite identify. It was Katherine's voice, but the intonation was foreign, expressionless.

"Atthowe and Krasner, 1968," she was saying. "Beh and Barratt, 1965. Delgado, 1969 . . ."

Just names and dates.

A bibliography.

It ran for forty-five seconds. Then the tape ended.

Chilton Public Library was at Sixth and Oak, a large frame house that didn't look at all like a library from the outside. It was after seven-thirty when Kenner got there, but he knew it would be open. They'd have kept the place open for him. They'd be waiting, expecting him. They'd know he was coming.

He ran up the steps and tried the door. It was locked. He hammered on it with his fists. Nothing happened at first. Then he heard a shuffling sound on the other side and the scraping of a bolt. The door opened a few inches. An old woman's head appeared in the crack.

"Closed," she said. "Open nine-thirty tomorrow."

"I'm Kenner," he said. "Didn't they tell you about me?"

"Who? Didn't who tell me?"

"Whoever, lady. Let me in, will you?"

She started to close the door, but Kenner put his weight against it and pushed it open. The woman took a step back then, but she didn't seem afraid. Even when Kenner closed the door behind him she showed no fear, only a kind of fretful disapproval, as if he'd merely raised his voice in the reading room. I'd be terrified in your place, lady, Kenner thought. Why aren't you afraid of me?

"This is an emergency," Kenner said.

"You want the hospital," the woman said. "This is the library."

"I need a book, not a doctor. So why don't you save us both some time and tell me what I want to know?"

"I don't know what you want to know," she said.

"Okay," he said, "we'll do it the slow way."

The library was small, and laid out like a private house. The entrance hallway led to two family-size rooms, one on each side, both book-lined, with wood floors. His shoes clacked on the floors as he went from room to room, wondering where to start.

"Do you have a catalogue? An index?"

"Don't need one."

"That figures," he said. Hell, why hadn't Kath given titles? He needed titles. "Do you have a Parapsychology section?"

"This is a small library, Mr. Kenner," the woman said. "A small town. All we have is what you see." She shuffled away across the wooden floor toward one of the private rooms. A voice behind one of the doors was saying, "Felix, I don't care what you paid for it. It goes or I go." Then there was audience laughter.

Kenner started looking at the books.

It didn't take him very long to go through the stock. Both rooms. There was a large Religion section, some American History, a lot of Sports, Gardening, Do-It-Yourself, a section full of cookbooks, another full of repair manuals, and plenty of popular fiction, mostly romance and detectives stories. But no occult, no parapsychology. No psychology of any kind.

He went back into the hallway, and the old woman was there waiting for him. "Find what you were looking for?" she said.

"What's upstairs?"

"Chilton Republics. Two rooms full. Forty years."

Kenner started up the stairs.

The doors were marked CR 1929–48 and CR 1949–68. He glanced inside both rooms, saw metal shelves filled with heavy bound volumes, thick with dust. The smell of mildew was strong.

He entered the room on the right, which covered 1948–68, located and pulled down the volume for 1967, and opened it at random. He got race riot in Newark and tax raises in Chilton. There was a picture of a regretful-looking Mayor Reynolds. What am I looking for? Kenner wondered. He studied the photograph, the layout of the page, the proportion of text to illustration. Neat layout; careful, painstaking spacing. Small-town pride in the appearance of its newspaper.

He sniffed the page. And suddenly he knew what had been wrong with the microfilm, why they were using microfilm at all. Paper aged. It smelled old, looked old. Microfilm didn't. Microfilm was small enough to conceal layout errors, alterations, inserts, deletions.

And he realized what it was that had worried him about the wide margins and the irrelevant pictures. Those pages had been remade. The page reporting Eddie Hensel's death, other pages; pages that falsified the past, distorted memories.

Looking forward.

Looking back wasn't possible in Chilton.

He drove to the motel and sat in his room waiting for the phone to ring. If Elaine had made it she would be arriving in Ithaca about now. If. If she hadn't been stopped. If she hadn't driven into a tree. If she called.

She had to call. He had to know.

He made coffee, bought a candy bar from the machine by the pool, and kept his stomach quiet with it, not wanting to go out to eat, not wanting to be that long away from the phone.

But waiting meant inactivity, and inactivity meant thinking, and he couldn't allow himself to think. Because if he allowed himself to think his mind might go places he didn't trust it to go. It might reason that if one thing was a lie, anything might be a lie; that if the newspaper records were unreliable, if any single report was false, any other report might be false. The twenty-eighth flu victim wasn't necessarily a doctor named Kenneth Frazer. The twenty-eighth flu victim could have been Katherine. So he wouldn't think. He'd made his mind blank, blank and white like the snow in that picture on the wall, still as the gray water of the harbor, and white, cool, and undisturbed as the snow on the roofs of the houses.

The phone woke him at 9:20.

It took him a few moments to remember where he was, even who he was. He'd dreamed he was somebody else, running in the snow. He didn't know who.

But when he picked up the phone and heard Elaine's voice, he remembered who he was and where he was.

"George?" Elaine sounded tentative, uncertain it was he.

"It's me," he confirmed. "I'm glad you made it."

"I'm not calling from home," she said. She hesitated. "Why have we got such a clear line?" she said then.

It was a fine, clear line. Too clear. Clear as the line he'd had to Andy Masterson.

"I read you," he said. "It doesn't matter."

It didn't matter. That was what the clear line meant. It no longer mattered how much he knew. Maybe it had never mattered. Somewhere, they were listening, assessing his progress, deciding when to end the game, whatever the game was. And when they were ready they'd cut the line, do whatever came after that.

"Go ahead, Elaine. I don't think it matters what we say now."

"You were right about Goodhart," she said. "He's

on the NSSRF payroll. And I got your list. Thirty-seven towns in thirty-seven states. Want to pick a state?"

"Montana," he said.

After a moment she said, "Cutler."

"Check," Kenner said. He wondered, almost idly, how long they'd give him now that he knew most of it. Maybe Bertha would know when checking-out time was. "They've been moving people in from other RAC's," Kenner said. "And *The Chilton Republic* re-writes history."

"I understand," she said. "Get out, George. They won't stop you. You're a good insurance man and I'm your policy. Anybody listening to this had better know that. Elaine Stromberg is George Kenner's insurance policy."

"Thanks," Kenner said, "but there's something I have to do first."

"What?"

"Would you believe I don't know?"

"Katherine?"

"Maybe. I found her biblio, by the way. Part of it. At the end of an Andy Williams tape."

"What was on it?"

"Moon River."

"You're unique, George. You know that? What was on the biblio?"

"Names and dates," he said. "If they'll let me I'll read them to you."

"Read the names."

He read her the names.

She didn't respond at first. Then he heard her let out a long, slow breath. "Oh, Jesus," she said. "You're in bad trouble."

"What the hell is it?"

"Atthowe and Krasner, 1968," she said. "That's a study they did in a VA hospital; contingent reinforcement procedures on chronic psychiatric patients."

"I still don't get it," he said.

"You really don't do you?" Elaine said. "It's behavior modification, George. Conditioning."

"Oh," he said. "Is that what it is?"

It seemed kind of dull. He felt let down, like a kid who'd watched a solar eclipse expecting the world to end; disappointed, like the Orson Welles radio audience when the Martians didn't land. He felt empty, numb, blank.

"You're in a goddamn Skinner box," Elaine was screaming at him down the line. "The whole town's a big Skinner box. Get the hell out of there!"

He put the phone down.

13

HE drove some way along Lakeshore, then parked and walked down to the beach. He didn't see anybody. He didn't know if anybody saw him.

Strange feeling.

It was nearly dark now. He stood watching the white flecks of the incoming tide, sniffing the wind. It was a cool wind, turning the humidity of the night around, breaking it, blowing the stench of dead fish through the twilight. A thin covering of clouds lay across the moon.

He began to walk, first across the pebbles, then over the grass dunes beyond. It didn't seem to matter which direction he took. A box had four sides, four walls. When he hit a wall he'd turn around and go back. If he got hungry he'd press a bar, pull a lever, and there would be food. That was what happened inside a Skinner box. He'd read about it in one of Katherine's college textbooks. If the rat made the right response it got rewarded; if it made the wrong response it got punished. Standard laboratory apparatus.

It's a big Skinner box. Not pigskin. Not paskin.

Not ESP. There were never any psychics in Chilton, nobody was psychic.

He started to jog, pulling his plaid shirt from inside his pants as he ran. Jog, jog, jog. The sound of glass breaking underfoot, blood pulsing through his head. No pain now, though. No more pain.

How do you feel about it, George? After three days in the box, how do you feel?

Numb. Tired. Apathetic.

Katherine's been here two years. How do you think she feels?

Numb. Dull. Apathetic.

He moved out of the grass and ran on the pebbles, breathing hard, his heart whirring like a cheap electric clock. Take it easy, he told himself. Time to quit. Take it easy.

He was getting tired now, slowing down. He stopped, squatted for a moment, then sat down on the beach and let the waves lick at his shoes. Quitting time. He was hungry, he remembered. Time to go back and eat, maybe get an early night . . .

George?

. . . but first get something to eat and drink, and after that maybe he'd watch TV awhile until he got really tired, and . . .

George? What the hell are you talking about?

. . . after a good night's sleep he'd feel fresher, could start to figure out what to do then, how to handle it, but right now it was definitely quitting time . . .

Say it again. Say "quitting time" again.

Quitting time.

Say it again. This time think about what it means.

Quitting time. It means I quit.

A long space. The sound of his own labored breathing and the lapping of waves.

Numb. Dull. Tired.

Apathetic. Acquiescent.

It was the wrong response.

It felt wrong, phony, unnatural. He shouldn't be calm, dull, apathetic. He shouldn't be jogging along the lakeshore, sitting on the beach with his feet in the water.

He should be mad as hell, scared and mad and running like hell, driving like hell, pumping out adrenaline like a four-barrel carburetor.

But he wasn't. Why wasn't he?

Because . . .

Yeah, dummy? Because?

Because the bastards had fixed him. Somehow. Somehow they'd drained him, taken the guts, the fight out of him, taken the anger out of him, somehow inhibited him, controlled him, maneuvered him, spiked his coffee, whatever, hypnotized him, somehow got at him, conditioned him, drugged him, boxed him in.

Fight it.

Get up.

He got up.

Now walk back to your car.

He started back along the beach toward his car.

What do I do then? What do I do when I get to the car?

Drive to 330 Elm Street. Don't stop on the way. Don't drink anything. Drive to 330 Elm and pick up Katherine.

Then what? What do I do after that? How do you get out of a box?

But he didn't like the answer he got, so he didn't listen to it.

Elm Street was the way he'd seen it Friday night. The streetlamps weren't lit yet, but there were lights in some of the houses, the same frame houses, with the same porches; and in some windows the paler light of illuminated fish tanks, television screens.

He drove slowly along until he reached 330, the Hensel house. David's station wagon was in the driveway. Kenner pulled in behind it.

Almost at once the porch light was turned on—the same subdued amber glow around which a cluster of moths fluttered—and the front door opened. Nobody came out, though.

Slowly, Kenner got out of the car and walked across

the lawn. He climbed the porch steps and pushed open the screen door, went through into the living room.

David Hensel was sitting in his armchair, eating an apple and watching television. Katherine wasn't in the room.

"Kathy isn't here," the boy said. He said it pleasantly, matter-of-factly. As if Kenner had just happened to stop by.

Kenner said, "Where is she, David?"

David shrugged. "Why don't you sit down, Mr. Kenner? Like an apple?"

Kenner stayed on his feet. "I know about the conditioning," he said.

"Sure you do," David said, without looking up. "You've been pretty slow, though. For an investigator, I mean. I hope you don't mind me saying that."

"I mind like hell. Where is she?"

"She had to go out," the boy said. "Sure about the apple? They're great apples. Local produce."

"I'll bet," Kenner said. "What's in them?"

"Nothing's in them except natural goodness. They spray some stuff on them, but you can't taste it." He picked an apple out of the bowl beside him and held it out to Kenner. "Want to try one?"

"What stuff? What do they spray on it?"

"I'm not into the technical side of it," David said, his eyes flicking from the TV to Kenner, then back again. "Makes you feel good, though. Same stuff they sprayed yesterday, down at the lake."

Kenner nodded. He'd been slow; the kid was right. He should have made that connection at least. Encephalitis had just been their excuse for spraying whatever shit they wanted to spray. He'd asked himself the wrong question at the cemetery. All along he'd been asking the wrong questions.

"How come you're eating it?" he asked. "If you know that."

The boy looked up at Kenner and smiled. "Makes you feel calm," he said. "I only know about it because I have a feedback role. Special status."

"Tell me about it," Kenner said. "I'm really interested."

"You don't have to patronize me, Mr. Kenner," David said, looking hurt. "I'm not a zombie. Where do you get your concept of BM? Out of comic books?"

"Behavior modification, right?"

"Don't humor me either. Not if you want me to tell you anything. Why don't you sit down, Mr. Kenner?"

Kenner sat on the plastic-covered sofa. "Okay," he said. "I'm listening."

"Special status," David said, as if there had been no interruption. "Basically I'm PR-coded, which is blue. I have a programmed-in predilection for blue things: packaging, clothes, etcetera. That's superficial, kind of an identifying tag. But it's functional, too, or will be once the experimental stage is over. Then I also have a green tag for being self-monitoring. I get to report how it feels." He grinned broadly.

"Fink status," Kenner said.

"Feedback, Mr. Kenner. It's an essential role at the lab stage. Want me to explain some more?"

Kenner wanted to back away. The boy was making his scalp itch. It was like finding a snake curled up in your bedroll and the snake saying, "Come on in. It's nice and warm." "What's PR?" Kenner said.

The boy chewed rhythmically at his apple. "Personality Reinforcement," he said. "That's one of the two individualized programs. Then there's a mass program, which is kind of a control thing. PR's self-explanatory."

"What color's the mass program?"

"Yellow. Everybody gets that. The other individualized one is CP. Counter Personality. That's pink. They've been having problems with it, but they'll get it right. Kathy's CP."

CP. Two initial letters. And there it was, his answer. His daughter, his witty, intelligent, life-loving child was CP. Counter Personality. In two years they'd wipe out twenty-three years of development, education, individuality, promise. With two letters of the alphabet and some shit sprayed from an airplane.

"Keep talking," Kenner said, and he thought: Keep talking, David. It's the only thing that's keeping you alive. Because the moment you finish talking, the moment you get through explaining, I'm going to tear you apart.

"Sure," the boy said. "The other category is administration, nonmedical. Green. Professor Lazarek, Chief Stratton, Mayor LoBianco—people like that. And then Dr. Goodhart's team runs the medical side. You'll like him. He's a nice guy."

"I'll bet they're all nice guys," Kenner said.

"You're being sarcastic again, Mr. Kenner. I guess you could use some more exposure to the control program. You'd like it. It promotes selflessness and passivity, the gentle virtues; and it combats willfulness, greed, antisocial characteristics like that." He shook his head earnestly. "I wouldn't go along with this if I didn't believe in it. But it's really going to produce a better society. Nobody needs all those drives nature put there, all that me-first pushiness the cities are so full of. You know? You see our figures at the school? Crime, divorce, auto fatalities. You don't get figures like that in an uncontrolled environment, Mr. Kenner. You get sociopaths, freaks, weirdos, muggers, killers, perverts. That isn't their fault. Put those same people in a controlled environment and they'd turn out to be pretty good citizens. You don't accept that, though, do you?"

Kenner thought: They're selling it. The whole goddamn package is for sale. They want me to volunteer, to join them, to live in this place. The boy had been inviting him all along. Bertha MacKintosh had been inviting him. See Chilton and die. And that was why he'd been allowed to know so much, see so much. They *wanted* him to know what was going on. They'd *let* him see the projections, Chilton's own private model of its future. They were selling him the town, the way retirement homes got sold, or grave plots. The entire visit had been a three-day sales pitch.

"You're telling it," Kenner said, "the way they tell it to you."

The boy looked sad, shook his head; a teacher saddened by a slow child refusing to grasp the simplest of lessons. "What do you think it is, Mr. Kenner?" he said. "A game of Simon Says? Do you think we're all being programmed to vote Republican or assassinate pinko presidents? You've been misled by alarmist liberals if you think that. Chilton isn't about power politics. It's about a better future, a safe, sane society, where people respect traditional values like neighborliness and goodness and decency. Those old-fashioned values are pretty hard to maintain without controls, but they can be maintained if responsible people are running things. And they will, sir. You'll see."

"You make it sound real utopian, David. Like *Brave New World*."

"Which is supposed to be a satire, right? Well, I don't happen to think that. I'd sooner live in Brave New World than in New York City."

Kenner looked into the boy's earnest pink face. It was difficult to hate a kid with that much utopian zeal, until you remembered what he'd helped do to Katherine, using the same seductive half-truths, the same simple-minded final solution to the world's social problems.

"Katherine didn't make that choice, did she?" Kenner said. "She didn't make any choice at all."

"That was a different situation. Things were just starting here then. It's kind of like a revolution, Mr. Kenner, what we have here. In the long run it's going to change society more than any revolution in history. At the start you have to do some drastic things, to protect what you're growing. It's like a seed. Kathy was fixing to dig up the seed."

ESP, she'd said. All those high school kids thinking uniform thoughts, plugged into the same program. Sure, it would have looked like telepathy. And their certain-

ty, their damned certainty about the future, that controlled, sealed environment they were planning—she'd
have taken that for precognition, the way he had. He'd
made the same mistakes as Kath, and now he was
where she'd been two years ago: about to be converted
to the faithful.

"And after the revolution," Kenner said, "everybody gets to be treated right. No more drastic action
needed, is that it? Like in Russia, David? Like that?"

"It won't be like that, sir. And it wasn't the way you
think with Kathy either. We liked each other before
they put her on the CP program. Maybe she wouldn't
have married me, but maybe I wouldn't have wanted to
marry her the way she was either. She's a much nicer
person the way she is now. We get along fine."

Kenner said, "She's nothing, the way she is now.
She's a big fat zero. Like this town, David. Like you.
Most especially like you."

The boy nodded. "I can understand you feeling like
that. You're talking about free will, right? I used to
think I needed that, too. Then they showed me I could
get along fine without it. It's like your appendix. It's
a lot less trouble to have it removed."

"How do they do it?" Kenner said. "They use brain
surgery?"

"Not a lot. Mostly it's drugs, ultrasonics, mass hyp-
nosis—things like that. Spraying, mass injections, food
additives. They're experimenting with animal feedstuffs,
but right now they do it mostly by repackaging, out at
the Paskin place near the fort. They repack branded
goods, put the additives in. It's fantastic how they can
reseal a can. Then there's Sentry beer—that's on a self-
selection-basis part of the control program. The barman monitors who drinks it, what effect it has, that
kind of thing. He's a psychologist."

Kenner's mind was whirling. Paskin, Sentry, the barman; the barman saying, "You have to be a psychologist in this job"—it was too much to take in, too
much to handle, too incredible.

And David, into his stride now, was saying, ". . . ultrasonics near Blanchette. It's supposed to be a sewage treatment plant. They use other methods I don't even know about. You'd have to ask Dr. Goodhart about that. Everything's still pretty experimental. Oh, the individualized programs are done through your own doctor, on a personal doctor-to-patient basis, which is a very important relationship here." He looked proud again. "Our doctors make house calls. I bet yours doesn't."

"What if people don't get sick?" Kenner said, feeling sick.

"Some of the drugs make you a little sick, but they cover that anyway, through dentists, people like that. Anywhere there's a one-to-one relationship. We do quite a bit of individualized programming at the school, in fact. But you only have to hypnotize a person once, and then you can reinforce the posthypnotic responses through the mass channels." He grinned broadly. "They're about to start on intrauterine programming over at the hospital."

"Jesus Christ," Kenner said. That was what the maternity unit was all about, the pink-and-blue nursery upstairs. Next it would be cloning, genetic engineering. And after that . . . what? They'd find something.

"Really, that's okay," David said soothingly. "It'll eliminate conflict entirely. Nothing to miss, right? No preconceptions in the womb." The boy smiled at his pun. Kenner was too stunned to react. "It was overdue," David went on. "Most of these techniques have been around for twenty years. And there's nothing new about conditioning. We're all conditioned all the time one way or another. Not just commercials. I mean the way they'll hype a movie or a book so we think it's something we mustn't miss out on. Moral values, social behavior, even patriotism. That's all conditioning, Mr. Kenner. We accept it, though. I've always gone along with what the government thought was best for me. They know better than an individual, right? Take TV."

He pointed to the TV set. Two cops were crouching behind a car, ducking bullets. "See if you can get around behind him," one cop was saying. The other cop said, "Cover me."

"It's really interesting," David said. "The way they do it."

The cop who'd said, ". . . get around behind him," was now talking through a bullhorn, saying, "Your partner's dead, Wilson. But he talked first. We know where the money is."

"What do you see?" David said.

"The bad old days," Kenner said. "Before everybody got neighborly."

"Two guys shooting at each other in a parking lot, right?"

"Good guys and bad guys," Kenner said. "A color show in black and white."

"What do you hear, Mr. Kenner?"

A woman's voice, shrill, yelling, "Pete, it's the truth. What he said is true. Angelo talked before he died."

"I hear a snake," Kenner said, "hissing in my ear."

"Concentrate real hard, Mr. Kenner. Listen real hard."

Gunshots. One of the cops yelling, "You haven't got a chance, Wilson. Throw your gun out and come out with your hands up."

"It takes a while," David said. "If you don't know it's there you never see or hear it."

"Subliminals," Kenner said. Something he should have been onto from day one, from the night in the moonlit room; and Saturday night, he remembered, he'd left the TV on all night. In the spaces. Flashes.

"Audio, too," David said. "They can trigger post-hypnotic responses with the audio. I don't know the technical name for that." He shook his head wonderingly, admiringly. "The set doesn't even have to be turned on."

And Kenner thought: I won't kill him. I won't even hurt the little creep. The kid's the product, like Kath. I want the factory. I'll find Kath, and then, somehow, I'll get out of this Skinner box of a town, and when I'm out, when I'm safe, I'll blow the whistle on it, blow it to hell, somehow. Somebody'll listen.

Who, Kenner? Who's going to listen?

Somebody. I'll find somebody.

Who, pal? The nutty newsstand guy on Lexington? Masterson? Who?

Kennedy's your remedy. Something-something energy.

What?

"Getting it?" David said, smiling. "No point in trying to run away, Mr. Kenner. Why don't you stay? You'll get to like it. This is where the future is."

Kenner stood up, started toward the door.

"Sir?" the boy said. "Why do you think they let me tell you all of this?"

"You're the official town guide, right?"

"Because it's too late, Mr. Kenner. You can't go home now."

"Who's going to stop me, kid? You?"

No, not him. The town. The bastards running the town. The TV people. Everybody with a TV set was going to stop him, everybody listening to the messages, seeing his picture flashed subliminally on the screen. Kennedy's your remedy, my ass. The message was: *Kenner, G.'s your enemy; watch the streets for Kenner, G.*

Military style.

His car wouldn't start. The engine turned over but wouldn't fire. Damp night air, he thought. Damp spark plugs, flooded carburetor.

Who're you trying to kid?

He got out and looked around. The street was empty and silent, the lamps lit now, throwing a sickly yellowish light except where the trees cast shadows. Nobody seemed to be watching the streets for him yet.

Stay calm, he told himself. Consider the options.

What options? I don't have any options.

Sure you do. Roll your heap out of the driveway and take the Hensel wagon. Shake the kid upside down till the key drops out; or hotwire it. Know how to hot-wire a car?

I'm an expert. Saw Steve McQueen do it once in a movie.

So hijack a car, a truck, anything that moves.

Nothing moves at night in Chilton. Take a look.

He took a look along Elm, and there was nothing; no cars, moving or stationary, no cars in the street or in any of the other driveways; they were all suddenly, coincidentally, locked away in garages.

A movement on the Hensel porch caught Kenner's eye. He looked up and saw David standing there.

"You could take my car, Mr. Kenner," the boy called. "Only I couldn't get mine started either."

Without replying, Kenner crossed the street and began to run.

He ran west on Fourth, toward the lake, black and cold but laced with moonshine; and as he ran, always a little ahead of him, lights started coming on in houses, in the windows of all the houses on both sides of the street; like a flare path for a plane that was landing. Then doors opened and people came out and stood in their gardens or on their driveways to watch him go past.

Nobody called out to him.

Nobody came out into the street.

They just stood in their doorways, in their gardens, in their driveways, and watched him as he ran past.

I don't have any options, he told himself.

You have options. One of the sides of this Skinner box is water. Steal a boat, if you can find a boat. If not, swim. Get out across the lake. Swim to where the shore curves past the point. You can swim, can't you?

No, not the lake. Not the numbing-cold, dark lake, with its currents and its poison. Not the lake.

And anyway, what about Kath? He owed Kath a try, a chance, owed her the chance to wake up from the nightmare. He could wake her, burst through the layers of their crap and reach her, get to the real Kath, deep inside, where she'd be new and fresh and untouched.

She didn't know. He had to find her, tell her. *She didn't even know, dammit.*

Oak Street now, and he was a block from Lakeshore. The friendly block, the block where old men walked their dogs and kids pulled over to let a stranger pass and people waved. The same people, now silhouetted in their lighted doorways, watching the streets for Kenner, G. Measure out your breathing, Kenner, G. It was maybe a mile and a half along Lakeshore to the clinic, to Katherine. Easy jogging on a cool summer's night. If they let you get that far. If she's there. She's there. If she is. If.

But he had options. Letting her go was an option. Saving himself and writing her off; insurance loss, bad debt; forgetting her. That was an option. Forget her, Kenner. Go home and forget her.

No way.

He looked ahead to the dark water of the lake, where the tide was running forcefully now, the white foam surging. Something else was there, too. Lights. A lot of moving lights, thin beams of white light, pointing in his direction, waving.

Flashlights. A bunch of people lining Lakeshore, all with flashlights, lining the track, all waiting for him, last man home, watching the streets for him. You were right, David. You're no zombie. None of these good citizens of Chilton is a zombie. Zombies have character. Next to these dumb programmed bastards a zombie is an independent thinker, a zombie's Tom Paine.

Turning right, he ran parallel with Lakeshore, along a narrow street whose name he couldn't see, whose trees were thin and sparse, unidentifiable, dead-looking. But there were houses here, too, and people in the houses, and lighted doorways, and people standing in the lighted doorways, lining the route to watch him go by, the runner, the guy doing the lap of honor, the Presidential motorcade; and Kenner, going past, yelled, "Where are your flags, you sons-of-bitches? Why aren't you waving flags?"

That's the way, he thought. Get mad. Get good and

angry, Kenner. Angry's what you're good at, remember?

I remember. Angry. Right.

A box has four sides, four walls. Also four corners. Remember that, too, if they corner you. A cornered rat does what, Kenner?

Fights.

Remember that if they corner you.

But they weren't going to corner him. He was going to find Kath and then he was going to get hold of a car and smash his way out of the box, through a wall if he had to.

First, though, there was something else he had to do.

If only he could think what it was.

He ran between two houses and across somebody's garden, trampling flowers, then climbed a low fence, and he was in the vacant lot behind the motel. It was dark here, dark as a rathole. But at least there were no zombies with flashlights watching him as he picked his way across the lot, getting entangled once in a wire, extracting himself, swearing softly in the darkness. Then he rounded the side of a cabin and there was the pool, glowing pale green from its underwater lighting, surrounded by its wire-mesh fence. POOL HOURS—9:30 A.M.—10:00 P.M. the notice said. It was nearly eleven o'clock. Nobody was in the pool.

Kenner rested a moment to control his breathing. He was breathing noisily, harshly, gasping, panting. Take it easy, he told himself.

His cabin was on the far side of the pool area. He could either cross out in the open, where it was light, or he could use the covered walkway around the edge and risk being heard by somebody in one of the cabins. The walkway to the right passed close to the motel office. He removed his shoes and took the path to the left, thinking: What if they changed the lock? What if they relet the room? What if they're waiting?

They wouldn't be waiting. This was the last place they'd expect him to come. They'd be watching Lakeshore, the woods behind the clinic, maybe, the roads out of Chilton. This was the rathole. They'd flushed him out of here. They wouldn't expect him to return. And he wasn't going to stay long. Just long enough to do what he had to do.

Most of the cabins were either in darkness or had the shades pulled down, but Cabin Seven was lighted and the shade was up. He could hear the TV playing inside. He stopped again, listening. Music, the closing theme of the police show David had been watching. And what else? Kenner wondered. His picture again? Some message at the edge of human hearing? *Kenner, G. in Lake Lodge, see?* Were all their stupid messages in rhyme for easy memorability?

He crouched below window level and eased his way past the cabin, then straightened up and passed the next two, both dark, Elaine's unoccupied, expecting lights to come on everywhere suddenly, doors to open, people to come out and point gleefully to him, chanting, "We found him, we found him." The image almost made him smile.

He went around to the back of the cabin where the parking spaces were. Nobody was there. A red Pinto was parked outside Cabin Seven. Kenner made a mental note of it. Sluggish, but wheels, in case nothing better came along. Cabin occupied, key available.

Then he fitted his key very slowly, very carefully into the lock of his cabin door and turned it. The door opened with a soft click.

No lights came on. Nobody jumped at him out of the dark interior.

Kenner stepped inside and closed the door gently behind him.

He sat in the darkness, trying to remember what it was he'd intended to do. The darkness wasn't total. There was a little moonlight filtering in, but it was dark enough to make him uneasy, dark and silent enough. He sat in the plastic armchair in front of the blank TV screen, tying his shoes and wondering how messages could come through if the set wasn't turned on. Maybe if he unplugged it. . . .

No, leave it. If messages were going out he wanted to be included. It occurred to him, also, as he sat there, that the room was probably wired for sound, that he might even have tripped an alarm, broken a beam, that the cops might be on their way even now.

It didn't matter.

And the sprinklers. They'd be bugs, some of them, or miniature camera lenses. Twenty-four-hour monitoring.

No matter. Too late for it to matter.

And the courtesy coffee—drugged. That, too. Very discourteous.

Too bad. Too late.

The last of the clouds must have dispersed, because the room was almost bright now; white, luminous light slanting in through the window, falling on the little snow scene on the wall, the little winter harbor scene familiar from so many hotel rooms across the country, snow from San Diego to Augusta, Maine. He got out of the chair and walked over to the painting, looked at it. Snow on the roofs of the little frame houses by the shore, the dull gray water, the curving beach with its pebbles and grassy dunes where he'd jogged . . .

Jog, jog.

Remember?

Jog, jog, jog.

They were doing things to his head again. Somehow. The guy inside was picking at the bone, or was it a rat gnawing through? It hurt, though, however it was being done.

How had they done it in Taquanna?

He couldn't remember how they'd done it in Taquanna, and it hurt when he tried, hurt the way electric shocks hurt the rats in the Skinner boxes, the rats they punished for pressing the wrong bar.

Memory was punishable.

More pain, punishment for remembering that.

Fight it. Fight the pain. Remember more. Jog your

memory. Jog as you've jogged every day since Taquanna. Jog, jog. Remember. The hospital in Taquanna. Darkness and pain. Silence and darkness and pain . . .

And before that? What was before that? Before that was the accident. The wreck was before that. And before the wreck? Before the rainstorm? Driving.

Driving where, George? Where were you going?

Home. I was going home.

From where, George?

From Scranton. Home from Scranton.

Sure? Sure it was Scranton?

My head. My goddamn head.

Screw your head. From Scranton?

I was in Scranton. Then . . .

Then?

Then I turned north, figured I could make it to Chilton before dark, surprise Katherine . . .

Then?

Then it started to rain heavily, slowing me up, and I was tired, and . . .

And what? What happened on the way to Chilton?

Nothing.

Nothing?

Nothing happened on the way to Chilton.

It happened on the way back.

14

He turned on the light and looked around the room, trying to remember, fighting the pain that was blurring his vision and forcing his eyes closed so that he could hardly see.

But he could guess. Christ, it wasn't hard to guess what they'd done. Refurnished the cabin, refurbished it, given it a paint job, new bedcovers, new carpet, installed sprinklers; the old cabin, the same cabin, with its little snow scene on the wall, the harbor that wasn't a harbor but a lakeside town, this town, Chilton, recognized not from motor lodges all over the country but from Lake Lodge, this cabin, eleven months ago.

He could handle the pain now, didn't need to remember now, could guess that his dreams, his visions of the future had been memories of the past, of a past visit to a town that looked forward because it couldn't look back, because memory caused pain, was fixed to cause pain; could guess that in this Skinner box the only kind of second sight was the kind you got from a second run in the box, through the maze. To see if you repeated your mistakes. To see if you'd learned.

Kenner already had the matches in his hand when he heard the siren, still some way off but coming closer, fast, though not fast enough, because a minute was all he would need. He had it planned this time, wasn't going to repeat his mistakes, whatever they'd been. This time it was going to be different.

Striking a match, he touched the flame to the bed-covers, to the drapes, dropped the match, ran into the other bedroom and did the same thing there. Arson, Kenner, he told himself. Beautiful, isn't it? The siren was close now, but he had a little time yet, time to watch the flames grow and spread, consuming the soft delicacies first, then starting on the furniture, the walls, the window frames, sucking at the bones. No, this wasn't the kind of arson he was used to, the kind done for profit, the destruction of spoiled warehouse stock or of an overinsured home; this was the other kind, the white-hot, angry, South Bronx kind that he'd never really understood until now.

The sprinklers started up in the other room, like sudden rain, and above their hiss he could hear the siren trailing off outside and a bell ringing somewhere, probably in the office. One last thing to do, he thought, running back into the main room. Red and blue lights were flashing, a car door closing. Only one car, one cop. Kenner knew, before he saw him, who that was going to be.

He had time to swing his foot into the TV screen, smashing it, a moment to enjoy the hiccup of implosion, the wisps of gas emerging, a brief, fulfilling high, and then the door was kicked open and the cop, the young cop, Larry, was through the doorway and shoulder-tackling like a ball player in a single un-broken movement, catching Kenner in the chest, knock-ing the breath out of him and his feet out from under him on the sodden, slippery carpet.

The cop went down, too, on top of Kenner, and for a while they writhed and grunted in the smoke-filled room, both steaming from the heat and the spray, both slippery, unable to grip each other's flesh, jab-bing and punching instead. Then the cop's weight settled evenly and he got Kenner's arms pinned and started using his knees, seeking the groin, trying to hurt, to maim, and Kenner, twisting under Larry's

weight, trying to avoid his knees, felt the cop's breath
sour in his face, pickle-sour, and he turned his head
away, recognizing the sourness, recognizing the power
of Larry's body, knowing suddenly that he'd fought
this bastard before, not here, not in this room, but
someplace, and knowing that this time it was for
keeps, which explained why Larry had come alone,
why he'd tackled, why his gun was still holstered,
because this time the sonofabitch wanted him dead.
And now the cop's forearm was across Kenner's wind-
pipe, cutting off his air, and his ears went out so
that he couldn't hear the hiss of the sprinklers anymore or the cop's harsh breathing, or his own anymore.
In desperation he tried to roll over, roll on top of
Larry, pin him, but Larry had anchorage, had his foot
hooked around the leg of the bed, like a shark fisher-
man strapped to his chair. Kenner tried to bring his
knees up into the cop's belly, but the cop grinned and
moved forward to straddle Kenner's chest, out of knee
range, then pushed down harder with his forearm on
Kenner's throat. No way you're going to take this
sonofabitch, Kenner. He's settling an old score and
you don't even remember the score he's settling. He's
going to finish you, claim the smoke got you. MAN
DIES IN MOTEL FIRE, the headline will say, and the
death certificate: Asphyxiation.

But the pressure on Kenner's throat was easing, and
through the smoke and the spots and flashes of his
vision, he could see that the cop was having trouble,
too. He was coughing, sucking air and coughing, breathing through his mouth. The dumb sonofabitch was getting more of the smoke up there and didn't know how
to breathe. Kenner knew how. He was filtering the
air through his nose, then letting it dribble out between
clenched teeth, the way he'd trained himself to do it.
But the dumb cop was gulping, making himself retch
on the fumes from the smoldering mattress, getting
weaker by the second. And his concentration was
going, his will was going. He wanted to breathe more
than he wanted to kill.

And suddenly, Kenner wanted to kill more than he wanted to breathe. With a violent twist of his body, arching his back and bringing up his knees, he threw the cop, threw him easily, rolling out from under his bulk at the same time, rolling on the slick carpet, then making it to his knees, slowly, but faster than the cop was making it to his, and then he turned back, away from the open doorway and the air, and moved on his knees to where Larry was gasping and shaking his head, not wanting to fight anymore, just wanting to breathe. Kenner's throat was burning and he was coughing himself now, deep, lung-racking coughs, and the carpet made squelching sounds as he moved across it, but he kept going because Larry was worse. Larry's face was dark red, contorted with the effort to find air where there was no air. He waved his hand feebly at Kenner, asking for help or aiming a blow—Kenner couldn't tell, didn't have the strength to help in any case, or the strength to fight. All he could manage was to reach out and pull the cop's gun from his holster. Larry didn't try to stop him, just lay looking up at him, and Kenner pointed the gun, holding it with both hands because he couldn't keep it steady with one hand, pointed it at Larry's head, telling himself he had to finish the sonofabitch, finish him so history, whatever it was, could never repeat itself.

But the gun was too heavy. Or the need for air was too great. Or something. He turned, and still holding the cop's gun, crawled his way, splashed his way over the carpet toward the door.

A group of people waited outside, Bertha among them. She was the only one Kenner recognized. Nobody spoke to him or moved toward him as he crawled out of the cabin, dizzy from the smoke, sick, choking on the sweetness of the outside air. He gestured toward the cabin with the gun and two men went inside and brought out the cop. Kenner wondered if it was the gun that made them compliant or whether they were used to doing what they were told. It didn't matter. Only getting away mattered now. He couldn't help Katherine, not on his own, not against the whole town. He had to get away. Fast. Somehow. Now.

Larry's cruiser was still in front of the cabin, engine idling, lights still flashing, gas tank full; the hard-sprung, highly tuned Le Sabre that he'd tried to outrun a few hours ago, the flier that laid its own track through curves and accelerated like a dragster. If he took that machine, if he could get a start in that, nothing could catch him before he hit the Interstate. And he had Larry's gun. With the cop's car and the cop's gun he had a chance.

The dizziness was beginning to pass, though not the nausea. His throat burned, tasted of charcoal, as if he'd been smoking wood shavings. His shirt clung to his back and he felt hot and clammy, weak, exhausted, sick. But he still had something left. Enough. Reserves. This was what he'd trained for without knowing it, this day, this moment. Eleven months in preparation, jogging, jogging his memory and toughening his body, for this.

He got to his feet, quivering all over. His body didn't want to move but Kenner forced it to move and it did. He walked slowly to the car, opened the door, eased himself into the driver's seat.

Then, as he was closing the door, he heard Bertha call out to him, "Don't forget to stop by and pay your bill, Mr. Kenner. Before you leave town."

He didn't answer. He laid the gun on the seat beside him, then hit the throttle. With a deep power-growl that reverberated among the cabins, the car lurched forward, tires screeching, and Kenner, nobody but Kenner, was in control.

Despite its power the car was easy, satisfying to handle; responsive to the throttle, positive to steer. He turned left onto Maple, using the full width of the road, then swung right onto First. There was no other traffic. The car's lights picked out the road half a mile ahead, but there was nothing in the beams except mosquitoes. By the time he reached the intersection with Main he was doing sixty, and the gas pedal was only halfway to the floor. It didn't make sense, but it was the only explanation. They'd know he was driving Larry's cruiser. They'd know he'd be taking First Street toward the Interstate, heading for New York City. Why were they letting him go?

Don't question it. Just drive.

The square flashed past on his left, the square where he'd rested on the bench yesterday afternoon, where the police cruisers had been parked, and the black Lincoln. No cars were parked there now. Lights were on in City Hall, though. Something was happening in there.

Don't think about it. Concentrate on the road. Drive.

The sidewalk ended and the trees began. He had the car up to eighty now, as fast as he dared go on a tree-lined two-laner at night, unless they came after him, and then he'd go the limit. But the rearview mirror stayed dark. There was nothing behind but empty road, nothing in front except blacktop and trees, white-fringed in the headlights, as if touched by frost.

Then something went ahead.

Four spots of light, growing fast; one at each edge of the road and two together in the center. Kenner braked hard even before he realized what the lights were, knowing only that he had to stop and stop fast. The cruiser slued all over the road, coming down to fifty-five in a few seconds before brake fade made him ease up on the pedal a moment; then he pushed down hard again, and now the lights were dazzling, close, and Kenner could make out the dark outlines of the two trucks, big rigs, side by side, taking up the width of the road, closing on him at maybe thirty-five; and he was closing on them at forty-five, with maybe half a minute left before they met head-on. The trucks weren't going to stop; they were going to slam into him, chew him up, ride right over him, and there wasn't a thing he could do, nowhere he could go; no time, no road, no way.

He acted out of instinct, doing what he'd never done or seen done before, but something he'd read about, heard about; wrenched the wheel hard over and pulled on the hand brake at the same time. The back wheels of the car locked and the tail whipped, dry-skidded around 180 degrees in a perfect bootlegger turn. The trucks were so close now that Kenner could smell the stink of their exhaust fumes through the open window; their lights were dazzling in his mirror, their engines deafening. He pushed down hard, but smoothly on the throttle, powering the cruiser back toward town, losing ground to the rigs before he could gain any, unable to hear his own engine for the noise of the trucks, the car interior flooded by their lights. And then the cruiser's acceleration started to pull him away, and the lights in his mirror dwindled to dime-size and the noise diminished, and he was clear.

There was an alternative route. The county road north, the continuation of Main Street, the road to the cemetery and the country club. It met the Interstate further north. The kid, Newstead, had been hitching on that road yesterday. Two, three minutes ago, he'd passed that intersection and it had been clear.

The first frame houses were coming into view, and Kenner brought his speed down to fifty, ready to make his turn at the intersection. There was the square again, still quiet, still empty; and there, a couple of hundred yards ahead, was the corner where yesterday he'd sat talking to Jerry Newstead. The cop, Larry, had pulled over in this car, the car Kenner was now trying to get away in. Christ, it was weird. Everything was so goddamn weird. Yesterday, he thought, turning right. That was yesterday.

The street was blocked by two patrol cars, nose to tail. Kenner had time for a glance, an impression, as he braked, time to judge that there wasn't room to squeeze through on either side, time to note the cop sitting in the driver's seat of each car, waiting, and then he was into a squealing U-turn, bumping roughly over the curb, uprooting a mailbox, and surging back toward First before the rigs could cut him off.

Ahead, Main Street was blocked by a Paskin truck. Paskin, Kenner suddenly realized, was half Pavlov, half Skinner: the fathers of conditioning. Another clue he'd missed. Too late. Always too late.

Right was his only option, right toward Lakeshore, three blocks away. Even as he made the right he could hear the rigs approaching, rumbling slowly through the quiet streets of Chilton, time no longer a problem. Kenner drove in the center of the road, ready to take any exit, but knowing which exit they'd leave him, knowing there was only one route through the maze.

Maple, the street that led to the motel, was barred by a tan and cream station wagon. Kenner couldn't see a driver inside it.

Only Lakeshore now.

Right or left? Which way through the maze?

He tried left, hoping, hoping they'd neglect the town side, but he wasn't surprised to find the road block there: another patrol car and a tow truck, parked in arrow formation, noses together in a point, headlights blinding him. He corrected, swung right, skidding a little, then opened up along the Lakeshore straightaway, repeating history again; in a different car; fast instead of slow; night instead of day; but the same road, in the same town, always the same.

There were lights in his rearview mirror now, headlights and red and blue flashing lights—the cruiser that had blocked Lakeshore South—and behind it more headlights, more flashing red and blue, as the two patrol cars from the roadblock at the intersection joined it, channeling him, funneling him, showing him the way through the maze; not the way out but the way to the center, where the monitors lived, in the center of the laboratory.

And ahead there were oncoming patrol cars, three of them abreast, dazzling him with their lights; and he was hitting the brakes again, knowing he mustn't brake, mustn't lose control of the wheel, but having no more options, none at all. Only the lake to the left; only one way he could go now, and that, he thought, had to be why they called it Hope; because at the end of it all, at the very end, that was all there was.

The iron gates were open. They were making it easy for him.

But he wasn't going to make it easy for them.

He made a sliding turn, wrenching the wheel to the right and giving the car gas so as to lose no impetus, launching the cruiser through the gates and onto the long, curving gravel driveway. The wheels spun momentarily on the loose surface, whipping up gravel, scrabbling for purchase like a cat on glass; and then the car found a line, and Kenner aimed it, a weapon, at the clinic entrance.

He had a clear run to the two smooth-edged stone steps and the heavy double wooden doors beyond, but the black Lincoln was parked outside, a little to the right of the steps, and Kenner angled his approach, not wanting to miss the limo, Harcourt's gleaming limo with its fresh Mac's Exxon wax job. The cruiser struck it a glancing blow, caving in the side, then took the steps like a ramp, lifting, smashing through the two oak doors at knee height, engine screaming; and Kenner was screaming, with exhilaration and anger and the sweet joy of destruction. The windshield had shattered, but he could still see, though he didn't need to see, could remember the long, wide corridor beyond the doors, wide enough to drive a car through, and the stairway at the end of the corridor, and a lot more, but too late, always too damn late.

He touched the brakes lightly, cautiously, and that was wise because the impact had put the brakes out and he had to pull on the hand brake, which threw the car off line, bouncing it from wall to wall, but slowing it so that when it hit the wooden stairway at the end of the corridor it only climbed three of the stairs before rolling slowly back to settle against a wall.

The driver's door was buckled. He had to kick it

hard several times to get it open, and then, gun in hand, he was out and running, in the right place this time, along the corridors from his dream, the clinic's corridors, not the hospital's, running and calling Kath's name. There were doors, and beyond the doors wards, beds, like a regular clinic, but a psychiatric clinic, because some of the people Kenner saw were in restraint, and some of the doors were steel-lined, with heavy bolts and covered peepholes. He stopped at one of the metal-lined doors, thinking: It's like the psycho ward of a prison hospital. He slid back the cover on the peephole and looked in. He saw a small, windowless room with a bed in it; and on the bed, electrodes attached to his scalp, his body in spasm, older now, hollow-eyed but recognizable, Edward Palmer Hensel.

"We'll answer all your questions now, Mr. Kenner," a man's voice said behind him.

Kenner swung around, leveling the gun. There were three men in the corridor, two big guys in orderlies' greens and a smaller man in a white doctor's coat.

"Goodhart," Kenner said. "Nice Dr. Goodhart, right?"

The man in the white coat nodded. "Let's help you relax a little first," he said. He raised his hand and Kenner saw that he was holding a hypodermic needle. Goodhart pressed the plunger and a thin arc of pale liquid rose feebly in the air.

Kenner pointed the gun at Goodhart's upper chest, steadying his aim with both hands. "Don't," he said. "I'm not a nice guy."

Goodhart took a step closer, smiling. "You don't remember that, do you?"

"Back off. I remember enough. If you're crazy enough to think I'm conditioned not to kill, you'd better read up on your Pavlov."

"That's Larry Folsom's gun," Goodhart said. "It isn't loaded."

"Don't play poker either, asshole. Back off."

Goodhart took another step forward. "Test it empirically," he said. "Try it."

Kenner tried it. The hammer clicked on an empty chamber.

Then the orderlies grabbed him, one on either side, and Goodhart, pushing at his sleeve, was saying conversationally, "That's how I got my job here. You shot Dr. Frazer on Sunday, February 13, 1977."

As the needle went in, Kenner found himself thinking, quite casually, with almost idle interest: How many times? How many times has this happened to me?

He was strapped to a bed in a darkened room. The only light in the room was the green glow of some monitoring instrument in one corner. He felt relaxed, unworried. Voices reached him from a long way off, as if in a dream, and there were faces. Goodhart's face, and a face Kenner recognized from a newspaper photograph, a face with a topping of white, fuzzy hair, benevolent-looking, trustworthy. That was Senator Harcourt. "Senator Harcourt's been waiting to see you all weekend, Mr. Kenner," Goodhart was saying. "We thought you'd put it together sooner. That's why we went to the trouble of having the equipment delivered yesterday." He clicked his tongue. "Sunday rates."

Kenner tried to talk, but his mouth was too dry, his lips sticky. "It's an established technique," Goodhart was telling the Senator, "but this new variant should be quicker, more reliable. I'm not going to predict, though. Kenner's built up a lot of resistance over three runs."

"Why go on using him?" Harcourt asked. "If he's violent."

"He has a lot going for him," Goodhart said. "He's well motivated to keep coming here—his daughter lives in Chilton, which is how it got started, how we selected him. Then we use him as Memory Dissolution subject and Stratton uses him as a security control. The two functions are pretty neatly interrelated, in fact. The less he remembers, the more he has to investigate. Kenner's a trained investigator. We'll have to process a lot of Kenners when we start scaling up, Senator; we can't put half the American population in cold storage. DM's one of the short-term answers. Until we stabilize."

"Does he get to make a fourth run?" Harcourt wanted to know.

"Not on the same basis as before. His retention factor's too unpredictable. But we think we've found a way to handle that. It's part of his new program." Goodhart walked over to the bed and smiled down at Kenner. "Listen, it won't be painful," he said. "That operant/aversion stuff you've had the last couple of times is in the museum now. Medieval Chinese torture. This new technique's a lot more sophisticated, believe me. Electrochemical basically, with microwave frills; plus new drug combinations. You'll love it." Then he said, "Look, I'm sorry. That wasn't funny, okay?"

Kenner stared at him.

A door opened, letting light into the room, and there were soft footsteps across the floor. "He's calm enough now," Goodhart said. "You want to run the movie?" There was a whispered reply, and then the soft footsteps came closer to the bed, and a voice Kenner knew said, "I gave you every chance in the book, George. Then I threw away the book and gave you some more chances. I'd like you to know that."

"We'll leave you two lovers alone," Goodhart said. "Call us after he's seen the film, Elaine."

"I really care about you, George," Elaine said. "I don't suppose that's easy for you to believe." Kenner closed his eyes, not wanting to see her, but her voice went on, saying, "I never lied to you. I gave you everything you needed to put it all together. Okay, ESP was our mistake. There was never any ESP. We shouldn't have let you keep that memory. You got hung up on it." She sighed. "You know something?

This may sound crazy, but I really wanted you to get away this time. Please look at me."

Kenner tried to turn his head away.

"Who do you think fixed that tape?" Elaine said. "David Doublethink? *I* fixed that tape. Kath recorded the biblio from memory one night last August, in one of her regressive phases. I had to erase it. But I put the songs in that order for *you,* and then I helped you find the tape, didn't I? And I really had that dream about judges and jail. Old Testament was the key. You should have looked in your Gideon Bible, in Judges 4: Jael hammering a nail through Sisera's head while he was sleeping. My conscience. I was expressing my guilt in dream terms—puns and pictures, remember? I wanted you to try and protect your mind that way in our last DM session, but you didn't. So don't blame me for the fact that you're a three-time loser, George. I'm the one who got you your fourth chance."

She reached out, touched his face. "Go fuck a zombie," Kenner said, and she pulled her hand back.

"Okay," she said, "so you're bitter. You'll forget, though. By Thursday you won't remember any of this. Count on it."

She cranked up the bed, raising Kenner to a half-upright position facing a screen. Then she went to start the projector.

The film was called *Tomorrow America.* It opened with some aerial shots of Chilton, and there was a commentary by Dr. Goodhart. The commentary began: "Welcome to the future."

"The movie's a little corny," Elaine said, taking a seat by the bed. "It was made for people like Harcourt. The part you'll find interesting comes later."

". . . a living laboratory," Goodhart was saying, "functioning at present within the larger, uncontrolled environment of the United States . . ."

"It's the logical extension of all religious and ideological thinking, George. Diminished but still functional ego, ensuring a measure of individuality, but submergence of the self into State, God, whatever. The Greater. It's the Zen ideal, and the Christian, and the Marxist. A basic human need fulfilled."

The screen showed a collage of TV commercials, presidential speeches, scenes from courtrooms, award dinners, graduation ceremonies. And Goodhart was saying, ". . . always conditioned its citizens through reward and punishment, toward favored and away from unfavored behavior. Now it is possible to do that with scientific rigor."

Kenner felt no revulsion, no fear, no outrage. Nothing but a glow of well-being, the comfortable warmth of a sick child half-watching TV while being talked to by its mother.

"Watergate didn't change that," Elaine was saying. "NSSRF still got its appropriations and security cover. America still trusts its politicians, its agencies."

Goodhart was into methodology now: electronic stimulation of the brain, narcohypnosis, ultrasonics, microwave radiation; listing drugs already tried or about to be tried: scopolamine, chloral hydrate, morphine hydrochloride; discussing the logistics of narcotizing entire populations through water supply and animal feedstuffs; there were interiors of the Paskin warehouse and the sewage treatment plant, shots of chicken farms and dairy farms and orchards. Goodhart saying: "Once the feasibility of large-scale BM is established experimentally, the programs may be adjusted to suit current needs."

"Love will be possible, George, once the ego drive is controlled. There won't be conflicts of will. People are going to start caring about other people: their wives and children, friends, neighbors, strangers. Tell me what's wrong with that."

Kenner shook his head. He felt there ought to be something wrong with it, but he couldn't think what it was. Something, though.

". . . resistant, unmodifiable percentage will be small but significant . . ." Exteriors of the clinic, then inte-

riors: rooms, corridors. And Goodhart saying, "Our
short-term solution was to isolate resistant and over-
modified subjects for periods of extended treatment . . ."

Elaine saying, "Those are Chilton's 'dead,' George.
Unmodifiables. The resistant and the overexposed, the
psychomimetics. Some recover and go to other RAC's,
start over. Linda Ballinger's here, but there's hope
for her. She remembered you. The car you saw Saturday night was the ambulance bringing her here from
the hospital. The old guy who kept bugging you for
a ride. He remembered something about you, too. That
needed a surgical procedure."

Cold, clinical, Kenner thought. A surgical procedure.
A knife in the cortex. "And the kid who was engaged
to Lazarek's daughter?" he said.

"An unmodifiable," she said.

"Dead like Eddie," Kenner said.

"Katherine was here in February 1977. We made
our sole exception in her case and let her out again.
Only you and David knew she was supposed to be
dead, and we erased that memory. But Kath remembered seeing Eddie."

"Chilton has accepted recoveries from Cutler, Montana," Goodhart was saying, "from South Fork, Ore-
gon . . ."

"Eddie Hensel was a special case," Elaine went on.
"He'd spent a year in a North Vietnamese POW camp
and two postwar years in the psychiatric ward of a VA
hospital. He was overconditioned. Two months after
he came back here, in October 1976, he went into a
catatonic state. We could have handled that routinely,
of course, hospitalized him again, but Eddie gave us
a chance to work on mass DM, erasing the memory
of an entire community. A particularly strong memory
at that. So we simply put the clock back. We fixed the
army records and backdated Eddie's 'death' four years.
It was a lot more ambitious and a lot tougher than
erasing Chilton's memory of you."

Kenner's attention was drawn to the screen by a
series of jerky monochrome shots in place of the color

images. Snowy streets and people bundled up against the cold; even an old battered Chevy like the one he'd totaled in Pennsylvania. And then he saw himself, walking toward the old Chevy, climbing in; the old Kenner; a black and white memory; the other guy inside his head: himself.

And Goodhart's voice-over: "February 12, 1977. The subject is George Kenner, an insurance investigator . . ."

"Smile, George," Elaine said. "You're on *Candid Camera.*"

They had it on film; not all, but most of it. The lost weekend after Katherine's marriage, the binge that never happened; and the second visit, last July, on the way back from Pennsylvania. Two almost identical visits. Now three.

The first time had been accidental. According to Elaine, he'd been sharper then. It had taken him forty-eight hours to get through the maze. Katherine had helped a lot that time.

Kenner watched the first restaurant scene, Kath sobbing, saying, "It's a big Skinner box, Daddy." He hadn't understood the reference, but Elaine had. That was when she'd decided to make Katherine the twenty-eighth flu victim.

"It wasn't the crab, George. It was the coffee. A simple emetic."

But when David had called in the night to tell him Katherine was dead, Kenner hadn't been convinced. He'd gone back to the hospital, beaten hell out of the doctor with tinted eyeglasses, Dr. Diamond. That scene wasn't on the film, but Kenner remembered it. And he remembered other things now. Diamond saying, "It won't do you any good to know where she is." Running into the cop, Larry Folsom, in the woods behind the clinic. Taking the cop's gun and pistol-whipping him with it. Breaking into the clinic.

That part was there, in a series of short, disjointed shots taken from crazy camera angles, like newsfilm of a riot. Kenner watched with detachment what Good-hart called "the tragic accident," himself putting two bullets into Dr. Frazer's upper chest.

Afterward he'd tried to get out by water across the icy lake. There was film of the boats searching for him, cops struggling with him in the water, hauling him out. Then the scene switched back to the clinic, to the room he was in now. He was strapped to the same bed, watching the same black and white images, mirrors in mirrors. Only then the film had caused him pain.

"Aversion therapy," Elaine said. "It's primitive and ineffective. We don't use it anymore."

Ineffective. He'd had the flashes of memory, the dreams, the headaches for five months. Then he'd made his second trip to Chilton.

This time nothing was accidental. Everything was programmed to happen the way it did. He'd run as if on tracks along the same paths, speaking the same lines; every situation, every phrase triggering the next, mechanically.

"You were getting *déjà vu* a lot then," Elaine said. "You ran a different course, though. Watch."

There was film of him calling Masterson, the old Masterson, a helpful, concerned Masterson. Masterson had called back with the information Kenner wanted, and that had given it to him, on the third day this time. The whole, incredible setup.

There was film of him setting the fire.

Film of the elaborately staged accident in northern Pennsylvania.

Film of the hospital in Taquanna, where he'd watched more movies, suffered more pain, for three weeks.

"We had to erase part of Masterson's memory," Elaine said casually. "Then we programmed him to answer your questions. It was the only way we could handle him. He didn't have security clearance for this project. He functions normally most of the time. A call from you, from Chilton, triggers him."

She stood up, went to the back of the room, and turned off the projector. "I guess that's it, George. You know how it went this time."

"Where's Kath?" Kenner asked.

"She's fine," Elaine said. "She's staying over at her in-laws'. The CP program's working out, I think. All you have to think about now is yourself. Now you remember it all, George, how does it feel?"

"Nothing," Kenner said. "It feels nothing."

"Okay, George. Now that you remember it all we're going to make you forget again."

First they put him in the dark, windowless room, in the silent, dark room. They put earphones on his ears and through the earphones they played silence. Sometimes white sound. Mostly silence.

That went on for a very long time.

A year, maybe.

He sang all the songs he knew. Sang them inside his head.

He recited all the poems he knew.

He told himself stories.

All of that used up the first day.

They were trying to break him, break his will. He wasn't going to let that happen. He mustn't break. He must hold on to his will.

He used dream language: puns and pictures. Saw his will as the wheel of a car, imagined himself driving on a slick road. Don't brake, he told himself. Whatever happens, whatever they do, don't break.

And he devised codes, private codes, little messages to himself.

Key words, personal triggers, words that would help him remember. He searched a long time for the right words, the right triggers. They had to be words, or phrases, that he'd come across often; often but not too often.

"Trigger" itself was a good code word. He decided to use that.

He worked in an insurance office, didn't he? Why not a word like "insurance"?

Too common.

How about "life insurance"?

Better. Not perfect, though.

"Life insurance policy" was a good trigger phrase. He decided to use that.

And the conditioning, Kenner. How are you going to remember the conditioning?

Easy. "Air conditioning." Every time I see an air-conditioning unit or hear the words "air conditioning" I'll remember what they're doing in Chilton.

Okay. What else.

Rats. Maze. Laboratory. Can you find some way of triggering those memories?

Sure. "Laboratory" and "maze" gave me "labyrinth." "Monitor" gives me "Minotaur." I'll think of Theseus looking for the Minotaur in the labyrinth, and I'll remember what they're doing in Chilton.

And that used up the second day.

He'd stayed longer than he'd expected. A week instead of the long weekend he'd planned. But then two years was a long time to be away from your daughter. He'd owed her the time.

As he headed toward the Interstate, on that narrow country blacktop darkened on either side by thick trees, he rolled down his window to get the last of the green-smelling air. Six hours of gas fumes lay ahead, and then the stink of Manhattan. Jesus, he thought, why am I doing it? What the hell am I going back for?

He thought back over the week, possibly the most relaxed, pleasantest week of his life. On the Saturday they'd driven out to Kanga Falls, taken a boat, fished the lake. Then, on Sunday morning, he'd gone to church with the Hensels. Long time since he'd been in a church. Okay, so he was no religious nut, but you had to admit there was something comfortable about a cool church interior on a hot Sunday morning, people who knew each other singing hymns together. A little corny, maybe. But nice.

Like David and his family.

Like Chilton.

Okay, don't rush me. I'm thinking about it. I bought the Friday edition of *The Republic,* didn't I?

It lay open on the seat beside him, folded over at the Classified Ads. He'd even ringed one of the farms for sale. Something to think about, that was all. He hadn't decided anything yet.

He could do a lot worse, though, than quit his job and move upstate; buy an apple farm near Chilton, near Katherine; free-wheel the rest of his life, spraying apples, doing whatever it was apple farmers did.

Like the sign said: CHILTON—A GREAT LITTLE PLACE TO LIVE.

The long-awaited national bestseller
is coming in May in paperback!

It all began with
THE CHRONICLES OF THOMAS COVENANT THE UNBELIEVER—
Lord Foul's Bane, The Illearth War
and *The Power that Preserves.*

Now the story of Thomas Covenant continues...

THE WOUNDED LAND

27831 / $2.95

by Stephen R. Donaldson

• 2 months on *Time* bestseller list

"Comparable to Tolkien at his best...a true classic!"
—Washington Post

DEL REY BOOKS

No one who buys it,
survives it.

THE HOUSE NEXT DOOR

A terrifying novel
by
Anne Rivers Siddons

29330 $2.50

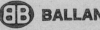 **BALLANTINE BOOKS**